PRAISE FOR ELLIS PETERS,
THE CHRONICLES OF BROTHER CADFAEL,
AND
THE DEVIL'S NOVICE

"A cult figure of crime fiction."
—*Financial Times* (London)

"Spellbinding . . . Peters has the matchless ability to make medieval England seem alive and vital."
—*Sacramento Bee*

"As usual, Miss Peters creates her magic, resurrecting a long-gone age and its people for our delight."
—*Washington Times*

"Brother Cadfael, hero of twenty novels by Ellis Peters and star of a new PBS Mystery series, is joining Sherlock Holmes, Father Brown, Hercule Poirot, Inspector Maigret, and Lord Peter Wimsey in the first rank of great fictional detectives. . . . The entire series is made up of intricately plotted whodunits peopled with compelling characters and a stunning array of sights and sounds."
—*World* magazine (NC)

"Ellis Peters makes us feel right at home in an England almost a millennium away. And she gives us a cracking good mystery."
—*Trenton Sunday Times*

"Highly enjoyable."
—*L.A. Life*

"The author, who is past eighty, brings the medieval world magnificently to life in this deservedly popular series."
—*Denver Post*

Please turn the page for more . . .

THE · DEVIL'S · NOVICE ·

ELLIS PETERS

THE · DEVIL'S
· NOVICE

THE MYSTERIOUS PRESS

Published by Warner Books

A Time Warner Company

MYSTERIOUS PRESS EDITION

Copyright © 1983 by Ellis Peters
All rights reserved.

Cover design and illustration by Bascove

This Mysterious Press edition is published
by arrangement with the author.

The Mysterious Press name and logo are registered trademarks of Warner Books, Inc.

 Mysterious Press Books are published by
Warner Books, Inc.
    1271 Avenue of the Americas
New York, NY 10020

Visit our Web site at
http://pathfinder.com/twep

W A Time Warner Company

Printed in the United States of America
ISBN 978-0-446-40515-7 ISBN -0446-40515-9

First published in Great Britain in 1983 by Macmillan London Limited
First U.S. Printing: February, 1997

10 9 8 7 6 5 4 3 2 1

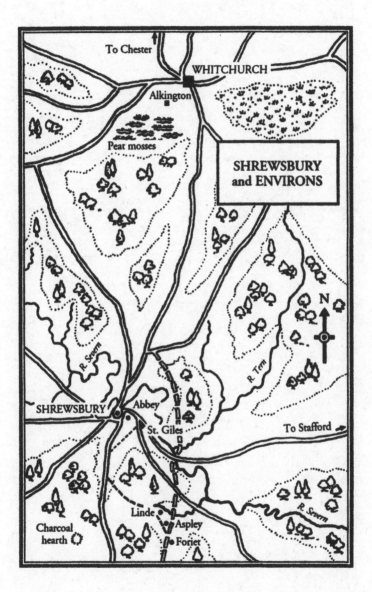

CHAPTER ONE

In the middle of September of that year of Our Lord, 1140, two lords of Shropshire manors, one north of the town of Shrewsbury, the other south, sent envoys to the abbey of Saint Peter and Saint Paul on the same day, desiring the entry of younger sons of their houses to the Order.

One was accepted, the other rejected. For which different treatment there were weighty reasons.

"I have called you few together," said Abbot Radulfus, "before making any decision in this matter, or opening it to consideration in chapter, since the principle here involved is at question among the masters of our order at this time. You, Brother Prior and Brother Sub-Prior, as bearing the daily weight of the household and family, Brother Paul as master of the boys and novices, Brother Edmund as an obedientiary and a child of the cloister from infancy, to advise upon the one hand, and Brother Cadfael, as a conversus come to the life at a ripe age and after wide venturings, to speak his mind upon the other."

So, thought Brother Cadfael, mute and passive on his stool in the corner of the abbot's bare, wood-scented parlour, I am to be the devil's lawman, the voice of the outer world. Mellowed through seventeen years or so of a vocation, but still sharpish in the cloistered ear. Well, we serve according to our skills, and in the degrees allotted to us, and this may be as good a way as any. He was more than a little sleepy, for he had been outdoors between the orchards of the Gaye and his own herb garden within the pale ever since morning, between the obligatory sessions of office and prayer, and was slightly drunk with the rich air of a fine, fat September, and ready for his bed as soon as Compline was over. But not yet so sleepy that he could not prick a ready ear when Abbot Radulfus declared himself in need of counsel, or even desirous of hearing counsel he yet would not hesitate to reject if his own incisive mind pointed him in another direction.

"Brother Paul," said the abbot, casting an authoritative eye round the circle, "has received requests to accept into our house two new devotionaries, in God's time to receive the habit and the tonsure. The one we have to consider here is from a good family, and his sire a patron of our church. Of what age, Brother Paul, did you report him?"

"He is an infant, not yet five years old," said Paul.

"And that is the ground of my hesitation. We have now only four boys of tender age among us, two of them not committed to the cloistral life, but here to be educated. True, they may well choose to remain with us and join the community in due time, but that is left to them to decide, when they are of an age to make such a choice. The other two, infant oblates given to God by their parents, are already twelve and ten years old, and are settled and happy among us, it would be ill-done to disturb their tranquillity. But I am not easy in my mind about accepting any more such oblates, when they can have no conception of what they are being offered or, indeed, of what they are being deprived. It is joy," said Radulfus, "to open the doors to a truly committed heart and mind, but the mind of a child barely out of nurse belongs with his toys, and the comfort of his mother's lap."

Prior Robert arched his silver eyebrows and looked dubiously down his thin, patrician nose. "The custom of offering children as oblates has been approved for centuries. The Rule sanctions it. Any change which departs from the Rule must be undertaken only after grave reflection. Have we the right to deny what a father wishes for his child?"

"Have we—has the father—the right to determine the course of a life, before the unwitting innocent has a voice to speak for himself? The practice, I know, is long established, and never before questioned, but it is being questioned now."

"In abandoning it," persisted Robert, "we may be depriving some tender soul of its best way to blessedness. Even in the years of childhood a wrong turning may be taken, and the way to divine grace lost."

"I grant the possibility," agreed the abbot, "but also I fear the reverse may be true, and many such children, better suited to another life and another way of serving God, may be shut into what must be for them a prison. On this matter I know only my own mind. Here we have Brother Edmund, a child of the cloister from his fourth year, and Brother Cadfael, conversus after an active and adventurous life and at a mature age. And both, as I hope and believe, secure in commitment. Tell us, Edmund, how do you look upon this matter? Have you regretted ever that you were denied experience of the world outside these walls?"

Brother Edmund the infirmarer, only eight years short of Cadfael's robust sixty, and a grave, handsome, thoughtful creature who might have looked equally well on horseback and in arms, or farming a manor and keeping a patron's eye on his tenants, considered the question seriously, and was not disturbed. "No, I have had no regrets. But neither did I know what there might be worth regretting. And I have known those who did rebel, even wanting that knowledge. It may be they imagined a better world without than is possible in this life, and it may be that I lack that gift of imagination. Or it may be only that I was fortunate in finding work here within to my liking and within my scope, and have been too busy to repine. I would not change. But my choice would have been the same if I had grown to puberty here, and made my vows only when I was grown. I have cause to know that others would have chosen differently, had they been free."

"That is fairly spoken," said Radulfus, "Brother Cadfael, what of you? You have ranged over much of the world, as far as the Holy Land, and borne arms. Your choice was made late and freely, and I do not think you have looked back. Was that gain, to have seen so much, and yet chosen this small hermitage?"

Cadfael found himself compelled to think before he spoke, and beneath the comfortable weight of a whole day's sunlight and labour thought was an effort. He was by no means certain what the abbot wanted from him, but had no doubt whatever of his own indignant discomfort at the notion of a babe in arms being swaddled willy-nilly in the habit he himself had assumed willingly.

"I think it was gain," he said at length, "and moreover, a better gift I brought, flawed and dinted though it might be, than if I had come in my innocence. For I own freely that I had loved my life, and valued high the warriors I had known, and the noble places and great actions I had seen, and if I chose in my prime to renounce all these, and embrace this life of the cloister in preference to all other, then truly I think I paid the best compliment and homage I had to pay. And I cannot believe that anything I hold in my remembrance makes me less fit to profess this allegiance, but rather better fits me to serve as well as I may. Had I been given in infancy, I should have rebelled in manhood, wanting my rights. Free from childhood, I could well afford to sacrifice my rights when I came to wisdom."

"Yet you would not deny," said the abbot, his lean face lit briefly by a smile, "the fitness of certain others, by nature and grace, to come in early youth to the life you discovered in maturity?"

"By no means would I deny it! I think those who do so, and with certainty, are the best we have. So they make the choice of their own will, and by their own light."

"Well, well!" said Radulfus, and mused with his chin in his hand, and his deep-set eyes shadowed. "Paul, have you any view to lay before us? You have the boys in charge, and I am well aware they seldom complain of you." For Brother Paul, middle-aged, conscientious and anxious, like a hen with a wayward brood, was known for his indulgence to the youngest, for ever in defence of mischief, but a good teacher for all that, instilling Latin without pain on either part.

"It would be no burden to me," said Paul slowly, "to care for a little lad of four, but it is of no merit that I should take pleasure in such a charge, or that he should be content. That is not what the Rule requires, or so it seems to me. A good father could do as much for a little son. Better if he come in knowledge of what he does, and with some inkling of what he may be leaving behind him. At fifteen or sixteen years, well taught . . . "

Prior Robert drew back his head and kept his austere countenance, leaving his superior to make up his own mind as he would. Brother Richard the sub-prior had held his tongue throughout, being a good man at managing day-to-day affairs, but indolent at attempting decisions.

"It has been in my mind, since studying the reasonings of Archbishop Lanfranc," said the abbot, "that there must be a change in our thoughts on this matter of child dedication, and I am now convinced that it is better to refuse all oblates until they are able to consider for themselves what manner of life they desire. Therefore, Brother Paul, it is my view that you must decline the offer of this boy, upon the terms desired. Let his father know that in a few years' time the boy will be welcome, as a pupil in our school, but not as an oblate entering the order. At a suitable age, should he so wish, he may enter. So tell his parent." He drew breath and stirred delicately in his chair, to indicate that the conference was over. "And you have, as I understand, another request for admission?"

Brother Paul was already on his feet, relieved and smiling. "There will be no difficulty there, Father. Leoric Aspley of Aspley desires to bring to us his younger son Meriet. But the young man is past his nineteenth birthday, and he comes at his own earnest wish. In his case, Father, we need have no qualms at all."

* * *

"Not that these are favourable times for recruitment,"
owned Brother Paul, crossing the great court to Compline with Cadfael at his side, "that we can afford to
turn postulants away. But for all that, I'm glad Father
Abbot decided as he did. I have never been quite
happy about the young children. Certainly in most
cases they may be offered out of true love and fervour. But sometimes a man must wonder . . . With
lands to keep together, and one or two stout sons already, it's a way of disposing profitably of the third."

"That can happen," said Cadfael drily, "even where
the third is a grown man."

"Then usually with his full consent, for the cloister
can be a promising career, too. But the babes in
arms—no, that way is too easily abused."

"Do you think we shall get this one in a few years,
on Father Abbot's terms?" wondered Cadfael.

"I doubt it. If he's placed here to school, his sire
will have to pay for him." Brother Paul, who could
discover an angel within every imp he taught, was
nevertheless a sceptic concerning their elders. "Had
we accepted the boy as an oblate, his keep and all else
would be for us to bear. I know the father. A decent
enough man, but parsimonious. But his wife, I fancy,
will be glad enough to keep her youngest."

They were at the entrance to the cloister, and the
mild green twilight of trees and bushes, tinted with
the first tinge of gold, hung still and sweet-scented on
the air. "And the other?" said Cadfael. "Aspley—that

should be somewhere south, towards the fringes of the Long Forest. I've heard the name, but no more. Do you know the family?

"Only by repute, but that stands well. It was the manor steward who came with the word, a solid old countryman, Saxon by his name—Fremund. He reports the young man lettered, healthy and well taught. Every way a gain to us."

A conclusion with which no one had then any reason to quarrel. The anarchy of a country distracted by civil war between cousins had constricted monastic revenues, kept pilgrims huddled cautiously at home, and sadly diminished the number of genuine postulants seeking the cloister, while frequently greatly increasing the numbers of indigent fugitives seeking shelter there. The promise of a mature entrant already literate, and eager to begin his novitiate, was excellent news for the abbey.

Afterwards, of course, there were plenty of wiseacres pregnant with hindsight, listing portents, talking darkly of omens, brazenly asserting that they had told everyone so. After every shock and reverse, such late experts proliferate.

It was only by chance that Brother Cadfael witnessed the arrival of the new entrant, two days later. After several days of clear skies and sunshine for harvesting the early apples and carting the new-milled flour, it was a day of miserable downpour, turning the roads to mud, and every hollow in the great court into a treacherous puddle. In the carrels of the scriptorium copiers and craftsmen worked thankfully at their desks. The boys kicked their heels discontentedly indoors, baulked of their playtime, and the few invalids in the infirmary felt their spirits sink as the daylight dimmed and went into mourning. Of guests there were few at that time. There was a breathing-space in the civil war, while earnest clerics tried to bring both sides together in agreement, but most of England preferred to stay at home and wait with held breath, and only those who had no option rode the roads and took shelter in the abbey guest-halls.

Cadfael had spent the first part of the afternoon in his workshop in the herbarium. Not only had he a number of concoctions working there, fruit of his autumn harvest of leaves, roots and berries, but he had also got hold of a copy of Aelfric's list of herbs and trees from the England of a century and a half earlier, and wanted peace and quiet in which to study it. Brother Oswin, whose youthful ardour was Cadfael's sometime comfort and frequent anxiety in this his private domain, had been excused attendance, and gone to pursue his studies in the liturgy, for the time of his final vows was approaching, and he needed to be word-perfect.

The rain, though welcome to the earth, was disturbing and depressing to the mind of man. The light lowered; the leaf Cadfael studied darkened before his eyes. He gave up his reading. Literate in English, he had learned his Latin laboriously in maturity, and though he had mastered it, it remained unfamiliar, an alien tongue. He went the round of his brews, stirred here and there, added an ingredient in a mortar and ground until it blended into the cream within, and went back in scurrying haste through the wet gardens to the great court, with his precious parchment in the breast of his habit.

He had reached the shelter of the guest-hall porch, and was drawing breath before splashing through the puddles to the cloister, when three horsemen rode from the Foregate, and halted under the archway of the gatehouse to shake off the rain from their cloaks. The porter came out in haste to greet them, slipping sidelong in the shelter of the wall, and a groom came running from the stable-yard, splashing through the rain with a sack over his head.

So that must be Leoric Aspley of Aspley, thought Cadfael, and the son who desires to take the cowl here among us. And he stood to gaze a moment, partly out of curiosity, partly out of a vain hope that the downpour would ease, and let him cross to the scriptorium without getting wetter than he need.

A tall, erect, elderly man in a thick cloak led the arrivals, riding a big grey horse. When he shook off his hood he uncovered a head of bushy, grizzled hair and a face long, austere and bearded. Even at that distance, across the wide court, he showed handsome, unsmiling, unbending, with a high-ridged, arrogant nose and a grimly proud set to his mouth and jaw, but his manner to porter and groom, as he dismounted, was gravely courteous. No easy man, probably no easy parent to please. Did he approve his son's resolve, or was he accepting it only under protest and with displeasure? Cadfael judged him to be in the mid-fifties, and thought of him, in all innocence, as an old man, forgetting that his own age, to which he never gave much thought, was past sixty.

He gave rather closer attention to the young man who had followed decorously a few respectful yards behind his father, and lighted down from his black pony quickly to hold his father's stirrup. Almost excessively dutiful, and yet there was something in his bearing reminiscent of the older man's stiff self-awareness, like sire, like son. Meriet Aspley, nineteen years old, was almost a head shorter than Leoric when they stood together on the ground; a well-made, neat, compact young man, with almost nothing to remark about him at first sight. Dark-haired, with his forelocks plastered to his wet forehead, and rain streaking his smooth cheeks like tears. He stood a little apart, his head submissively bent, his eyelids lowered, attentive like a servant awaiting his lord's orders; and when they moved away into the shelter of the gatehouse he followed at heel like a well-trained hound. And yet there was something about him complete, solitary and very much his own, as though he paid observance to these formalities without giving away anything more, an outward and scrupulous observance that touched no part of what he carried within. And such distant glimpses as Cadfael had caught of his face had shown it set and composed as austerely as his sire's and deep, firm hollows at the corners of a mouth at first sight full-lipped and passionate.

No, thought Cadfael, those two are not in harmony, that's certain. And the only way he could account satisfactorily for the chill and stiffness was by returning to his first notion, that the father did not approve his son's decision, probably had tried to turn him from it, and held it against him grievously that he would not be deterred. Obstinacy on the one hand and frustration and disappointment on the other held them apart. Not the best of beginnings for a vocation, to have to resist a father's will. But those who have been blinded by too great a light do not see, cannot afford to see, the pain they cause. It was not the way Cadfael had come into the cloister, but he had known it happen to one or two, and understood its compulsion.

They were gone, into the gatehouse to await Brother Paul, and their formal reception by the abbot. The groom who had ridden in at their heels on a shaggy forest pony trotted down with their mounts to the stables, and the great court was empty again under the steady rain. Brother Cadfael tucked up his habit and ran for the shelter of the cloister, there to shake off the water from his sleeves and cowl, and make himself comfortable to continue his reading in the scriptorium. Within minutes he was absorbed in the problem of whether the "dittanders" of Aelfric was, or was not, the same as his own "dittany". He gave no more thought then to Meriet Aspley, who was so immovably bent on becoming a monk.

The young man was introduced at chapter next day, to make his formal profession and be made welcome by those who were to be his brothers. During their probation novices took no part in the discussions in chapter, but might be admitted to listen and learn on occasions, and Abbot Radulfus held that they were entitled to be received with brotherly courtesy from their entry.

In the habit, newly donned, Meriet moved a little awkwardly, and looked strangely smaller than in his own secular clothes, Cadfael reflected, watching him thoughtfully. There was no father beside him now to freeze him into hostility, and no need to be wary of those who were glad to accept him among them; but still there was a rigidity about him, and he stood with eyes cast down and hands tightly clasped, perhaps overawed by the step he was taking. He answered questions in a low, level voice, quickly and submissively. A face naturally ivory-pale, but tanned deep gold by the summer sun, the flush of blood beneath his smooth skin quick to mantle on high cheekbones. A thin, straight nose, with fastidious nostrils that quivered nervously, and that full, proud mouth that had so rigorous a set to it in repose, and looked so vulnerable in speech. And the eyes he hid in humility, large-lidded under clear, arched brows blacker than his hair.

"You have considered well," said the abbot, "and now have time to consider yet again, without blame from any. Is it your wish to enter the cloistered life here among us? A wish truly conceived and firmly maintained? You may speak out whatever is in your heart."

The low voice said, rather fiercely than firmly: "It is my wish, Father." He seemed almost to start at his own vehemence, and added more warily: "I beg that you will let me in, and I promise obedience."

"That vow comes later," said Radulfus with a faint smile. "For this while, Brother Paul will be your instructor, and you will submit yourself to him. For those who come into the Order in mature years a full year's probation is customary. You have time both to promise and to fulfil."

The submissively bowed head reared suddenly at hearing this the large eyelids rolled back from wide, clear eyes of a dark hazel flecked with green. So seldom had he looked up full into the light that their brightness was startling and disquieting. And his voice was higher and sharper, almost dismayed, as he asked: "Father, is that needful? Cannot the time be cut short, if I study to deserve? The waiting is hard to bear."

The abbot regarded him steadily, and drew his level brows together in a frown, rather of speculation and wonder than of displeasure. "The period can be shortened, if such a move seems good to us. But impatience is not the best counsellor, nor haste the best advocate. It will be made plain if you are ready earlier. Do not strain after a perfection."

It was clear that the young man Meriet was sensitive to all the implications of both words and tone. He lowered his lids again like shutters over the brightness, and regarded his folded hands. "Father, I will be guided. But I do desire with all my heart to have the fullness of my commitment, and be at peace." Cadfael thought that the guarded voice shook for an instant. In all probability that did the boy no harm with Radulfus, who had experience both of passionate enthusiasts and those gradually drawn like lambs to the slaughter of dedication.

"That can be earned," said the abbot gently.

"Father, it shall!" Yes, the level utterance did quiver, however briefly. He kept the startling eyes veiled.

Radulfus dismissed him with somewhat careful kindness, and closed the chapter after his departure. A model entry? Or was it a shade too close to the feverish fervour an abbot as shrewd as Radulfus must suspect and deplore, and watch very warily hereafter? Yet a high-mettled, earnest youth, coming to his desired haven, might well be over-eager and in too much of a hurry. Cadfael, whose two broad feet had always been solidly planted on earth, even when he took his convinced decision to come into harbour for the rest of a long life, had considerable sympathy with the ardent young, who overdo everything, and take wing at a line of verse or a snatch of music. Some who thus take fire burn to the day of their death, and set light to many others, leaving a trail of radiance to generations to come. Other fires sink for want of fuel, but do no harm to any. Time would discover what young Meriet's small, desperate flame portended.

Hugh Beringar, deputy-sheriff of Shropshire, came down from his manor of Maesbury to take charge in Shrewsbury, for his superior, Gilbert Prestcote, had departed to join King Stephen at Westminster for his half-yearly visit at Michaelmas, to render account of his shire and its revenues. Between the two of them they had held the county staunch and well-defended, reasonably free from the disorders that racked most of the country, and the abbey had good cause to be grateful to them, for many of its sister houses along the Welsh marches had been sacked, pillaged, evacuated, turned into fortresses for war, some more than once, and no remedy offered. Worse than the armies of King Stephen on the one hand and his cousin the empress on the other—and in all conscience they were bad enough—the land was crawling with private armies, predators large and small, devouring everything wherever they were safe from any force of law strong enough to contain them. In Shropshire the law had been strong enough, thus far, and loyal enough to care for its own.

When he had seen his wife and baby son installed comfortably in his town house near St. Mary's church, and satisfied himself of the good order kept in the castle garrison, Hugh's first visit was always to pay his respects to the abbot. By the same token, he never left the enclave without seeking Brother Cadfael in his workshop in the garden. They were old friends, closer than father and son, having not only that easy and tolerant relationship of two generations, but shared experiences that made of them contemporaries. They sharpened minds, one upon the other, for the better protection of values and institutions that needed defence with every passing day in a land so shaken and disrupted.

Cadfael asked after Aline, and smiled with pleasure even in speaking her name. He had seen her won by combat, along with high office for so young a man as his friend, and he felt almost a grandsire's fond pride in their firstborn son, to whom he had stood godfather at his baptism in the first days of this same year.

"Radiant," said Hugh with high content, "and asking after you. When time serves I'll make occasion to carry you off, and you shall see for yourself how she's blossomed."

"The bud was rare enough," said Cadfael. "And the imp Giles? Dear life, nine months old, he'll be quartering your floors like a hound-pup! They're on their feet almost before they're out of your arms."

"He's as fast on four legs," said Hugh proudly, "as his slave Constance is on two. And has a grip on him like a swordsman born. But God keep that time well away from him many years yet, his childhood will be all too short for me. And God willing, we shall be clear of this shattered time before ever he comes to manhood. There was a time when England enjoyed a settled rule, there must be another such to come."

He was a balanced and resilient creature, but the times cast their shadow on him when he thought on his office and his allegiance.

"What's the word from the south?" asked Cadfael, observing the momentary cloud. "It seems Bishop Henry's conference came to precious little in the end."

Henry of Blois, bishop of Winchester and papal legate, was the king's younger brother, and had been his staunch adherent until Stephen had affronted, attacked and gravely offended the church in the persons of certain of its bishops. Where Bishop Henry's personal allegiance now rested was matter for some speculation, since his cousin the Empress Maud had actually arrived in England and ensconced herself securely with her faction in the west, based upon the city of Gloucester. An exceedingly able, ambitious and practical cleric might well feel some sympathy upon both sides, and a great deal more exasperation with both sides; and it was consistent with his situation, torn between kin, that he should have spent all the spring and summer months of this year trying his best to get them to come together sensibly, and make some arrangement for the future that should appease, if not satisfy, both claims, and give England a credible government and some prospect of the restoration of law. He had done his best, and even managed to bring representatives of both parties to meet near Bath only a month or so ago. But nothing had come of it.

"Though it stopped the fighting," said Hugh wryly, "at least for a while. But no, there's no fruit to gather."

"As we heard it," said Cadfael, "the empress was willing to have her claim laid before the church as judge, and Stephen was not."

"No marvel!" said Hugh, and grinned briefly at the thought. "He is in possession, she is not. In any submission to trail, he has all to lose, she has nothing at stake, and something to gain. Even a hung judgement would reflect she is no fool. And my king, God give him better sense, has affronted the church, which is not slow to avenge itself. No, there was nothing to be hoped for there. Bishop Henry is bound away into France at this moment, he hasn't given up hope, he's after the backing of the French King and Count Theobald of Normandy. He'll be busy these next weeks, working out some propositions for peace with them, and come back armed to accost both these enemies again. To tell the truth, he hoped for more backing here than ever he got, from the north above all. But they held their tongues and stayed at home."

"Chester?" hazarded Cadfael.

Earl Ranulf of Chester was an independent-minded demi-king in a strong northern palatine, and married to a daughter of the earl of Gloucester, the empress's half-brother and chief champion in this fight, but he had grudges against both factions, and had kept a cautious peace in his own realm so far, without committing himself to arms for either party.

"He and his half-brother, William of Roumare. Roumare has large holdings in Lincolnshire, and the two between them are a force to be reckoned with. They've held the balance, up there, granted, but they could have done more. Well, we can be grateful even for a passing truce. And we can hope."

Hope was in no very generous supply in England during these hard years, Cadfael reflected ruefully. But do him justice, Henry of Blois was trying his best to bring order out of chaos. Henry was proof positive that there is a grand career to be made in the world by early assumption of the cowl. Monk of Cluny, abbot of Glastonbury, bishop of Winchester, papal legate—a rise as abrupt and spectacular as a rainbow. True, he was a king's nephew to start with, and owed his rapid advancement to the old king Henry. Able younger sons from lesser families, choosing the cloister and the habit could not all expect the mitre, within or without their abbeys. That brittle youngster with the passionate mouth and the green-flecked eyes, for instance—how far was he likely to get on the road to power?

"Hugh," said Cadfael, damping down his brazier with a turf to keep it live but sleepy, in case he should want it later, "what do you know of the Aspleys of Aspley? Down the fringe of the Long Forest, I fancy, no great way from the town, but solitary."

"Not so solitary," said Hugh, mildly surprised by

the query. "There are three neighbour manors there, all grown from what began as one assart. They all held from the great earl, they all hold from the crown now. He's taken the name Aspley. His grandsire was Saxon to the finger-ends, but a solid man, and Earl Roger took him into favour and left him his land. They're Saxon still, but they'd taken his salt, and were loyal to it and went with the earldom when it came to the crown. This lord took a Norman wife and she brought him a manor somewhere to the north, beyond Nottingham, but Aspley is still the head of his honour. Why, what's Aspley to you?"

"A shape on a horse in the rain," said Cadfael simply. "He's brought us his younger son, heaven-bent or hell-bent on the cloistered life. I wondered why, that's the truth of it."

"Why?" Hugh shrugged and smiled. "A small honour, and an elder brother. There'll be no land for him, unless he has the martial bent and sets out to carve some for himself. And cloister and church are no bad prospects. A sharp lad could get farther that way than hiring out a sword. Where's the mystery?"

And there, vivid in Cadfael's mind, was the still young and vigorous figure of Henry of Blois to point the judgement. But was that stiff and quivering boy the stuff of government?

"What like is the father?" he asked, sitting down beside his friend on the broad bench against the wall of his workshop.

"From a family older than Ethelred, and proud as

the devil himself, for all he has but two manors to his
name. Princes kept their own local courts in content,
then. There are such houses still, in the hill lands and
the forests. I suppose he must be some years past
fifty," said Hugh, pondering placidly enough over his
dutiful studies of the lands and lords under his vigi-
lance in these uneasy times. "His reputation and word
stand high. I never saw the sons. There'd be five or
six years between them, I fancy. Your sprig would be
what age?"

"Nineteen, so he's reported."

"What frets you about him?" asked Hugh, undisturbed though perceptive; and he slanted a brief
glance along his shoulder at Brother Cadfael's blunt
profile, and waited without impatience.

"His tameness," said Cadfael, and checked himself
at finding his imagination, rather than his tongue, so
unguarded. "Since by nature he is wild," he went on
firmly, "with a staring eye on him like a falcon or a
pheasant, and a brow like an overhanging rock. And
folds his hands and clips his lids like a maidservant
scolded!"

"He practises his craft," said Hugh easily, "and
studies his abbot. So they do, the sharp lads. You've
seen them come and go."

"So I have." Ineptly enough, some of them, ambitious young fellows gifted with the means to go so far
and no farther, and bidding far beyond their abilities.
He had no such feeling about this one. That hunger
and thirst after acceptance, beyond rescue, seemed to

him an end in itself, a measure of desperation. He doubted if the falcon-eyes looked beyond at all, or saw any horizon outside the enclosing wall of the enclave. "Those who want a door to close behind them, Hugh, must be either escaping into the world within or from the world without. There is a difference. But do you know a way of telling one from the other?"

CHAPTER TWO

❧

THERE WAS A FAIR CROP OF OCTOBER APPLES THAT year in the orchards along the Gaye, and since the weather had briefly turned unpredictable, they had to take advantage of three fine days in succession that came in the middle of the week, and harvest the fruit while it was dry. Accordingly they mustered all hands to the work, choir monks and servants, and all the novices except the schoolboys. Pleasant work enough, especially for the youngsters who were allowed to climb trees with approval, and kilt their habits to the knee, in a brief return to boyhood.

One of the tradesmen of the town had a hut close to the corner of the abbey lands along the Gaye, where he kept goats and bees, and he had leave to cut fodder for his beasts under the orchard trees, his own grazing being somewhat limited. He was out there that day with a sickle, brushing the longer grass, last cut of the year, from round the boles, where the scythe could not be safely used. Cadfael passed the time of day with him pleasantly, and sat down with him under an apple tree to exchange the leisured civilities proper to such a meeting. There were very few burgesses in Shrewsbury he did not know, and this good man had a flock of children to ask after.

Cadfael had it on his conscience afterwards that it might well have been his neighbourly attentions that caused his companion to lay down his sickle under the tree, and forget to pick it up again when his youngest son, a frogling knee-high, came hopping to call his father to his midday bread and ale. However that might be, leave it he did, in the tussocky grass braced against the bole. And Cadfael rose a little stiffly, and went to the picking of apples, while his fellow-gossip hoisted his youngest by standing leaps back to the hut, and listened to his chatter all the way.

The straw baskets were filling merrily by then. Not the largest harvest Cadfael had known from this orchard, but a welcome one all the same. A mellow, half-misty, half-sunlit day, the river running demure and still between them and the high, turretted silhouette of the town, and the ripe scent of harvest, compounded of fruit, dry grasses, seeding plants and summer-warmed trees growing sleepy towards their rest, heavy and sweet on the air and in the nose; no marvel if constraints were lifted and hearts lightened. The hands laboured and the minds were eased. Cadfael caught sight of Brother Meriet working eagerly, heavy sleeves turned back from round, brown, shapely young arms, skirts kilted to smooth brown knees, the cowl shaken low on his shoulders, and his untonsured head shaggy and dark and vivid against the sky. His profile shone clear, the hazel eyes wide and unveiled. He was smiling. No shared, confiding smile, only a witness to his own content, and that, perhaps, brief and vulnerable enough.

Cadfael lost sight of him, plodding modestly ahead with his own efforts. It is perfectly possible to be spiritually involved in private prayer while working hard at gathering apples, but he was only too well aware that he himself was fully absorbed in the sensuous pleasure of the day, and from what he had seen of Brother Meriet's face, so was that young man. And very well it suited him.

It was unfortunate that the heaviest and most ungainly of the novices should choose to climb the very tree beneath which the sickle was lying, and still more unfortunate that he should venture to lean out too far in his efforts to reach one cluster of fruit. The tree was of the tip-bearing variety, and the branches weakened by a weighty crop. A limb broke under the strain, and down came the climber in a flurry of falling leaves and crackling twigs, straight on to the upturned blade of the sickle.

It was a spectacular descent, and half a dozen of his fellows heard the crashing fall and came running, Cadfael among the first. The young man lay motionless in the tangle of his habit, arms and legs thrown broadcast, a long gash in the left side of his gown, and a bright stream of blood dappling his sleeve and the grass under him. If ever a man presented the appearance of sudden and violent death, he did. No wonder the unpracticed young stood aghast with cries of dismay on seeing him.

Brother Meriet was at some distance, and had not heard the fall. He came in innocence between the trees, hefting a great basket of fruit towards the riverside path. His gaze, for once open and untroubled, fell upon the sprawled figure, the slit gown, the gush of blood. He baulked like a shot horse, starting back with heels stuttering in the turf. The basket fell from his hands and spilled apples all about the sward.

He made no sound at all, but Cadfael, who was kneeling beside the fallen novice, looked up, startled by the rain of fruit, into a face withdawn from life and daylight into the clay-stillness of death. The fixed eyes were green glass with no flame behind them. They stared and stared unblinking at what seemed a stabbed man, dead in the grass. All the lines of the mask shrank, sharpened, whitened, as though they would never move or live again.

"Fool boy!" shouted Cadfael, furious at being subjected to such alarm and shock when he already had one fool boy on his hands. "Pick up your apples and get them and yourself out of here, and out of my light, if you can do nothing better to help. Can you not see the lad's done no more than knock his few wits out of his head against the bole, and skinned his ribs on the sickle? If he does bleed like a stuck pig, he's well alive, and will be."

And indeed, the victim proved it by opening one dazed eye, staring round him as if in search of the enemy who had done this to him, and becoming voluble in complaint of his injuries. The relieved circle closed round him, offering aid, and Meriet was left to gather what he had spilled, in stiff obedience, still without word or sound. The frozen mask was very slow to melt, the green eyes were veiled before ever the light revived behind them.

The sufferer's wound proved to be, as Cadfael had said, a messy but shallow graze, soon staunched and bound close with a shirt sacrificed by one of the novices, and the stout linen band from the repaired handle of one of the fruit-baskets. His knock on the head had raised a bump and given him a headache, but no worse than that. He was despatched back to the abbey as soon as he felt inclined to rise and test his legs, in the company of two of his fellows big enough and brawny enough to make a chair for him with their interlaced hands and wrists if he foundered. Nothing was left of the incident but the trampling of many feet about the patch of drying blood in the grass, and the sickle which a frightened boy came timidly to reclaim. He hovered until he could approach Cadfael alone, and was cheered and reassured at being told there was no great harm done, and no blame being urged against his father for an unfortunate oversight. Accidents will happen, even without the assistance of forgetful goat-keepers and clumsy and overweight boys.

As soon as everyone else was off his hands, Cadfael looked round for the one remaining problem. And there he was, one black-habited figure among the rest, working away steadily; just like the others, except that he kept his face averted, and while all the rest were talking shrilly about what had happened, the subsiding excitement setting them twittering like starlings, he said never a word. A certain rigour in his movements, as if a child's wooden doll had come to life; and always the high shoulder turned if anyone came near. He did not want to be observed; not, at least, until he recovered the mastery of his own face.

They carried their harvest home, to be laid out in trays in the lofts of the great barn in the grange court, for these later apples could keep until Christmas. On the way back, in good time for Vespers, Cadfael drew alongside Meriet, and kept pace with him in placid silence most of the way. He was adept at studying people while seeming to have no interest in them beyond a serene acceptance that they were in the same world with him.

"Much ado, back there," said Cadfael, essaying a kind of apology, which might have the merit of being surprising, "over a few inches of skin. I spoke you rough, brother, in haste. Bear with me! He might as easily have been what you thought him. I had that vision before me as clear as you had. Now we can both breathe the freer."

The head bent away from him turned ever so swiftly and warily to stare along a straight shoulder. The flare of the green-gold eyes was like very brief lighting, sharply snuffed out. A soft, startled voice said: "Yes, thank God! And thank you, brother!" Cadfael thought the "brother" was a dutiful but belated afterthought, but valued it none the less. "I was small use, you were right. I . . . am not accustomed . . ." said Meriet lamely.

"No, lad, why should you be? I'm well past double your age, and came late to the cowl, not like you. I have seen death in many shapes, I've been soldier and sailor in my time; in the east, in the Crusade, and for ten years after Jerusalem fell. I've seen men killed in battle. Come to that, I've killed men in battle. I never took joy in it, that I can remember, but I never drew back from it, either, having made my vows." Something was happening there beside him, he felt the young body braced to sharp attention. The mention, perhaps, of vows other than the monastic, vows which had also involved the matter of life and death? Cadfael, like a fisherman with a shy and tricky bite on his line, went on paying out small-talk, easing suspicion, engaging interest, exposing, as he did not often do, the past years of his own experience. The silence favoured by the Order ought not to be allowed to stand in the way of its greater aims, where a soul was tormenting itself on the borders of conviction. A garrulous old brother, harking back to an adventurous past, ranging half the known world—what could be more harmless, or more disarming?

"I was with Robert of Normandy's company, and a mongrel lot we were, Britons, Normans, Flemings, Scots, Bretons—name them, they were there! After the city was settled and Baldwin crowned, the most of us went home, over a matter of two or three years, but I had taken to the sea by then, and I stayed. There were pirates ranged those coasts, we had always work to do."

The young thing beside him had not missed a word of what had been said, he quivered like an untrained but thoroughbred hound hearing the horn, though he said nothing.

"And in the end I came home, because it was home and I felt the need of it," said Cadfael. "I served here and there as a free man-at-arms for a while and then I was ripe, and it was time. But I had had my way through the world."

"And now, what do you do here?" wondered Meriet.

"I grow herbs, and dry them, and make remedies for all the ills that visit us. I physic a great many souls besides those of us within."

"And that satisfies you?" It was a muted cry of protest; it would not have satisfied him.

"To heal men, after years of injuring them? What could be more fitting? A man does what he must do," said Cadfael carefully, "whether the duty he has taken on himself is to fight, or to salvage poor souls from the fighting, to kill, to die or to heal. There are many will claim to tell you what is due from you, but only one who can shear through the many, and reach the truth. And that is you, by what light falls for you to show the way. Do you know what is hardest for me here of all I have vowed? Obedience. And I am old."

And have had my fling, and a wild one, was implied. And what am I trying to do now, he wondered, to warn him off pledging too soon what he cannot give, what he has not got to give?

"It is true!" said Meriet abruptly. "Every man must do what is laid on him to do and not question. If that is obedience?" And suddenly he turned upon Brother Cadfael a countenance altogether young, devout and exalted, as though he had just kissed, as once Cadfael had, the crossed hilt of his own poniard, and pledged his life's blood to some cause as holy to him as the deliverance of the city of God.

Cadfael had Meriet on his mind the rest of that day, and after Vespers he confided to Brother Paul the uneasiness he felt in recalling the day's disaster; for Paul had been left behind with the children, and the reports that had reached him had been concerned solely with Brother Wolstan's fall and injuries, not with the unaccountable horror they had aroused in Meriet.

"Not that there's anything strange in shying at the sight of a man lying in his blood, they were all shaken by it. But he—what he felt was surely extreme."

Brother Paul shook his head doubtfully over his difficult charge. "Everything he feels is extreme. I don't find in him the calm and the certainty that should go with a true vocation. Oh, he is duty itself, whatever I ask of him he does, whatever task I set him he performs, he's greedy to go faster than I lead him. I never had a more diligent student. But the others don't like him, Cadfael. He shuns them. Those who have tried to approach him say he turns from them, and is rough and short in making his escape. He'd rather go solitary. I tell you, Cadfael, I never knew a postulant pursue his novitiate with so much passion, and so little joy. Have you once seen him smile since he entered here?"

Yes, once, thought Cadfael; this afternoon before Wolstan fell, when he was picking apples in the orchard, the first time he's left the enclave since his father brought him in.

"Do you think it would be well to bring him to chapter?" he wondered dubiously.

"I did better than that, or so I hoped. With such a nature, I would not seem to be complaining where I have no just cause for complaint. I spoke to Father Abbot about him. 'Send him to me,' says Radulfus, 'and reassure him,' he says, 'that I am here to be open to any who need me, the youngest boy as surely as any of my obedientiaries, and he may approach me as his own father, without fear.' And send him I did, and told him he could open his thoughts with every confidence. And what came of it? 'Yes, Father, no, Father,

I will, Father!' And never a word blurted out from the heart. The only thing that opens his lips freely is the mention that he might be mistaken in coming here, and should consider again. That brings him to his knees fast enough. He begs to have his probation shortened, to be allowed to take his vows soon. Father Abbot read him a lecture on humility and the right use of the year's novitiate, and he took it to heart, or seemed to, and promised patience. But still he presses. Books he swallows faster than I can feed them to him, he's bent on hurrying to his vows at all costs. The slower ones resent him. Those who can keep pace with him, having the start of him by two months or more, say he scorns them. That he avoids I've seen for myself. I won't deny I'm troubled for him."

So was Cadfael, though he did not say how deeply.

"I couldn't but wonder . . ." went on Paul thoughtfully. "Tell him he may come to me as to his father, without fear, says the abbot. What sort of reassurance should that be to a young fellow new from home? Did you see them, Cadfael, when they came? The pair of them together?"

"I did," said Cadfael cautiously, "though only for moments as they lighted down and shook off the rain, and went within."

"When did you need more than moments?" said Brother Paul. "As to his own father, indeed! I was present throughout, I saw them part. Without a tear, with few words and hard, his sire went hence and left him to me. Many, I know, have done so before, fearing the parting as much as their young could fear it, perhaps more." Brother Paul had never engendered, christened, nursed, tended young of his own, and yet there had been some quality in him that the old Abbot Heribert, no subtle nor very wise man, had rightly detected, and confided to him the boys and the novices in a trust he had never betrayed. "But I never saw one go without the kiss," said Paul. "Never before. As Aspley did."

In the darkness of the long dortoir, almost two hours past Compline, the only light was the small lamp left burning at the head of the night stairs into the church, and the only sound the occasional sigh of a sleeper turning, or the uneasy shifting of a wakeful brother. At the head of the great room Prior Robert had his cell, commanding the whole length of the open corridor between the two rows of cells. There had been times when some of the younger brothers, not yet purged of the old Adam, had been glad of the fact that the prior was a heavy sleeper. Sometimes Cadfael himself had been known to slip out by way of the night stairs, for reasons he considered good enough. His first encounters with Hugh Beringar, before that young man won his Aline or achieved his office, had been by night, and without leave. And never regretted! What Cadfael did not regret, he found grave difficulty in remembering to confess. Hugh had been a puzzle to him then, an ambiguous young man who might be either friend or enemy. Proof upon proof since then sealed him friend, the closest and dearest.

In the silence of this night after the apple-gathering, Cadfael lay awake and thought seriously, not about Hugh Beringar, but about Brother Meriet, who had recoiled with desperate revulsion from the image of a stabbed man lying dead in the grass. An illusion! The injured novice lay sleeping in his bed now, not more than three or four cells from Meriet, uneasily, perhaps, with his ribs swathed and sore, but there was not a sound from where he lay, he must be fathoms deep. Did Meriet sleep half as well? And where had he seen, or why had he so vividly imagined, a dead man in his blood?

The quiet, with more than an hour still to pass before midnight, was absolute. Even the restless sleepers had subsided into peace. The boys, by the abbot's orders separated from their elders, slept in a small room at the end of the dortoir, and Brother Paul occupied the cell that shielded their private place. Abbot Radulfus knew and understood the unforseen dangers that lurked in ambush for celibate souls, however innocent.

Brother Cadfael slept without quite sleeping, much as he had done many a time in camp and on the battlefield, or wrapped in his sea-cloak on deck, under the stars of the Midland Sea. He had talked himself back into the east and the past, alerted to danger, even where no danger could possibly be.

The scream came rendingly, shredding the darkness

and the silence, as if two demoniac hands had torn
apart by force the slumbers of all present here, and
the very fabric of the night. It rose into the roof, and
fluttered ululating against the beams of the ceiling,
starting echoes wild as bats. There were words in it,
but no distinguishable word, it gabbled and stormed
like a malediction, broken by sobbing pauses to draw
in breath.

Cadfael was out of his bed before it rose to its
highest shriek, and groping into the passage in the direction from which it came. Every soul was awake by
then, he heard a babble of terrified voices and a frantic gabbling of prayers, and Prior Robert, slow and
sleepy, demanding querulously who dared so disturb
the peace. Beyond where Brother Paul slept, children's voices joined in the cacophony; the two
youngest boys had been startled awake and were
wailing their terror, and no wonder. Never had their
sleep here been so rudely shattered, and the youngest
was no more than seven years old. Paul was out of his
cell and flying to comfort them. The clamour and
complaint continued, loud and painful, by turns
threatening and threatened. Saints converse in
tongues with God. With whom did this fierce, violent
voice converse, against whom did it contend, and in
what language of pain, anger and defiance?

Cadfael had taken his candle out with him, and
made for the lamp by the night-stairs to kindle it,
thrusting his way through the quaking darkness and
shoving aside certain aimless, agitated bodies that

blundered about in the passage, blocking the way. The din of shouting, cursing and lamenting, still in the incoherent tongue of sleep, battered at his ears all the way, and the children howled piteously in their small room. He reached the lamp, and his taper flared and burned up steadily, lighting staring faces, openmouthed and wide-eyed, and the lofty beams of the roof above. He knew already where to look for the disturber of the peace. He elbowed aside those who blundered between, and carried his candle into Meriet's cell. Less confident souls came timidly after, circling and staring, afraid to approach too near.

Brother Meriet sat bolt upright in his bed, quivering and babbling, hands clenched into fists in his blanket, head reared back and eyes tight-closed. There was some reassurance in that, for however tormented, he was still asleep, and if the nature of his sleep could be changed, he might wake unscathed. Prior Robert was not far behind the starers now, and would not hesitate to seize and shake the rigid shoulder readiest to his hand, in peremptory displeasure. Cadfael eased an arm cautiously round the braced shoulders instead and held him close. Meriet shuddered and the rhythm of this distressful crying hiccuped and faltered. Cadfael set down his candle, and spread his palm over the young man's forehead, urging him gently down to his forsaken pillow. The wild crying subsided into a child's querulous whimper, stuttered and ceased. The stiff body yielded, softened, slid down into the bed. By the time Prior Robert reached the bedside, Meriet lay in limp innocence, fast asleep and free of his incubus.

Brother Paul brought him to chapter next day, as needing guidance in the proper treatment of one so clearly in dire spiritual turmoil. For his own part, Paul would have been inclined to content himself with paying special attention to the young man for a day or two, trying to draw him what inward trouble could have caused him such a nightmare, and accompanying him in special prayers for his peace of mind. But Prior Robert would have no delays. Granted the novice had suffered a shocking and alarming experience the previous day, in the accident to his fellow, but so had all the rest of the labourers in the orchard, and none of them had awakened the whole dortoir with his bellowings in consequence. Robert held that such manifestations, even in sleep, amounted to wilful acts of self-display, issuing from some deep and tenacious demon within, and the flesh could be best eased of its devil by the scourge. Brother Paul stood between him and the immediate use of the discipline in this case. Let the matter go to the abbot.

Meriet stood in the centre of the gathering with eyes cast down and hands folded, while his involuntary offence was freely discussed about his ears. He had awakened like the rest, such as had so far recovered their peace as to sleep again after the disturbance, when the bell roused them for Matins, and because of the enjoined silence as they filed down the night-stairs he had known of no reason why so many and such wary eyes should be turned upon him, or why his companions should so anxiously leave a great gap between themselves and him. So he had pleaded when finally enlightened about his misbehaviour, and Cadfael believed him.

"I bring him before you, not as having knowingly committed any offence," said Brother Paul, "but as being in need of help which I am not fitted to attempt alone. It is true, as Brother Cadfael has told us—for I myself was not with the party yesterday—that the accident to Brother Wolstan caused great alarm to all, and Brother Meriet came upon the scene without warning, and suffered a severe shock, fearing the poor young man was dead. It may be that this alone preyed upon his mind, and came as a dream to disturb his sleep, and no more is needed now than calm and prayer. I ask for guidance."

"Do you tell me," Radulfus, with a thoughtful eye on the submissive figure before him, "that he was asleep throughout? Having roused the entire dortoir?"

"He slept through all," said Cadfael firmly. "To have shaken him awake in that state might have done him great harm, but he did not wake. When persuaded, with care, he sank into a deeper level of sleep, and was healed from his distress. I doubt if he recalls anything of his dream, if he did dream. I am sure he knew nothing of what had happened, and the flurry he had caused, until he was told this morning."

"That is true, Father," said Meriet, looking up

briefly and anxiously. "They have told me what I did, and I must believe it, and God knows I am sorry. But I swear I knew nothing of my offence. If I had dreams, evil dreams, I recall nothing of them. I know no reason why I should so disturb the dortoir. It is as much a mystery to me as to any. I can but hope it will not happen again."

The abbot frowned and pondered. "It is strange that so violent a disturbance should arise in your mind without cause. I think, rather, that the shock of seeing Brother Wolstan lying in his blood does provide a source of deep distress. But that you should have so little power to accept, and to control your own spirit, does that bode well, son, for a true vocation?"

It was the one suggested threat that seemed to alarm Meriet. He sank to his knees, with an abrupt and agitated grace that brought the ample habit swirling about him like a cloak, and lifted a strained face and pleading hands to the abbot.

"Father, help me, believe me! All my wish is to enter here and be at peace, to do all that the Rule asks of me, to cut off all the threads that bind me to my past. If I offend, if I transgress, willingly or no, wittingly or no, medicine me, punish me, lay on me whatever penance you see fit, only don't cast me out!"

"We do not easily despair of a postulant," said Radulfus, "or turn our backs on one in need of time and help. There are medicines to soothe a too-fevered mind. Brother Cadfael has such. But they are aids that should be used only in grave need, while you seek better cures in prayer, and in the mastery of yourself."

"I could better come to terms," said Meriet vehemently, "if you would but shorten the period of my probation, and let me in to the fullness of this life. Then there would be no more doubt or fear . . ."

Or hope? Wondered Cadfael, watching him; and went on to wonder if the same thought had not entered the abbot's mind.

"The fullness of this life," said Radulfus sharply, "must be deserved. You are not ready yet to take vows. Both you and we must practise patience some time yet before you will be fit to join us. The more hotly you hasten, the more will you fall behind. Remember that, and curb your impetuosity. For this time, we will wait. I accept that you have not offended willingly, I trust that you may never again suffer or cause such disruption. Go now, Brother Paul will tell you our will for you."

Meriet cast one flickering glance round all the considering faces, and departed, leaving the brothers to debate what was best to be done with him. Prior Robert, on his mettle, and quick to recognize a humility in which there was more than a little arrogance, felt that the mortification of the flesh, whether by hard labour, a bread and water diet, or flagellation, might help to concentrate and purify a troubled spirit. Several took the simplest line: since the boy had never intended wrong, and yet was a menace to others, punishment was undeserved, but segregation from his fellows might be considered justified, in the interests of the general peace. Yet even that might seem to him a punishment, Brother Paul pointed out.

"It may well be," said the abbot finally, "that we trouble ourselves needlessly. How many of us have never had one ill night, and broken it with night-mares? Once is but once. We have none of us come to any harm, not even the children. Why should we not trust that we have seen both the first and the last of it? Two doors can be closed between the dortoir and the boys, should there again be need. And should there again be need, then further measures can be taken."

Three nights passed peacefully, but on the fourth there was another commotion in the small hours, less alarming than on the first occasion, but scarcely less disturbing. No wild outcry this time, but twice or thrice, at intervals, there were words spoken loudly and in agitation, and such as were distinguishable were deeply disquieting, and caused his fellow-novices to hold off from him with even deeper suspicion.

"He cried out, 'No, no, no!' several times," reported his nearest neighbour, complaining to Brother Paul next morning. "And then he said, 'I will, I will!' and something about obedience and duty . . . Then after all was quiet again he suddenly cried out, 'Blood!' And I looked in, because he had started me awake again, and he was sitting up in bed wringing his hands. After that he sank down again, there was nothing more. But to whom was he talking? I dread there's a devil has hold of him. What else can it be?"

Brother Paul was short with such wild suppositions, but could not deny the words he himself had heard, nor the disquiet they aroused in him. Meriet again was astonished and upset at hearing that he had troubled the dortoir a second time, and owned to no recollection of any bad dream, or even so small and understandable a thing as a belly-ache that might have disrupted his own rest.

"No harm done this time," said Brother Paul to Cadfael, after High Mass, "for it was not loud, and we had the door closed on the children. And I've damped down their gossip as best I can. But for all that, they go in fear of him. They need their peace, too, and he's a threat to it. They say there's a devil at him in his sleep, and it was he brought it here among them, and who knows which of them it will prey on next? The devil's novice, I've heard him called. Oh, I put a stop to that, at least aloud. But it's what they're thinking."

Cadfael himself had heard the tormented voice, however subdued this time, had heard the pain and desperation in it, and was assured beyond doubt that for all these things there was a human reason. But what wonder if these untravelled young things, credulous and superstitious, dreaded a reason that was not human?

That was well into October and the same day that Canon Eluard of Winchester, on his journey south from Chester, came with his secretary and his groom to spend a night or two for repose in Shrewsbury. And not for simple reasons of religious policy or courtesy, but precisely because the novice Meriet Aspley was housed within the walls of Saint Peter and Saint Paul.

CHAPTER THREE

ELUARD OF WINCHESTER WAS A BLACK CANON OF
considerable learning and several masterships, some
from French schools. It was this wide scholarship and
breadth of mind which had recommended him to
Bishop Henry of Blois, and raised him to be one of the
three highest ranking and best trusted of that great
prelate's household clergy, and left him now in charge
of much of the bishop's pending business while his
principal was absent in France.

Brother Cadfael ranked too low in the hierarchy to be
invited to the abbot's table when there were guests of
such stature. That occasioned him no heart-burning, and
cost him little in first-hand knowledge of what went on,
since it was taken for granted that Hugh Beringar, in the
absence of the sheriff, would be present at any meeting
involving political matters, and would infallibly acquaint
his other self with whatever emerged of importance.

Hugh came to the hut in the herb garden, yawning, after accompanying the canon to his apartment in the guest-hall.

"An impressive man, I don't wonder Bishop Henry values him. Have you seen him, Cadfael?"

"I saw him arrive." A big, portly, heavily-built man who nonetheless rode like a huntsman from his childhood and a warrior from puberty; a rounded, bushy tonsure on a round, solid head, and a dark shadow about the shaven jowls when he lighted down in early evening. Rich, fashionable but austere clothing, his only jewellery a cross and ring, but both of rare artistry. And he had a jaw on him and an authoritative eye, shrewd but tolerant. "What's he doing in these parts, in his bishop's absence overseas?"

"Why, the very same his bishop is up to in Normandy, soliciting the help of every powerful man he can get hold of, to try and produce some plan that will save England from being dismembered utterly. While he's after the support of king and duke in France, Henry wants just as urgently to know where Earl Ranulf and his brother stand. They never paid heed to the meeting in the summer, so it seems Bishop Henry sent one of his men north to be civil to the pair of them and make sure of their favour, just before he set off for France—one of his own household clerics, a young man marked for advancement, Peter Clemence. And Peter Clemence has not returned. Which could mean any number of things, but with time lengthening out and never a word from him or from either of that pair in the north concerning him, Canon Eluard began to be restive. There's a kind of truce in the south and west, while the two sides wait and watch each other, so Eluard felt he might as well set off in person to Chester, to find out what goes on up there, and what's become of the bishop's envoy."

"And what *has* become of him?" asked Cadfael shrewdly. "For his lordship, it seems, is now on his way south again to join King Stephen. And what sort of welcome did he get in Chester?"

"As warm and civil as heart could wish. And for what my judgement is worth, Canon Eluard, however loyal he may be to Bishop Henry's efforts for peace, is more inclined to Stephen's side than to the empress, and is off back to Westminster now to tell the King he might be wise to strike while the iron's hot, and go north in person and offer a few sweetmeats to keep Chester and Roumare as well-disposed to him as they are. A manor or two and a pleasant title—Roumare is as good as earl of Lincoln now, why not call·him so?— could secure his position there. So, at any rate, Eluard seems to have gathered. Their loyalty is pledged over and over. And for all his wife is daughter to Robert of Gloucester, Ranulf did stay snug at home when Robert brought over his imperial sister to take the field a year and more ago. Yes, it seems the situation there could hardly be more to the canon's satisfaction, now that it's stated. But as for why it was not stated a month or so ago, by the mouth of Peter Clemence returning . . .

Simple enough! The man never got there, and they never got his embassage."

"As sound a reason as any for not answering it," said Cadfael, unsmiling, and eyed his friend's saturnine visage with narrowed attention. "How far did he get on his way, then?" There were wild places enough in this disrupted England where a man could vanish, for no more than the coat he wore or the horse he rode. There were districts where manors had been deserted and run wild, and forests had been left unmanned, and whole villages, too exposed to danger, had been abandoned and left to rot. Yet the north had suffered less than the south and west by and large, and lords like Ranulf of Chester had kept their lands relatively stable thus far.

"That's what Eluard has been trying to find out on his way back, stage by stage along the most likely route a man would take. For certainly he never came near Chester. And stage by stage our canon has drawn blank until he came into Shropshire. Never a trace of Clemence, hide, hair or horse, all through Cheshire."

"And none as far as Shrewsbury?" For Hugh had more to tell, he was frowning down thoughtfully into the beaker he held between his thin, fine hands.

"Beyond Shrewsbury, Cadfael, though only just beyond. He's turned back a matter of a few miles to us, for reason enough. The last he can discover of Peter Clemence is that he stayed the night of the eighth day of September with a household to which he's a distant cousin on the wife's side. And where do you think that was? At Leoric Aspley's manor, down in the edge of the Long Forest."

"Do you tell me!" Cadfael stared, sharply attentive now. The eighth of the month, and a week or so later comes the steward Fremund with his lord's request that the younger son of the house should be received, at his own earnest wish, into the cloister. *Post hoc* is not *propter hoc*, however. And in any case, what connection could there possibly be between one man's sudden discovery that he felt a vocation, and another man's overnight stay and morning departure? "Canon Eluard knew he would make one of his halts there? The kinship was known?"

"Both the kinship and his intent, yes, known both to Bishop Henry and to Eluard. The whole manor saw him come, and have told freely how he was entertained there. The whole manor, or very near, saw him off on his journey next morning. Aspley and his steward rode the first mile with him, with the household and half the neighbors to see them go. No question, he left there whole and brisk and well-mounted."

"How far to his next night's lodging? And was he expected there?" For if he had announced his coming, then someone should have been enquiring for him long since.

"According to Aspley, he intended one more halt at Whitchurch, a good halfway to his destination, but he knew he could find easy lodging there and had not sent word before. There's no trace to be found of him there, no one saw or heard of him."

"So between here and Whitchurch the man is lost?"

"Unless he changed his plans and his route, for which, God knows, there could be reasons, even here in my writ," said Hugh ruefully, "though I hope it is not so. We keep the best order anywhere in this realm, or so I claim, challenge me who will, but even so I doubt it good enough to make passage safe everywhere. He may have heard something that caused him to turn aside. But the bleak truth of it is, he's lost. And all too long!"

"And Canon Eluard wants him found?"

"Dead or alive," said Hugh grimly. "For so will Henry want him found, and an account paid by someone for his price, for he valued him."

"And the search is laid upon you?" said Cadfael.

"Not in such short terms, No. Eluard is a fair-minded man, he takes a part of the load upon him, and doesn't grudge. But this shire is my business, under the sheriff, and I pick up my share of the burden. Here is a scholar and a cleric vanished where my writ runs. That I do not like," said Hugh, in the ominously soft voice that had a silver luster about it like bared steel.

Cadfael came to the question that was uppermost in his mind. "And why, then, having the witness of Aspley and all his houses at his disposal, did Canon Eluard feel it needful to turn back these few miles to Shrewsbury?" But already he knew the answer.

"Because, my friend, you have here the younger son of that house, new in his novitiate. He is thorough, this Canon Eluard. He wants word from even the stray from that tribe. Who knows which of all that manor may not have noticed the one thing needful?"

It was a piercing thought; it stuck in Cadfael's mind, quivering like a dart. Who knows, indeed? "He has not questioned the boy yet?"

"No, he would not disrupt the evening offices for such a matter—nor his good supper, either," added Hugh with a brief grin. "But tomorrow he'll have him into the guests' parlour and go over the affair with him, before he goes on southward to join the king at Westminster, and prompt him to go and make sure of Chester and Roumare, while he can."

"And you will be present at that meeting," said Cadfael with certainty.

"I shall be present. I need to know whatever any man can tell me to the point, if a man has vanished by foul means within my jurisdiction. This is now as much my business as it is Eluard's."

"You'll tell me," said Cadfael confidently, "what the lad has to say, and how he bears himself?"

"I'll tell you," said Hugh, and rose to take his leave.

As it turned out, Meriet bore himself with stoical calm during that interview in the parlour, in the presence of Abbot Radulfus, Canon Eluard and Hugh Beringar, the powers here of both church and state. He answered questions simply and directly, without apparent hesitation.

Yes, he had been present when Master Clemence came to break his journey at Aspley. No, he had not been expected, he came unheralded, but the house of his kinsmen was open to him whenever he would. No, he had not been there more than once before as a guest, some years ago, he was now a man of affairs, and kept about his lord's person. Yes, Meriet himself had stabled the guest's horse, and groomed, watered and fed him, while the women had made Master Clemence welcome within. He was the son of a cousin of Meriet's mother, who was some two years dead now—the Norman side of the family. And his entertainment? The best they could lay before him in food and drink, music after the supper, and one more guest at the table, the daughter of the neighbouring manor who was affianced to Meriet's elder brother Nigel. Meriet spoke of the occasion with wide-open eyes and clear, still countenance.

"Did Master Clemence say what his errand was?" asked Hugh suddenly. "Tell where he was bound and for what purpose?"

"He said he was on the bishop of Winchester's business. I don't recall that he said more than that while I was there. But there was music after I left the hall, and they were still seated. I went to see that all was done properly in the stable. He may have said more to my father."

"And in the morning?" asked Canon Eluard.

"We had all things ready to serve him when he rose, for he said he must be in the saddle early. My father and Fremund, our steward, with two grooms, rode with him the first mile of his way, and I, and the servants, and Isouda . . ."

"Isouda?" said Hugh, pricking his ears at a new

name. Meriet had passed by the mention of his brother's betrothed without naming her.

"She is not my sister, she is heiress to the manor of Fortei, that borders ours on the southern side. My father is her guardian and manages her lands, and she lives with us." A younger sister of small account, his tone said, for once quite unguarded. "She was with us to watch Master Clemence from our doors with all honour, as is due."

"And you saw no more of him?"

"I did not go with them. But my father rode a piece more than is needful, for courtesy, and left him on a good track."

Hugh had still one more question. "You tended his horse. What like was it?"

"A fine beast, not above three years old, and mettlesome." Meriet's voice kindled into enthusiasm. "A tall dark bay, with white blaze on his face from forehead to nose, and two white forefeet."

Noteworthy enough, then, to be readily recognized when found, and moreover, to be a prize for someone. "If somebody wanted the man out of this world, for whatever reason," said Hugh to Cadfael afterwards in the herb garden, "he would still have a very good use for such a horse as that. And somewhere between here and Whitchurch that beast must be, and where he is there'll be threads to take up and follow. If the worst comes to it, a dead man can be hidden, but a live horse is going to come within some curious soul's sight, sooner or later, and sooner or later I shall get wind of it."

Cadfael was hanging up under the eaves of his hut the rustling bunches of herbs newly dried out at the end of the summer, but he was giving his full attention to Hugh's report at the same time. Meriet had been dismissed without, on the face of it, adding anything to what Canon Eluard had already elicited from the rest of the Aspley household. Peter Clemence had come and gone in good health, well-mounted, and with the protection of the bishop of Winchester's formidable name about him. He had been escorted civilly a mile on his way. And vanished.

"Give me, if you can, the lad's answers in his very words," requested Cadfael. "Where there's nothing of interest to be found in the content, it's worth taking a close look at the manner."

Hugh had an excellent memory, and reproduced Meriet's replies even to the intonation. "But there's nothing there, barring a very good description of the horse. Every question he answered and still told us nothing, since he knows nothing."

"Ah, but he did not answer every question," said Cadfael. "And I think he may have told us a few notable things, though whether they have any bearing on Master Clemence's vanishing seems dubious. Canon Eluard asked him: 'And you saw no more of him?' And the lad said: *'I did not go with them.'* But he did not say he had seen no more of the departed guest. And again, when he spoke of the servants and this Foriet girl, all gathered to speed the departure with him, he did not say 'and my brother'. Nor did he say that his brother had ridden with the escort."

"All true," agreed Hugh, not greatly impressed. "But none of these need mean anything at all. Very few of us watch every word, to leave no possible detail in doubt."

"That I grant. Yet it does no harm to note such small things, and wonder. A man not accustomed to lying, but brought up against the need, will evade if he can. Well, if you find your horse in some stable thirty miles or more from here, there'll be no need for you or me to probe behind every word young Meriet speaks, for the hunt will have outrun him and all his family. And they can forget Peter Clemence—barring the occasional Mass, perhaps, for a kinsman's soul."

Canon Eluard departed for London, secretary, groom, baggage and all, bent on urging King Stephen to pay a diplomatic visit to the north before Christmas, and secure his interest with the two powerful brothers who ruled there almost from coast to coast. Ranulf of Chester and William of Roumare had elected to spend the feast at Lincoln with their ladies, and a little judicious flattery and the dispensing of a modest gift or two might bring in a handsome harvest. The canon had paved the way already, and meant to make the return journey in the king's party.

"And on the way back," he said, taking leave of Hugh in the great court of the abbey, "I shall turn aside from his Grace's company and return here, in the hope

that by then you will have some news for me. The
bishop will be in great anxiety."

He departed, and Hugh was left to pursue the search
for Peter Clemence, which had now become, for all
practical purposes, the search for his bay horse. And
pursue it he did, with vigour, deploying as many men
as he could muster along the most frequented ways
north, visiting lords of manors, invading stables, questioning travellers. When the more obvious halting
places yielded nothing, they spread out into wilder
country. In the north of the shire the land was flatter,
with less forest but wide expanses of heath, moorland
and scrub, and several large tracts of peat-moss, deso-
late and impossible to cultivate, though the locals who
knew the safe dykes cut and stacked fuel there for their
winter use.

The manor of Alkington lay on the edge of this
wilderness of dark-brown pools and quaking mosses
and tangled bush, under a pale, featureless sky. It was
sadly run down from its former value, its ploughlands
shrunken, no place to expect to find, grazing in the tenant's paddock, a tall bay thoroughbred fit for a prince to
ride. But it was there that Hugh found him, white-
blazed face, white forefeet and all, grown somewhat
shaggy and ill-groomed, but otherwise in very good
condition.

There was as little concealment about the tenant's
behaviour as about his open display of his prize. He
was a free man, and held as subtenant under the lord of

Wem, and he was willing and ready to account for the unexpected guest in his stable.

"And you see him, my lord, in better fettle than he was when he came here, for he'd run wild some time, by all accounts, and devil a man of us knew whose he was or where he came from. There's a man of mine has an assart west of here, an island on the moss, and cuts turf there for himself and others. That's what he was about when he caught sight of yon creature wandering loose, saddle and bridle and all, and never a rider to be seen, and he tried to catch him, but the beast would have none of it. Time after time he tried, and began to put out feed for him, and the creature was wise enough to come for his dinner, but too clever to be caught. He'd mired himself to the shoulder, and somewhere he tore loose the most of his bridle, and had the saddle ripped round half under his belly before ever we got near him. In the end I had my mare fit, and we staked her out there and she fetched him. Quiet enough, once we had him, and glad to shed what was left of his harness, and feel a currier on his sides again. But we'd no notion whose he was. I sent word to my lord at Wem, and here we keep him till we know what's right."

There was no need to doubt a word, it was all above board here. And this was but a mile or two out of the way to Whitchurch, and the same distance from the town.

"You've kept the harness? Such as he still had?"

"In the stable, to hand when you will."

"But no man. Did you look for a man afterwards?"

The mosses were no place for a stranger to go by night, and none too safe for a rash traveller even by day. The peat-pools, far down, held bones enough.

"We did, my lord. There are fellows hereabouts who know every dyke and every path and every island that can be trodden. We reckoned he'd been thrown, or foundered with his beast, and only the beast won free. It has been known. But never a trace. And that creature there, though soiled as he was, I doubt if he'd been in above the hocks, and if he'd gone that deep, with a man in the saddle, it would have been the man who had the better chance."

"You think," said Hugh, eyeing him shrewdly, "he came into the mosses riderless?"

"I do think so. A few miles south there's woodland. If there were footpads there, and got hold of the man, they'd have trouble keeping their hold of this one. I reckon he made his own way here."

"You'll show my sergeant the way to your man on the mosses? He'll be able to tell us more, and show the places where the horse was straying. There's a clerk of the bishop of Winchester's household lost," said Hugh, electing to trust a plainly honest man, "and maybe dead. This was his mount. If you learn of anything more send to me, Hugh Beringar, at Shrewsbury castle, and you shan't be the loser."

"Then you'll be taking him away. God knows what his name was, I called him Russet." The free lord of this poor manor leaned over his wattle fence and snapped his fingers, and the bay came to him confidently and sank his muzzle into the extended palm. "I'll miss him. His coat has not its proper gloss yet, but it will come. At least we got the burs and the rubble of heather out of it."

"We'll pay you his price," said Hugh warmly. "It's well earned. And now I'd best look at what's left of his accoutrements, but I doubt they'll tell us anything more."

It was pure chance that the novices were passing across the great court to the cloister for the afternoon's instruction when Hugh Beringar rode in at the gatehouse of the abbey, leading the horse, called for convenience Russet, to the stable-yard for safe-keeping. Better here than at the castle, since the horse was the property of the bishop of Winchester, and at some future time had better be delivered to him.

Cadfael was just emerging from the cloister on his way to the herb garden, and was thus brought face to face with the novices entering. Late in the line came Brother Meriet, in good time to see the lofty young bay that trotted into the courtyard on a leading-rein, and arched his copper neck and brandished his long, narrow white blaze at strange surroundings, shifting white-sandalled forefeet delicately on the cobbles.

Cadfael saw the encounter clearly. The horse tossed its narrow, beautiful head, stretched neck and nostril, and whinnied softly. The young man blanched white as the blazoned forehead, and jerked strongly back in his careful stride, and brief sunlight found the green in his eyes. Then he remembered himself and passed hurriedly on, following his fellows into the cloister.

In the night, an hour before Matins, the dortoir was shaken by a great, wild cry of:"Barbary ... Barbary ... " and then a single long, piercing whistle, before Brother Cadfael reached Meriet's cell, smoothed an urgent hand over brow and cheek and pursed lips, and eased him back, still sleeping, to his pillow. The edge of the dream, if it was a dream, was abruptly blunted, the sounds melted into silence. Cadfael was ready to frown and hush away the startled brothers when they came, and even Prior Robert hesitated to break so perilous a sleep, especially at the cost of inconveniencing everyone else's including his own. Cadfael sat by the bed long after all was silence and darkness again. He did not know quite what he had been expecting, but he was glad he had been ready for it. As for the morrow, it would come, for better or worse.

CHAPTER FOUR

MERIET AROSE FOR PRIME HEAVY-EYED AND SOMbre, but seemingly quite innocent of what had happened during the night, and was saved from the immediate impact of the brothers' seething dread, disquiet and displeasure by being summoned forth, immediately the office was over, to speak with the deputy-sheriff in the stables. Hugh had the torn and weathered harness spread on a bench in the yard, and a groom was walking the horse called Russet appreciatively about the cobbles to be viewed clearly in the mellow morning light.

"I hardly need to ask," said Hugh pleasantly, smiling at the way the white-fired brow lifted and the wide nostrils dilated at sight of the approaching figure, even in such unfamiliar garb. "No question but he knows *you* again, I must needs conclude that you know him just as well." And as Meriet volunteered nothing, but continued to wait to be asked: "Is this the horse Peter Clemence was riding when he left your father's house?"

"Yes my lord, the same." He moistened his lips and kept his eyes lowered, but for one spark of a glance for the horse; he did not ask anything.

"Was that the only occasion when you had to do with him? He comes to you readily. Fondle him if you will, he's asking for your recognition."

"It was I stabled and groomed and tended him, that night," said Meriet, low-voiced and hesitant. "And I saddled him in the morning. I never had his like to care for until then. I . . . I am good with horses."

"So I see. Then you have also handled his gear." It had been rich and fine, the saddle inlaid with coloured leathers, the bridle ornamented with silver-work now dinted and soiled. "All this you recognize?"

Meriet said: "Yes. This was his." And at last he did ask, almost fearfully: "Where did you find Barbary?"

"Was that his name? His master told you? A matter of twenty miles and more north of here, on the peat-hags near Whitchurch. Very well, young sir, that's all I need from you. You can go back to your duties now."

Round the water-troughs in the lavatorium, over their ablutions, Meriet's fellows were making the most of his absence. Those who went in dread of him as a soul possessed, those who resented his holding himself apart, those who felt his silence to be nothing short of disdain for them, all raised their voices clamorously to air their collective grievance. Prior Robert was not there, but his clerk and shadow, Brother Jerome, was, and with ears pricked and willing to listen.

"Brother, you heard him yourself! He cried out again in the night, he awoke us all . . . "

"He howled for his familiar. I heard the demon's name, he called him Barbary! And his devil whistled back to him . . . we all know it's devils that hiss and whistle!"

"He's brought an evil spirit in among us, we're not safe for our lives. And we get no rest at night . . . Brother, truly, we're afraid!"

Cadfael, tugging a comb through the thick bush of grizzled hair ringing his nut-brown dome, was in two minds about intervening, but thought better of it. Let them pour out everything they had stored up against the lad, and it might be seen more plainly how little it was. Some genuine superstitious fear they certainly suffered, such night alarms do shake simple minds. If they were silenced now they would only store up their resentment to breed in secret. Out with it all, and the air might clear. So he held his peace, but he kept his ears pricked.

"It shall be brought up again in chapter," promised Brother Jerome, who thrived on being the prime channel of appeal to the prior's ears. "Measures will surely be taken to secure rest at nights. If necessary, the disturber of the peace must be segregated."

"But, brother," bleated Meriet's nearest neighbour in the dortoir, "if he's set apart in a separate cell, with no one to watch him, who knows what he may not get up to? He'll have greater freedom there, and I dread his devil will thrive all the more and take hold on others. He could bring down the roof upon us or set fire to the cellars under us . . ."

"That is want of trust in divine providence," said Brother Jerome, and fingered the cross on his breast as he said it. "Brother Meriet has caused great trouble, I grant, but to say that he is possessed of the devil—"

"But, brother, it's true! He has a talisman from his demon, he hides it in his bed. I know! I've seen him slip some small thing under his blanket, out of sight, when I looked in upon him in his cell. All I wanted was to ask him a line in the psalm, for you know he's learned, and he had something in his hand, and slipped it away very quickly, and stood between me and the bed, and wouldn't let me in further. He looked black as thunder at me, brother, I was afraid! But I've watched since. It's true, I swear, he has a charm hidden there, and at night he takes it to him to his bed. Surely this is the symbol of his familiar, and it will bring evil on us all!"

"I cannot believe . . ." began Brother Jerome, and broke off there, reconsidering the scope of his own credulity. "You have *seen* this? In his *bed*, you say? Some alien thing hidden away? That is not according to the Rule." For what should there be in a dortoir cell but cot and stool, a small desk for reading, and the books for study? These, and the privacy and quiet which can exist only by virtue of mutual consideration, since mere token partitions of wainscot separate cell from cell. "A novice entering here must give up all worldly possessions," said Jerome, squaring his meagre shoulders and scenting a genuine infringement of the approved order of things. Grist to the mill! Nothing he loved better than an occasion for admonition. "I shall speak to Brother Meriet about this."

Half a dozen voices, encouraged, urged him to more immediate action. "Brother, go now, while he's away, and see if I have not told you truth! If you take away his charm the demon will have no more power over him."

"And we shall have quiet again . . ."

"Come with me!" said Brother Jerome heroically, making up his mind. And before Cadfael could stir, Jerome was off, out of the lavatorium and surging towards the dortoir stairs, with a flurry of novices hard on his heels.

Cadfael went after them hunched with resigned disgust, but not foreseeing any great urgency. The boy was safely out of this hobnobbing with Hugh in the stables, and of course they would find nothing in his cell to give them any further hold on him, malice being a great stimulator of the imagination. The flat disappointment might bring them down to earth. So he hoped! But for all that, he made haste on the stairs.

But someone else was in an even greater hurry. Light feet beat a sharp drum-roll on the wooden treads at Cadfael's back, and an impetuous body overtook him in the doorway of the long dortoir, and swept him several yards down the tiled corridor between the cells. Meriet thrust past with long, indignant strides, his habit flying.

"I heard you! I heard you! Let my things alone!"

Where was the low, submissive voice now, the modestly lowered eyes and folded hands? This a furious young lordling peremptorily ordering hands off his possessions, and homing on the offenders with fists clenched and eyes flashing. Cadfael, thrust off-balance for a moment, made a grab at a flying sleeve, but only to be dragged along in Meriet's wake.

The covey of awed, inquisitive novices gathered round the opening of Meriet's cell, heads thrust cautiously within and rusty black rumps protruding without, whirled in alarm at hearing this angry apparition bearing down on them, and broke away with agitated clucking like so many flurried hens. In the very threshold of his small domain Meriet came nose to nose with Brother Jerome emerging.

On the face of it it was a very uneven confrontation: a mere postulant of a month or so, and one who had already given trouble and been cautioned, facing a man in authority, the prior's right hand, a cleric and confessor, one of the two appointed for the novices. The check did give Meriet pause for one moment, and Cadfael leaned to his ear to whisper breathlessly: "Hold back, you fool! He'll have your hide!" He might have saved the breath of which he was short, for Meriet did not even hear him. The moment when he might have come to his senses was already past, for his eye had fallen on the small, bright thing Jerome dangled before him from outraged fingers, as though it were unclean. The boy's face blanched, not with the pallor of fear, but the blinding whiteness of pure anger, every line of bone in a strongly-boned countenance chiselled in ice.

"That is mine," he said with soft and deadly authority, and held out his hand. "Give it to me!"

Brother Jerome rose on tiptoe and swelled like a turkey-cock at being addressed in such tones. His thin nose quivered with affronted rage. "And you openly avow it? Do you not know, impudent wretch, that in asking for admittance here you have forsworn 'mine,' and may not possess property of any kind? To bring in any personal things here without the lord abbot's permission is flouting the Rule. It is a sin! But wilfully to bring with you this—*this!*—is to offend foully against the very vows you say you desire to take. And to cherish it in your bed is a manner of fornication. Do you dare? Do you dare? You shall be called to account for it!"

All eyes but Meriet's were on the innocent cause of offence; Meriet maintained a burning stare upon his adversary's face. And all the secret charm turned out to be was a delicate linen ribbon, embroidered with flowers in blue and gold and red, such a band as a girl would use to bind her hair, and knotted into its length a curl of that very hair, reddish gold.

"Do you so much as know the meaning of the vows you say you wish to take?" fumed Jerome. "Celibacy, poverty, obedience, stability—is there any sign in you of any of these? Take thought now, while you may, renounce all thought of such follies and pollutions as this vain thing implies, or you cannot be accepted here.

Penance for this backsliding you will not escape, but you have time to amend, if there is any grace in you."

"Grace enough, at any rate," said Meriet, unabashed and glittering, "to keep my hands from prying into another man's sheets and stealing his possessions. Give me," he said through his teeth, very quietly, "what is mine!"

"We shall see, insolence, what the lord abbot has to say of your behaviour. Such a vain trophy as this you may not keep. And as for your insubordination, it shall be reported faithfully. Now let me pass!" ordered Jerome, supremely confident still of his dominance and his rightness.

Whether Meriet mistook his intention, and supposed that it was simply a matter of sweeping the entire issue into chapter for the abbot's judgement, Cadfael could never be sure. The boy might have retained sense enough to accept that, even if it meant losing his simple little treasure in the end; for after all, he had come here of his own will, and at every check still insisted that he wanted with all his heart to be allowed to remain and take his vows. Whatever his reason, he did step back, though with a frowning and dubious face, and allowed Jerome to come forth into the corridor.

Jerome turned towards the night-stairs, where the lamp was still burning, and all his mute myrmidons followed respectfully. The lamp stood in a shallow bowl on a bracket on the wall, and was guttering towards its end. Jerome reached it, and before either Cadfael or Meriet realized what he was about, he had drawn the gauzy ribbon through the flame. The tress of hair hissed and vanished in a small flare of gold, the ribbon fell apart in two charred halves, and smouldered in the bowl. And Meriet, without a sound uttered, launched himself like a hound leaping, straight at Brother Jerome's throat. Too late to grasp at his cowl and try to restrain him, Cadfael lunged after.

No question but Meriet meant to kill. This was no noisy brawl, all bark and no bite, he had his hands round the scrawny throat, bringing Jerome crashing to the floor-tiles under him, and kept his grip and held to his purpose though half a dozen of the dismayed and horrified novices clutched and clawed and battered at him, themselves ineffective, and getting in Cadfael's way. Jerome grew purple, heaving and flapping like a fish out of water, and wagging his hands helplessly against the tiles. Cadfael fought his way through until he could stoop to Meriet's otherwise oblivious ear, and bellow inspired words into it.

"For shame, son! An old man!"

In truth, Jerome lacked twenty of Cadfael's own sixty years, but the need justified the mild exaggeration. Meriet's ancestry nudged him in the ribs. His hands relaxed their grip, Jerome halsed in breath noisily and cooled from purple to brick-red, and a dozen hands hauled the culprit to his feet and held him, still breathing fire and saying no word, just as Prior Robert, tall and awful as though he wore the mitre already, came sailing down the tiled corridor, blazing like a bolt of the wrath of God.

In the bowl of the lamp, the two ends of flowered ribbons smouldered, giving off a dingy and ill-scented smoke, and the stink of the burned ringlet still hung upon the air.

Two of the lay servants, at Prior Robert's orders, brought the manacles that were seldom used, shackled Meriet's wrists, and led him away to one of the punishment cells isolated from all the communal uses of the house. He went with them, still wordless, too aware of his dignity to make any resistance, or put them to any anxiety on his account. Cadfael watched him go with particular interest, for it was as if he saw him for the first time. The habit no longer hampered him, he strode disdainfully, held his head lightly erect, and if it was not quite a sneer that curled his lips and his still roused nostrils, it came very close to it. Chapter would see him brought to book, and sharply, but he did not care. In a sense he had had his satisfaction.

As for Brother Jerome, they picked him up, put him to bed, fussed over him, brought him soothing draughts which Cadfael willingly provided, bound up his bruised throat with comforting oils, and listened dutifully to the feeble, croaking sounds he soon grew wary of assaying, since they were painful to him. He had taken no great harm, but he would be hoarse for some while, and perhaps for a time he would be careful and civil in dealing with the still unbroken sons of the nobility who came to cultivate the cowl. Mistakenly? Cadfael brooded over the inexplicable predilection of Meriet Aspley. If ever there was a youngster bred for the manor and the field of honour, for horse and arms, Meriet was the man.

"For shame, son! An old man!" And he had opened his hands and let his enemy go, and marched off the field prisoner, but with all the honours.

The outcome at chapter was inevitable; there was nothing to be done about that. Assault upon a priest and confessor could have cost him excommunication, but that was set aside in clemency. But his offence was extreme, and there was no fitting penalty but the lash. The discipline, there to be used only in the last resort, was nevertheless there to be used. It was used upon Meriet. Cadfael had expected no less. The criminal, allowed to speak, had contented himself with saying simply that he denied nothing of what was alleged against him. Invited to plead in extenuation, he refused, with impregnable dignity. And the scourge he endured without a sound.

In the evening, before Compline, Cadfael went to the abbot's lodging to ask leave to visit the prisoner, who was confined to his solitary cell for some ten days of penance.

"Since Brother Meriet would not defend himself," said Cadfael, "and Prior Robert, who brought him before you, came on the scene only late, it is as well that you should know all that happened, for it may bear on the manner in which this boy came to us." And he recounted his sad history of the keepsake Meriet had concealed in his cell and fondled by night. "Father, I don't claim to know. But the elder brother of our most troublous postulant is affianced, and is to marry soon, as I understand."

"I take your meaning," said Radulfus heavily, leaning linked hands upon his desk, "and I, too, have thought of this. His father is a patron of our house, and the marriage is to take place here in December. I had wondered if the younger son's desire to be out of the world . . . It would, I think, account for him." And he smiled wryly for all the plagued young who believe that frustration in love is the end of their world, and there is nothing left for them but to seek another. "I have been wondering for a week or more," he said, "whether I should not send someone with knowledge to speak with his sire, and examine whether we are not all doing this youth a great disservice, in allowing him to take vows very ill-suited to his nature, however much he may desire them now."

"Father," said Cadfael heartily, "I think you would be doing right."

"The boy has qualities admirable in themselves, even here," said Radulfus half-regretfully, "but alas, not at home here. Not for thirty years, and after satiety with the world, after marriage, and child-getting and child-rearing, and the transmission of a name and a pride of birth. We have our ambience, but they—they are necessary to continue both what they know, and what we can teach them. These things you understand, as do all too few of us who harbour here and escape the tempest. Will you go to Aspley in my behalf?"

"With all my heart, Father," said Cadfael.

"Tomorrow?"

"Gladly, if you so wish. But may I, then, go now and see both what can be done to settle Brother Meriet, mind and body, and also what I can learn from him?"

"Do so, with my goodwill," said the abbot.

In his small stone penal cell, with nothing in it but a hard bed, a stool, a cross hung on the wall, and the necessary stone vessel for the prisoner's bodily needs, Brother Meriet looked curiously more open, easy and content than Cadfael had yet seen him. Alone, unobserved and in the dark, at least he was freed from the necessity of watching his every word and motion, and fending off all such as came too near. When the door was suddenly unlocked, and someone came in with a tiny lamp in hand, he certainly stiffened for a moment, and reared his head from his folded arms to stare; and Cadfael took it as a compliment and an encouragement that on recognizing him the young man just as spontaneously sighed, softened, and laid his cheek back on his forearms, though in such a way that he could watch the newcomer. He was lying on his belly on the pallet, shirtless, his habit stripped down to the waist to leave his weals open to the air. He was defiantly calm, for his blood was still up. If he had confessed to all that was charged against him, in perfect honesty, he had regretted nothing.

"What do they want of me now?" he demanded directly, but without noticeable apprehension.

"Nothing. Lie still, and let me put this lamp somewhere steady. There, you hear? We're locked in together. I shall have to hammer at the door before you'll be rid of me again." Cadfael set his light on the bracket below the cross, where it would shine upon the bed. "I've brought what will help you to a night's sleep, within and without. If you choose to trust my medicines? There's a draught can dull your pain and put you to sleep, if you want it?"

"I don't," said Meriet flatly, and lay watchful with his chin on his folded arms. His body was brown and lissom and sturdy, the bluish welts on his back were not too gross a disfigurement. Some lay servant had held his hand; perhaps he himself had no great love for Brother Jerome. "I want wakeful. This is quiet here."

"Then at least keep still and let me salve this copper hide of yours. I told you he would have it!" Cadfael sat down on the edge of the narrow pallet, opened his jar, and began to anoint the slender shoulders that rippled and twitched to his touch. "Fool boy," he said chidingly, "you could have spared yourself."

"Oh, that!" said Meriet indifferently, nevertheless passive under the soothing fingers. "I've had worse," he said, lax and easy on his spread arms. "My father, if he was roused, could teach them something here."

"He failed to teach you much sense, at any rate. Though I won't say," admitted Cadfael generously, "that I haven't sometimes wanted to strangle Brother Jerome myself. But on the other hand, the man was only doing his duty, if in a heavy-handed fashion. He is a confessor to the novices, of whom I hear—can I be-

lieve it?—you are one. And if you do so aspire, you are
held to be renouncing all ado with women, my friend,
and all concern with personal property. Do him justice
he had grounds for complaint of you."

"He had no grounds for stealing from me," flared
Meriet hotly.

"He had a right to confiscate what is forbidden
here."

"I still call it stealing. And he had no right to destroy
it before my eyes—nor to speak as though women were
unclean!"

"Well, if you've paid for your offences, so has he for
his," said Cadfael tolerantly. "He has a sore throat will
keep him quiet for a week yet, and for a man who likes
the sound of his own sermons that's no mean revenge.
But as for you, lad, you've a long way to go before
you'll ever make a monk, and if you mean to go
through with it, you'd better spend your penance here
doing some hard thinking."

"Another sermon?" said Meriet into his crossed
arms, and for the first time there was almost a smile in
his voice, if a rueful one.

"A word to the wise."

That caused him to check and hold his breath, lying
utterly still for one moment, before he turned his head
to bring one glittering, anxious eye to bear on Cadfael's
face. The dark-brown hair coiled and curled agreeably
in the nape of his summer-browned neck, and the neck
itself had still the elegant, tender shaping of boyhood.
Vulnerable still to all manner of wounds, on his own

behalf, perhaps, but certainly on behalf of others all too fiercely loved. The girl with the red-gold hair?

"They have not said anything? Demanded Meriet, tense with dismay. "They don't mean to cast me out? He wouldn't do that—the abbot? He would have told me openly!" He turned with a fierce, lithe movement, drawing up his legs and rising on one hip, to seize Cadfael urgently by the wrist and stare into his eyes. "What is it you know? What does he mean to do with me? I can't, I won't, give up now."

"You've put your own vocation in doubt," said Cadfael bluntly, "no other has had any hand in it. If it had rested with me, I'd have clapped your pretty trophy back in your hand, and told you to be off out of here, and find either her or another as like her as one girl is to another equally young and fair, and stop plaguing us who ask nothing more than a quiet life. But if you still want to throw your natural bent out of door, you have that chance. Either bend your stiff neck, or rear it, and be off!"

There was more to it than that, and he knew it. The boy sat bolt upright, careless of his half-nakedness in a cell stony and chill, and held him by the wrist with strong, urgent fingers, staring earnestly into his eyes, probing beyond into his mind, and not afraid of him, or even wary.

"I will bend it," he said. "You doubt if I can, but I can, I will. Brother Cadfael, if you have the abbot's ear, help me, tell him I have not changed, tell him I do want to be received. Say I will wait, it I must, and learn and be patient, but I will deserve! In the end he shall not be able to complain of me. Say so to him! He won't reject me."

"And the gold-haired girl?" said Cadfael, purposely brutal.

Meriet wrenched himself away and flung himself down again on his breast. "She is spoken for," he said no less roughly, and would not say one word more of her.

"There are others," said Cadfael. "Take thought now or never. Let me tell you, child, as one old enough to have a son past your age, and with a few regrets in his own life, if he had time to brood on them—there's many a young man has got his heart's dearest wish, only to curse the day he ever wished for it. By the grace and good sense of our abbot, you will have time to make certain before you're bound past freeing. Make good use of your time, for it won't return once you're pledged."

A pity, in a way, to frighten a young creature so, when he was already torn many ways, but he had ten days and nights of solitude before him now, a low diet, and time both for prayer and thought. Being alone would not oppress him, only the pressure of uncongenial numbers around him had done that. Here he would sleep without dreams, not starting up to cry out in the night. Or if he did, there would be no one to hear him and add to his trouble.

"I'll come and bring the salve in the morning," said Cadfael, taking up his lamp. "No, wait!" He set it down again. "If you lie so, you'll be cold in the night. Put on your shirt, the linen won't trouble you too much, and you can bear the brychan over it."

"I'm well enough," said Meriet, submitting almost shamefacedly, and subsiding with a sigh into his folded arms again. "I . . . . I do thank you—brother!" he ended as an awkward afterthought, and very dubiously, as if the form of address did no justice to what was in his mind, though he knew it to be the approved one here.

"That came out of you doubtfully," remarked Cadfael judicially, "like biting on a sore tooth. There are other relationships. Are you still sure it's a brother you want to be?"

"I *must*," blurted Meriet, and turned his face morosely away.

Now why, wondered Cadfael, banging on the door of the cell for the porter to open and let him out, why must the one thing of meaning he says be said only at the end, when he's settled and eased, and it would be shame to plague him further? Not: I do! or: I will! but: I must! Must implies a resolution enforced, either by another's will, or by an overwhelming necessity. Now who has willed this sprig into the cloister, or what force of circumstance has made him choose this way as the best, the only one left open to him?

Cadfael came out from Compline that night to find Hugh waiting for him at the gatehouse.

"Walk as far as the bridge with me. I'm on my way home, but I hear from the porter here that you're off on

an errand for the lord abbot tomorrow, so you'll be out
of my reach day-long. You'll have heard about the
horse?"

"That you've found him, yes, nothing more. We've
been all too occupied with our own miscreants and
crimes this day to have much time or thought for anything outside," owned Cadfael ruefully. "No doubt
you've been told about that." Brother Albin, the porter,
was the most consummate gossip in the enclave. "Our
worries go side by side and keep pace, it seems, but
never come within touch of each other. That's strange
in itself. And now you find the horse miles away to the
north, or so I heard."

They passed through the gate together and turned left
towards the town, under a chill, dim sky of driving
clouds, though on the ground there was no more than a
faint breeze, hardly enough to stir the moist, sweet, rot-
ting smells of autumn. The darkness of trees on the
right of the road, the flat metallic glimmer of the mill-
pond on their left, and the scent and sound of the river
ahead, between them and the town.

"Barely a couple miles short of Whitchurch," said
Hugh, "where he had meant to pass the night, and have
an easy ride to Chester next day." He recounted the
whole of it; Cadfael's thoughts were always a welcome
illumination from another angle. But here their two
minds moved as one.

"Wild enough woodland short of the place," said
Cadfael sombrely, "and the mosses close at hand. If it
was done there, whatever was done, and the horse,

being young and spirited, broke away and could not be caught, then the man may be fathoms deep. Past finding. Not even a grave to dig."

"It's what I've been thinking myself," agreed Hugh grimly. "But if I have such footpads living wild in my shire, how is it I've heard no word of them until now?"

"A venture south out of Cheshire? You know how fast they can come and go. And even where your writ runs, Hugh, the times breed changes. But if these were masterless men, they were no skilled hands with horses. Any outlaw worth his salt would have torn out an arm by the shoulder rather than lose a beast like that one. I went to have a look at him in the stables," owned Cadfael, "when I was free. And the silver on his harness . . . only a miracle could have got it away from them once they clapped eyes on it. What the man himself had on him can hardly have been worth more than horse and harness together."

"If they're preying on travellers there," said Hugh, "they'll know just where to slide a weighted man into the peat-hags, where they're hungriest. But I've men there searching, whether or no. There are some among the natives there can tell if a pool has been fed recently—will you believe it? But I doubt, truly I doubt, if even a bone of Peter Clemence will ever be seen again."

They had reached the near end of the bridge. In the half-darkness the Severn slid by at high speed, close to them and silent, like a great serpent whose scales occasionally caught a gleam of starlight and flashed like silver, before that very coil had passed and was speeding downstream far too fast for overtaking. They halted to take leave.

"And you are bound for Aspley," said Hugh. "Where the man lay safely with his kin, a single day short of his death. If indeed he is dead! I forget we are no better than guessing. How if he had good reasons to vanish there and be written down as dead? Men change their allegiance these days as they change their shirts, and for every man for sale there are buyers. Well, use your eyes and your wits at Aspley for your lad—I can tell by now when you have a wing spread over a fledgling— but bring me back whatever you can glean about Peter Clemence, too, and what he had in mind when he left them and rode north. Some innocent there may be nursing the very word we need, and thinking nothing of it."

"I will so," said Cadfael, and turned back in the gloaming towards the gatehouse and his bed.

CHAPTER FIVE

HAVING THE ABBOT'S AUTHORITY ABOUT HIM, and something more than four miles to go, Brother Cadfael helped himself to a mule from the stables in preference to tackling the journey to Aspley on foot. Time had been when he would have scorned to ride, but he was past sixty years old, and minded for once to take his ease. Moreover, he had few opportunities now for riding, once a prime pleasure, and could not afford to neglect such as did come his way.

He left after Prime, having taken a hasty bite and drink. The morning was misty and mild, full of the heavy, sweet, moist melancholy of the season, with a thickly-veiled sun showing large and mellow through the haze. And the way was pleasant, for the first part on the highway.

The Long Forest, south and south-west of Shrews-bury, had survived unplundered longer than most of its kind, its assarts few and far between, its hunting coverts thick and wild, its open heaths home to all manner of creatures of earth and air. Sheriff Prestcote kept a weather eye on changes there, but did not interfere with what reinforced order rather than challenging it, and the border manors had been allowed to enlarge and improve their fields, provided they kept the peace there with a firm enough hand. There were very ancient holdings along the rim which had once been assarts deep in woodland, and now had hewn out good arable land from old upland, and fenced their intakes. The three old neighbour-manors of Linde, Aspley and Foriet guarded this eastward fringe, half-wooded, half-open. A man riding for Chester from this place would not need to go through Shrewsbury, but would pass it by and leave it to westward. Peter Clemence had done so, choosing to call upon his kinsfolk when the chance offered, rather than make for the safe haven of Shrewsbury abbey. Would his fate have been different, had he chosen to sleep within the pale of Saint Peter and Saint Paul? His route to Chester might even have missed Whitchurch, passing to westward, clear of the mosses. Too late to wonder!

Cadfael was aware of entering the lands of the Linde manor when he came upon well-cleared fields and the traces of grain long harvested, and stubble being culled by sheep. The sky had partially cleared by then, a mild and milky sun was warming the air without quite disseminating the mist, and the young man who came strolling along a headland with a hound at

his heel and a half-trained merlin on a creance on his
wrist had dew-darkened boots, and a spray of drops on
his uncovered light-brown hair from the shaken leaves
of some copse left behind him. A young gentleman
very light of foot and light of heart, whistling merrily
as he rewound the creance and soothed the ruffled
bird. A year or two past twenty, he might be. At sight
of Cadfael he came bounding down from the headland
to the sunken track, and having no cap to doff, gave
him a very graceful inclination of his fair head and a
blithe:

"Good-day, brother! Are you bound for us?"

"If by any chance your name is Nigel Aspley," said
Cadfael, halting to return the airy greeting, "then indeed I am." But this could hardly be the elder son who
had five or six years the advantage of Meriet, he was
too young, of too markedly different a colouring and
build, long and slender and blue-eyed, with rounded
countenance and ready smile. A little more red in the
fair hair, which had the elusive greenish-yellow of oak
leaves just budded in spring, or just turning in autumn,
and he could have provided the lock that Meriet had
cherished in his bed.

"Then we're out of luck," said the young man grace-
fully, and made a pleasant grimace of disappointment.
"Though you'd still be welcome to halt at home for a
rest and a cup, if you have the leisure for it? For I'm
only a Linde, not an Aspley, and my name is Janyn."

Cadfael recalled what Hugh had told him of
Meriet's replies to Canon Eluard. The elder brother

was affianced to the daughter of the neighbouring manor; and that could only be a Linde, since he had also mentioned without much interest the foster-sister who was a Foriet, and heiress to the manor that bordered Aspley on the southern side. Then this personable and debonair young creature must be a brother of Nigel's prospective bride.

"That's very civil of you," said Cadfael mildly, "and I thank you for the goodwill, but I'd best be getting on about my business. For I think I must have only a mile or so still to go."

"Barely that, sir, if you take the left-hand path below here where it forks. Through the copse and you're into their fields, and the track will bring you straight to their gate. If you're not in haste I'll walk with you and show you."

Cadfael was more than willing. Even if he learned little from his companion about this cluster of manors all productive of sons and daughters of much the same age, and consequently brought up practically as one family, yet the companionship itself was pleasant. And a few useful grains of knowledge might be dropped like seed, and take root for him. He let the mule amble gently, and Janyn Linde fell in beside him with a long, easy stride.

"You'll be from Shrewsbury, brother?" Evidently he had his share of human curiosity. "Is it something concerning Meriet? We were shaken, I can tell you, when he made up his mind to take the cowl, and yet, come to think, he went always his own ways, and would follow them. How did you leave him? Well, I hope?"

"Passably well," said Cadfael cautiously. "You must know him a deal better than we do, as yet, being neighbours, and much of an age."

"Oh, we were all raised together from pups, Nigel, Meriet, my sister and me—especially after both our mothers died—and Isouda, too, when she was left orphan, though she's younger. Meriet's our first loss from the clan, we miss him."

"I hear there'll be a marriage soon that will change things still more," said Cadfael, fishing delicately.

"Roswitha and Nigel?" Janyn shrugged lightly and airily. "It was a match our fathers planned long ago— but if they hadn't, they'd have had to come round to it, for those two made up their own minds almost from children. If you're bound for Aspley you'll find my sister somewhere about the place. She's more often there than here, now. They're deadly fond!" He sounded tolerantly amused, as brothers still unsmitten frequently are by the eccentricities of lovers. Deadly fond! Then if the red-gold hair had truly come from Roswitha's head, surely it had not been given? To a besotted younger brother of her bridegroom? Clipped on the sly, more likely, and the ribbon stolen. Or else it came, after all, from some very different girl.

"Meriet's mind took another way," said Cadfael, trailing his line. "How did his father take it when he chose the cloister? I think were I a father, and had but two sons, I should take no pleasure in giving up either of them."

Janyn laughed, briefly and gaily. "Meriet's father took precious little pleasure in anything Meriet ever did, and Meriet took precious little pains to please him. They waged one long battle. And yet I dare swear they loved each other as well as most fathers and sons do. Now and then they come like that, oil and water, and nothing they can do about it."

They had reached a point below the headland where the fields gave place to a copse, and a broad ride turned aside at a slight angle to thread the trees.

"There lies your best way," said Janyn, "straight to their manor fence. And if you should have time to step in at our house on your way back, brother, my father would be glad to welcome you."

Cadfael thanked him gravely, and turned into the green ride. At a turn of the path he looked back. Janyn was strolling jauntily back towards his headland and the open fields, where he could fly the merlin on his creance without tangling her in trees to her confusion and displeasure. He was whistling again as he went, very melodiously, and his fair head had the gloss and rare colour of young oak foliage, Meriet's contemporary, but how different by nature! This one would have no difficulty in pleasing the most exacting of fathers, and would certainly never vex his by electing to remove from a world which obviously pleased him very well.

The copse was open and airy, the trees had shed half

their leaves, and let in light to a floor still green and fresh. There were brackets of orange fungus jutting from the tree-boles, and frail bluish toadstools in the turf. The path brought Cadfael out, as Janyn had promised, to the wide, striped fields of the Aspley manor, carved out long ago from the forest, and enlarged steadily ever since, both to westward, into the forest land, and eastward, into richer, tamed country. The sheep had been turned into the stubble here, too, in greater numbers, to crop what they could from the aftermath, and leave their droppings to manure the ground for the next sowing. And along a raised track between strips the manor came into view, within an enclosing wall, but high enough to be seen over its crest; a long, stone-built house, a windowed hall floor over a squat undercroft, and probably some chambers in the roof above the solar end. Well built and well kept, worth inheriting, like the land that surrounded it. Low, wide doors made to accommodate carts and wagons opened into the undercroft, a steep stairway led up to the hall door. There were stables and byres lining the inside of the wall on two sides. They kept ample stock.

There were two or three men busy about the byres when Cadfael rode in at the gate, and a groom came out from the stable to take his bridle, quick and respectful at sight of the Benedictine habit. And out from the open hall door came an elderly, thickset, bearded personage who must, Cadfael supposed rightly, be the steward Fremund who had been Meriet's herald to the abbey. A well-run household.

Peter Clemence must have been met with ceremony on the threshold when he arrived unexpectedly. It would not be easy to take these retainers by surprise.

Cadfael asked for the lord Leoric, and was told that he was out in the back fields superintending the grubbing of a tree that had heeled into his stream from a slipping bank, and was fouling the flow, but he would be sent for at once, if Brother Cadfael would wait but a quarter of an hour in the solar, and drink a cup of wine or ale to pass the time. An invitation which Cadfael accepted willingly after his ride. His mule had already been led away, doubtless to some equally meticulous hospitality of its own. Aspley kept up the lofty standards of his forbears. A guest here would be a sacred trust.

Leoric Aspley filled the narrow doorway when he came in, his thick bush of greying hair brushing the lintel. Its colour, before he aged, must have been a light brown. Meriet did not favour him in figure or complexion, but there was a strong likeness in the face. Was it because they were too unbendingly alike that they fought and could not come to terms, as Janyn had said? Aspley made his guest welcome with cool immaculate courtesy, waited on him with his own hand, and pointedly closed the door upon the rest of the household.

"I am sent, said Cadfael, when they were seated, facing each other in a deep window embrasure, their cups on the stone beside them, "by Abbot Radulfus, to consult you concerning your son Meriet."

"What of my son Meriet? He has now, of his own will, a closer kinship with you, brother, than with me, and has taken another father in the lord abbot. Where is the need to consult me?"

His voice was measured and quiet, making the chill words sound rather mild and reasonable than implacable, but Cadfael knew then that he would get no help here. Still, it was worth trying.

"Nevertheless, it was you engendered him. If you do not wish to be reminded of it," said Cadfael, probing for a chink in this impenetrable armour, "I recommend you never look in a mirror. Parents who offer their babes as oblates do not therefore give up loving them. Neither, I am persuaded, do you."

"Are you telling me he has repented of his choice already?" demanded Aspley, curling a contemptuous lip. "Is he trying to escape from the Order so soon? Are you sent to herald his coming home with his tail between his legs?"

"Far from it! With every breath he insists on this one wish, to be admitted. All that can help to hasten his acceptance he does, with almost too much fervour. His every waking hour is devoted to achieving the same goal. But in sleep it is no such matter. Then, as it seems to me, his mind and spirit recoil in horror. What he desires, waking, he turns from, screaming, in his bed at night. It is right you should know this."

Aspley sat frowning at him in silence and surely, by his fixed stillness, in some concern. Cadfael pursued his first advantage, and told him of the disturbances in the dortoir, but for some reason which he himself did not fully understand he stopped short of recounting the attack on Brother Jerome, its occasion and its punishment. If there was a fire of mutual resentment between them, why add fuel? "When he wakes," said Cadfael, "he has no knowledge of what he has done in sleep. There is no blame there. But there is a grave doubt concerning his vocation. Father Abbot asks that you will consider seriously whether we are not, between us, doing Meriet a great wrong in allowing him to continue, however much he may wish it now."

"That he wants to be rid of him," said Aspley, recovering his implacable calm, "I can well understand. He was always an obdurate and ill-conditioned youth."

"Neither Abbot Radulfus nor I find him so," said Cadfael, stung.

"Then whatever other difficulties there may be, he is better with you than with me, for I have so found him from a child. And might not I as well argue that we should be doing him a great wrong if we turned him from a good purpose when he inclines to one? He has made his choice, only he can change it. Better for him he should endure these early throes, rather than give up his intent."

Which was no very surprising reaction from such a man, hard and steadfast in his own undertakings, certainly strict to his word, and driven to pursue his courses to the end as well by obstinacy as by honour. Nevertheless, Cadfael went on trying to find the joints in his armour, for it must be a strangely bitter resentment which could deny a distracted boy a single motion of affection.

"I will not urge him one way or the other," said Aspley finally, "nor confuse his mind by visiting him or allowing any of my family to visit him. Keep him, and let him wait for enlightenment, and I think he will still wish to remain with you. He has put his hand to the plough, he must finish his furrow. I will not receive him back if he turns tail."

He rose to indicate that the interview was over, and having made it plain that there was no more to be got out of him, he resumed the host with assured grace, offered the midday meal, which was as courteously refused, and escorted his guest out to the court.

"A pleasant day for your ride," he said, "though I should be the better pleased if you would take meat with us."

"I would and thank you," said Cadfael, "but I am pledged to return and deliver your answer to my abbot. It is an easy journey."

A groom led forth the mule. Cadfael mounted, took his leave civilly, and rode out at the gate in the low stone wall.

He had gone no more than two hundred paces, just enough to carry him out of sight of those he had left within the pale, when he was aware of two figures sauntering without haste back towards that same gateway. They walked hand in hand, and they had not yet perceived a rider approaching them along the pathway between the fields, because they had eyes only for each other. They were talking by broken snatches, as in a shared dream where precise expression was not needed, and their voices, mellowly male and silverly female, sounded even in the distance like brief peaks of laughter. Or bridle bells, perhaps, but that they came afoot. Two tolerant, well-trained hounds followed them at heel, nosing up the drifted scents from either side, but keeping their homeward line without distraction.

So these must surely be the lovers, returning to be fed. Even lovers must eat. Cadfael eyed them with interest as he rode slowly towards them. They were worth observing. As they came nearer, but far enough from him to be oblivious still, they became more remarkable. Both were tall. The young man had his father's noble figure, but lissome and light-footed with youth, and the light brown hair and ruddy, outdoor skin of the Saxon. Such a son as any man might rejoice in. Healthy from birth, as like as not, growing and flourishing like a hearty plant, with every promise of full harvest. A stocky dark second, following lamely several years later, might well fail to start any such spring of satisfied pride. One paladin is enough, besides being hard to match. And if he strides towards manhood without ever a flaw or a check, where's the need for a second?

And the girl was his equal. Tipping his shoulder, and slender and straight as he, she was the image of her brother, but everything that in him was comely and attractive was in her polished into beauty. She had the

same softly rounded, oval face, but refined almost into
translucence, and the same clear blue eyes, but a shade
darker and fringed with auburn lashes. And there beyond mistake was the reddish gold hair, a thick coil of
it, and curls escaping on either side of her temples.

Thus, then, was Meriet explained? Frantic to escape
from his frustrated love into a world without women,
perhaps also anxious to remove from his brother's happiness the slightest shadow of grief or reproach—did
that account for him? But he had taken the symbol of
his torment into the cloister with him—was that sensible?

The small sound of the mule's neat hooves in the
dry grass of the track and the small stones had finally
reached the ears of the girl. She looked up and saw the
rider approaching, and said a soft word into her companion's ear. The young man checked for a moment in
his stride, and stared with reared head to see a Benedictine monk in the act of riding away from the gates
of Aspley. He was very quick to connect and wonder.
The light smile faded instantly from his face, he drew
his hand from the girl's hold, and quickened his pace
with the evident intention of accosting the departing
visitor.

They drew together and halted by consent. The elder
son, close to, loomed even taller than his sire, and im-
probably good to look upon, in a world of imperfec-
tion. With a large but shapely hand raised to the mule's
bridle, he looked up at Cadfael with clear brown eyes

rounded in concern, and gave short greeting in his haste.

"From Shrewsbury, brother? Pardon if I dare question, but you have been to my father's house? There's news? My brother—he has not . . ." He checked himself there to make belated reverance, and account for himself. "Forgive such a rough greeting, when you do not even know me, but I am Nigel Aspley, Meriet's brother. Has something happened to him? He has not done—any foolishness?"

What should be said to that? Cadfael was by no means sure whether he considered Meriet's conscious actions to be foolish or not. But at least there seemed to be one person who cared what became of him, and by the anxiety and concern in his face suffered fears for him which were not yet justified.

"There's no call for alarm on his account," said Cadfael soothingly. "He's well enough and has come to no harm, you need not fear."

"And he is still set—he has not changed his mind?"

"He has not. He is as intent as ever on taking vows."

"But you've been with my father! What could there be to discuss with him? You are sure that Meriet . . ." He fell silent, doubtfully studying Cadfael's face. The girl had drawn near at her leisure and stood a little apart, watching them both with serene composure, and in a posture of such natural grace that Cadfael's eyes could not forbear straying to enjoy her.

"I left your brother in stout heart," he said, carefully truthful, "and of the same mind as when he came to us.

I was sent by my abbot only to speak with your father about certain doubts which have arisen rather in the lord abbot's mind than in Brother Meriet's. He is still very young to take such a step in haste, and his zeal seems to older minds excessive. You are nearer to him in years than either your sire or our officers," said Cadfael persuasively. "Can you not tell me why he may have taken this step? For what reason, sound and sufficient to him, should he choose to leave the world so early?"

"I don't know," said Nigel lamely, and shook his head over his failure. "Why do they do so? I never understood." As why should he, with all the reasons he had for remaining in and of this world? "He said he wanted it," said Nigel.

"He says so still. At every turn he insists on it."

"You'll stand by him? You'll help him to have his will? If that is truly what he wishes?"

"We're all resolved," said Cadfael sententiously, "on helping him to his desire. Not all young men pursue the same destiny, as you must know." His eyes were on the girl; she was aware of it, and he was aware of her awareness. Another coil of red-gold hair had escaped from the band that held it; it lay against her smooth cheek, casting a deep gold shadow.

"Will you carry him my dear remembrances, brother? Say he has my prayers, and my love always." Nigel withdrew his hand from the bridle, and stood back to let the rider proceed.

"And assure him of my love, also," said the girl in a

voice of honey, heavy and sweet. Her blue eyes lifted to Cadfael's face. "We have been playfellows many years, all of us here," she said, certainly with truth. "I may speak in terms of love, for I shall soon be his sister."

"Roswitha and I are to be married at the abbey in December," said Nigel, and again took her by the hand.

"I'll bear your messages gladly," said Cadfael, "and wish you both all possible blessing against the day."

The mule moved resignedly, answering the slight shake of the bridle. Cadfael passed them with his eyes still fixed on the girl Roswitha, whose infinite blue gaze opened on him like a summer sky. The slightest of smiles touched her lips as he passed, and a small, contented brightness flashed in her eyes. She knew that he could not but admire her, and even the admiration of an elderly monk was satisfaction to her. Surely the very motions she had made in his presence, so slight and so conscious, had been made in the knowledge that he was well aware of them, cobweb threads to entrammel one more unlikely fly.

He was careful not to look back, for it had dawned on him that she would confidently expect him to.

Just within the fringe of the copse, at the end of the fields, there was a stone-built sheepfold, close beside the ride, and someone was sitting on the rough wall, dangling crossed ankles and small bare feet, and nursing in her lap a handful of late hazelnuts, which she cracked in her teeth, dropping the fragments of shell into the long grass. From a distance Cadfael had been uncertain whether this was boy or girl, for her gown was kilted to the knee, and her hair cropped just short enough to swing clear of her shoulders, and her dress was the common brown homespun of the countryside. But as he drew nearer it became clear that this was certainly a girl, and moreover, busy about the enterprise of becoming a woman. There were high, firm breasts under the close-fitting bodice, and for all her slenderness she had the swelling hips that would some day make childbirth natural and easy for her. Sixteen, he thought, might be her age. Most curiously of all, it appeared that she was both expecting and waiting for him, for as he rode towards her she turned on her perch to look towards him with a slow, confident smile of recognition and welcome, and when he was close she slid from the wall, brushing off the last nutshells, and shook down her skirts with the brisk movements of one making ready for action.

"Sir, I must talk to you," she said with firmness, and put up a slim brown hand to the mule's neck. "Will you light down and sit with me?" She had still her child's face, but the woman was beginning to show through, paring away the puppy-flesh to outline the elegant lines of her cheekbones and chin. She was brown almost as her nutshells, with a warm rose-colour mantling beneath the tanned, smooth skin, and a mouth rose-red, and curled like the petals of a half-open rose. The short, thick mane of curling hair was richly russet-brown, and her eyes one shade darker, and black-lashed. No cottar's girl, if she did choose to go plain and scorning finery. She knew she was an heiress, and to be reckoned with.

"I will, with pleasure," said Cadfael promptly, and did so. She took a step back, her head on one side, scarcely having expected such an accommodating reception, without explanation asked or given; and when he stood on level terms with her, and barely half a head taller, she suddenly made up her mind, and smiled at him radiantly.

"I do believe we two can talk together properly. You don't question, and yet you don't even know me."

"I think I do," said Cadfael, hitching the mule's bridle to a staple in the stone wall. "You can hardly be anyone else but Isouda Foriet. For all the rest I've already seen, and I was told already that you must be the youngest of the tribe."

"He told you of me?" she demanded at once, with sharp interest, but no noticeable anxiety.

"He mentioned you to others, but it came to my ears."

"How did he speak of me?" she asked bluntly, jutting a firm chin. "Did that also come to your ears?"

"I did gather that you were a kind of young sister." For some reason, not only did he not feel it possible to lie to this young person, it had no value even to soften the truth for her.

She smiled consideringly, like a confident commander weighing up the odds in a threatened field. "As if he did not much regard me. Never mind! He will."

"If I had the ruling of him," said Cadfael with respect, "I would advise it now. Well, Isouda, here you have me, as you wished. Come and sit, and tell me what you wanted of me."

"You brothers are not supposed to have to do with women," said Isouda, and grinned at him warmly as she hoisted herself back on to the wall. "That makes him safe from *her*, at least, but it must not go too far with this folly of his. May I know your name, since you know mine?"

"My name is Cadfael, a Welshman from Trefriw."

"My first nurse was Welsh," she said, leaning down to pluck a frail green thread of grass from the fading stems below her, and set it between strong white teeth. "I don't believe you have always been a monk, Cadfael, you know too much."

"I have known monks, children of the cloister from the eight years old," said Cadfael seriously, "who knew more than I shall ever know, though only God knows how, who made it possible. But no, I have lived forty years in the world before I came to it. My knowledge is limited. But what I know you may ask of me. You want, I think, to hear of Meriet."

"Not 'Brother Meriet'?" she said, pouncing, light as a cat, and glad.

"Not yet. Not for some time yet."

"*Never!*" she said firmly and confidently. "It will not come to that. It must not." She turned her head and looked him in the face with a high, imperious stare. "He is mine," she said simply. "Meriet is mine, whether he knows it yet or no. And no one else will have him."

CHAPTER SIX

"ASK ME WHATEVER YOU WISH," SAID CADFAEL,
shifting to find the least spiky position on the stones of
the wall. "And then there are things I have to ask of
you."

"And you'll tell me honestly what I need to know?
Every part of it?" she challenged. Her voice had a
child's directness and high, clear pitch, but a lord's authority.

"I will." For she was equal to it, even prepared for it.
Who knew this vexing Meriet better?

"How far has he got towards taking vows? What enemies has he made? What sort of fool has he made of
himself, with his martyr's wish? Tell me everything
that has happened to him since he went from me."
"From me" was what she said, not "from us."

Cadfael told her. If he chose his words carefully, yet
he made them tell her the truth. She listened with so

contained and armed a silence, nodding her head, occasionally where she recognized necessity, shaking it
where she deprecated folly, smiling suddenly and
briefly where she understood, as Cadfael could not yet
fully understand, the proceedings of her chosen man.
He ended telling her bluntly of the penalty Meriet had
brought upon himself, and even, which was a greater
temptation to discretion, about the burned tress that was
the occasion of his fall. It did not surprise or greatly
dismay her, he noted. She thought about it not more
than a moment.

"If you but knew the whippings he has brought on
himself before! No one will ever break him that way.
And your Brother Jerome has burned her lure—that
was well done. He won't be able to fool himself for
long, with no bait left him." She caught, Cadfael
thought, his momentary suspicion that he had nothing
more to deal with here than women's jealousy. She
turned and grinned at him with open amusement. "Oh,
but I saw you meet them! I was watching, though they
didn't know it, and neither did you. Did you find her
handsome? Surely you did, so she is. And did she not
make herself graceful and pleasing for you? Oh, it was
for you, be sure—why should she fish for Nigel, she
has him landed, the only fish she truly wants. But she
cannot help casting her line. *She* gave Meriet that lock
of hair, of course! She can never quite let go of any
man."

It was so exactly what Cadfael had suspected, since
casting eyes on Roswitha, that he was silenced.

"I'm not afraid of *her*," said Isouda tolerantly. "I know her too well. He only began to imagine himself loving her because she belonged to Nigel. He must desire whatever Nigel desires, and he must be jealous of whatever Nigel possesses and he has not. And yet, if you'll trust me, there is no one he loves as he loves Nigel. No one. Not yet!"

"I think," said Cadfael, "you know far more than I about this boy who troubles my mind and engages my liking. And I wish you would tell me what he does not, everything about this home of his and how he has grown up in it. For he's in need of your help and mine, and I am willing to be your dealer in this, if you wish him well, for so do I."

She drew up her knees and wrapped her slender arms around them, and told him. "I am the lady of a manor, left young, and left to my father's neighbour as his ward, my Uncle Leoric, though he is not my uncle. He is a good man. I know my manor is as well-run as any in England, and my uncle takes nothing out of it. You must understand, this is a man of the old kind, stark upright. It is not easy to live with him, if you are his and a boy, but I am a girl, and he has been always indulgent and good to me. Madam Avota, who died two years back—well, she was his wife first, and only afterwards Meriet's mother. You saw Nigel—what more could any man wish for his heir? They never even needed or wished for Meriet. They did all their duty by him when he came, but they could not even see past Nigel to notice the second one. And he was so different."

She paused to consider the two, and probably had her finger on the very point where they went different ways.

"Do you think," she asked doubtfully, "that small children know when they are only second best? I think Meriet knew it early. He was different even to look at, but that was the least part. I think he always went the opposing way, whatever they wished upon him. If his father said white, Meriet said black; wherever they tried to turn him, he dug his heels hard and wouldn't budge. He couldn't help learning, because he was sharp and curious, so he grew lettered, but when he knew they wanted him a clerk, he went after all manner of low company, and flouted his father every way. He's always been jealous of Nigel," said the girl musing against her raised knees, "but always worshipped him. He flouts his father purposely, because he knows he's loved less, and that grieves him bitterly, and yet he can't hate Nigel for being loved more. How can he, when *he* loves him so much?"

"And Nigel repays his affection?" asked Cadfael, recollecting the elder brother's troubled face.

"Oh, yes, Nigel's fond of him, too. He always defended him. He's stood between him and punishment many a time. And he always would keep him with him, whatever they were about, when they all played together."

"They?" said Cadfael. "Not 'we'?"

Isouda spat out her chewed stem of late grass, and turned a surprised and smiling face. "I'm the youngest, three years behind even Meriet, I was the infant struggling along behind. For a little while, at any rate. There was not much I did not see. You know the rest of us? Those two boys, with six years between them, and the two Lindes, midway between. And me, come rather late and too young. You've seen Roswitha. I don't know if you've seen Janyn?"

"I have," said Cadfael, "on my way here. He directed me."

"They are twins. Had you guessed that? Though I think he got all the wits that were meant for both. She is only clever one way," said Isouda judicially, "in binding men to her and keeping them bound. She was waiting for you to turn and look after her, and she would have rewarded you with one quick glance. And now you think I am only a silly girl, jealous of one prettier," she said disconcertingly, and laughed at seeing him bridle. "I would like to be beautiful, why not? But I don't envy Roswitha. And after our cross-grained fashion we have all been very close here. Very close! All those years must count for something."

"It seems to me," said Cadfael, "that you of all people best know this young man. So tell me, if you can, why did he ever take a fancy for the cloistered life? I know as well as any, how he clings to that intent, but for my life I do not see why? Are you any wiser?"

She was not. She shook her head vehemently. "It goes counter to all I know of him."

"Tell me, then, everything you recall about the time when this resolve was made. And begin," said Cadfael, "with the visit to Aspley of the bishop's envoy, this Peter Clemence. You'll know by now—who does not!—that the man never got to his next night's lodging. And has not been seen since."

She turned her head sharply to stare. "And his horse is found, so they're saying now. Found near the Cheshire border. You don't think Meriet's whim has anything to do with that? How could it? And yet . . ." She had a quick and resolute mind, she was already making disquieting connections. "It was the eighth night of September that he slept as Aspley. There was nothing strange, nothing to remark. He came alone, very early in the evening. Uncle Leoric came out to greet him, and I took his cloak indoors and had the maids make ready a bed for him, and Meriet cared for his horse. He always makes easy friends with horses. We made good cheer for the guest. They were keeping it up in hall with music after I went to my bed. And the next morning he broke his fast, and Uncle Leoric and Fremund and two grooms rode with him the first part of his way."

"What like was he, this clerk?"

She smiled, between indulgence and mild scorn. "Very fine, and knew it. Only a little older than Nigel, I should guess, but so travelled and sure of himself. Very handsome and courtly and witty, not like a clerk at all. Too courtly for Nigel's liking! You've seen Roswitha, and what she is like. This young man was just as certain all women must be drawn to him. They were two who matched like hand and glove, and Nigel was not best pleased. But he held his tongue and minded his manners, at least while I was there. Meriet did not like their by-play, either, he took himself off early to the stable, he liked the horse better than the man."

"Did Roswitha bide overnight, too?"

"Oh, no, Nigel walked home with her when it was growing dark. I saw them go."

"Then her brother was not with her that night?"

"Janyn? No, Janyn has no interest in the company of lovers. He laughs at them. No, he stayed at home."

"And the next day . . . Nigel did not ride with the guest departing? Nor Meriet? What were they about that morning?"

She frowned over that, thinking back. "I think Nigel must have gone quite early back to the Lindes. He is jealous of her, though he sees no wrong in *her.* I believe he was away most of the day, I don't think he even came home to supper. And Meriet—I know he was with us when Master Clemence left, but after that I didn't see him until late in the afternoon. Uncle Leoric had been out with hounds after dinner, with Fremund and the chaplain and his kennelman. I remember Meriet came back with them, though he didn't ride out with them. He had his bow—he often went off solitary, especially when he was out of sorts with all of us. They went in, all. I don't know why, it was a very quiet evening, I supposed because the guest was gone, and there was no call for ceremony. I don't believe Meriet came to supper in hall that day. I didn't see him again all the evening."

"And after? When was it that you first heard of his wish to enter with us at Shrewsbury?"

"It was Fremund who told me, the night following. I hadn't seen Meriet all that day to speak for himself. But I did the next day. He was about the manor as usual then, he did not look different, not in any particular. He came and helped me with the geese in the back field," said Isouda, hugging her knees, "and I told him what I had heard, and that I thought he was out of his wits, and asked him why he should covet such a fruitless life . . ." She reached a hand to touch Cadfael's arm, and a smile to assure herself of his understanding, quite unperturbed. "You are different, you've had one life already, a new one halfway is a fresh blessing for you, but what has he had? But he stared me in the eye, straight as a lance, and said he knew what he was doing, and it was what he wanted to do. And lately he had outgrown me and gone away from me, and there was no possible reason he should pretend with me, or scruple to tell me what I asked. And I have none to doubt what he did tell me. He wanted this. He wants it still. But why? That he never told me."

"That," said Brother Cadfael ruefully, "he has not told anyone, nor will not if he can evade it. What is to be done, lady, with this young man who wills to destroy himself, shut like a wild bird in cage?"

"Well, he's not lost yet," said Isouda resolutely. "And I shall see him again when we come for Nigel's marriage in December, and after that Roswitha will be out of his reach utterly, for Nigel is taking her north to the manor near Newark, which Uncle Leoric is giving to them to manage. Nigel was up there in midsummer, viewing his lordship and making ready, Janyn kept him company on the visit. Every mile of distance will help. I shall look for you, Brother Cadfael, when we come. I'm not afraid, now I've talked to you. Meriet is mine, and in the end I shall have him. It may not be me he dreams of now, but his dreams now are devilish, I would not be in those. I want him well awake. If you love him, you keep him from the tonsure, and I will do the rest!"

If I love him—and if I love you, faun, thought Cadfael, riding very thoughtfully homeward after leaving her. For you may very well be the woman for him. And what you have told me I must sort over with care, for Meriet's sake, and for yours.

He took a little bread and cheese on his return, and a measure of beer, having forsworn a midday meal with a household where he felt no kinship; and that done, he sought audience with Abbot Radulfus in the busy quiet of the afternoon, when the great court was empty, and most of the household occupied in cloister or gardens or fields.

The abbot had expected him, and listened with acute attention to everything he had to recount.

"So we are committed to caring for this young man, who may be misguided in his choice, but still persists in it. There is no course open to us but to keep him, and give him every chance to win his way in among us. But we have also his fellows to care for, and they are in real fear of him, and of the disorders of his sleep. We have yet the nine remaining days of his imprisonment, which he seems to welcome. But after that, how can we best dispose of him, to allow him access to grace, and relieve the dortoir of its trouble?"

"I have been thinking of that same question," said Cadfael. "His removal from the dortoir may be as great a benefit to him as to those remaining, for he is a solitary soul, and if ever he takes the way of withdrawal wholly I think he will be hermit rather than monk. It would not surprise me to find that he has gained by being shut in a penal cell, having that small space and great silence to himself, and able to fill it with his own meditations and prayers, as he could not do in a greater place shared by many others. We have not all the same image of brotherhood."

"True! But we are a house of brothers sharing in common, and not so many desert fathers scattered in isolation," said the abbot drily. "Nor can the young man be left for ever in a punishment cell, unless he plans to attempt the strangling of my confessors and obedientiaries one by one to ensure it. What have you to suggest?"

"Send him to serve under Brother Mark at Saint Giles," said Cadfael. "He'll be no more private there, but he will be in the company and the service of creatures manifestly far less happy than himself, lepers and beggars, the sick and maimed. It may be salutary. In them he can forget his own troubles. There are advantages beyond that. Such a period of absence will hold back his instruction, and his advance towards taking vows, but that can only be good, since clearly he is in no fit mind to take them yet. Also, though Brother Mark is the humblest and simplest of us all, he has the gift of many such innocent saints, of making his way into the heart. In time Brother Meriet may open to him, and be helped from his trouble. At least it would give us all a breathing-space."

Keep him from the tonsure, said Isouda's voice in his mind, and I will do the rest.

"So it would," agreed Radulfus reflectively. "The boys will have time to forget their alarms, and as you say, ministering to men worse blessed than himself may be the best medicine for him. I will speak with Brother Paul, and when Brother Meriet has served out his penance he shall be sent there."

And if some among us take it that banishment to work in the lazar-house is a further penance, thought Cadfael, going away reasonably content, let them take satisfaction from it. For Brother Jerome was not the man to forget an injury, and any sop to his revenge might lessen his animosity towards the offender. A term of service in the hospice at the far edge of the town might also serve more turns than Meriet's, for Brother Mark, who tended the sick there, had been Cadfael's most valued assistant until a year or so ago, and he had recently suffered the loss of his favourite and much-indulged waif, the little boy Bran, taken into the household of Joscelin and Iveta Lucy on their marriage, and would be somewhat lost without a lame duck to cosset and care for. It wanted only a word in Mark's ear concerning the tormented record of the devil's novice, and his ready sympathy would be enlisted on Meriet's behalf. If Mark could not reach him, no one could; but at the same time he might also do much for Mark. Yet another advantage was that Brother Cadfael, as supplier of the many medicines, lotions and ointments that were in demand among the sick, visited Saint Giles every third week, and sometimes oftener, to replenish the medicine cupboard, and could keep an eye on Meriet's progress there.

Brother Paul, coming from the abbot's parlour before Vespers, was clearly relieved at the prospect of enjoying a lengthened truce even after Meriet was released from his prison.

"Father Abbot tells me the suggestion came from you. It was well thought of, there's need of a long pause and a new beginning, though the children will easily forget their terrors. But that act of violence—that will not be so easily forgotten."

"How is your penitent faring?" asked Cadfael. "Have you visited him since I was in there early this morning?"

"I have. I am not so sure of his penitence," said Brother Paul dubiously, "but he is very quiet and biddable, and listens to exhortation patiently. I did not try him too far. We are failing sadly if he is happier in a cell than out among us. I think the only thing that frets him is having no work to do, so I have taken him the sermons of Saint Augustine, and given him a better lamp to read by, and a little desk he can set on his bed. Better far to have his mind occupied, and he is quick at letters. I suppose you would rather have given him Palladius on agriculture," said Paul, mildly joking. "Then you could make a case for taking him into your herbarium, when Oswin moves on."

It was an idea that had occurred to Brother Cadfael, but better the boy should go clean away, into Mark's gentle stewardship, "I have not asked leave again," he said, "but if I may visit him before bed, I should be glad. I did not tell him of my errand to his father, I shall not tell him now, but there are two people there have sent him messages of affection which I have promised to deliver." There was also one who had not, and perhaps she knew her own business best.

"Certainly you may go in before Compline," said Paul. "He is justly confined, but not ostracized. To shun him utterly would be no way to bring him into our family, which must be the end of our endeavours."

It was not the end of Cadfael's but he did not feel it necessary or timely to say so. There is a right place for every soul under the sun, but it had already become clear to him that the cloister was no place for Meriet Aspley, however feverishly he demanded to be let in.

Meriet had his lamp lighted, and so placed as to illumine the leaves of Saint Augustine on the head of his cot. He looked round quickly but tranquilly when the door opened, and knowing the incomer, actually smiled. It was very cold in the cell, the prisoner wore

habit and scapular for warmth, and by the careful way
he turned his body, and the momentary wincing halt to
release a fold of his shirt from a tender spot, his weals
were stiffening as they healed.

"I'm glad to see you so healthily employed," said
Cadfael. "With a small effort in prayer, Saint Augustine
may do you good. Have you used the balm since this
morning? Paul would have helped you, if you had
asked him."

"He is good to me," said Meriet, closing his book
and turning fully to his visitor. And he meant it, that
was plain.

"But you did not choose to condescend to ask for
sympathy or admit to need—I know! Let me have off
the scapular and drop your habit." It had certainly not
yet become a habit in which he felt at home, he moved
naturally in it only when he was aflame, and forgot he
wore it. "There, lie down and let me at you."

Meriet presented his back obediently, and allowed
Cadfael to draw up his shirt and anoint the fading weals
that showed only here and there a dark dot of dried
blood. "Why do I do what you tell me?" he wondered,
mildly rebelling. "As though you were no brother at all,
but a father?"

"From all I've heard of you," said Cadfael, busy with
his balm, "you are by no means known for doing what
your own father tells you."

Meriet turned in his cradling arms and brought to
bear one bright green-gold eye upon his companion.
"How do you know so much of me? Have you been

there and talked with my father?" He was ready to bristle in distrust, the muscles of his back had tensed. "What are they trying to do? What business is there needs my father's words now? I am here! If I offend, I pay. No one else settles my debts."

"No one else has offered," said Cadfael placidly. "You are your own master, however ill you master yourself. Nothing is changed. Except that I have to bring you messages, which do not meddle with your lordship's liberty to save or damn yourself. Your brother sends you his best remembrances and bids me say he holds you in his love always."

Meriet lay very still, only his brown skin quivered very faintly under Cadfael's fingers.

"And the lady Roswitha also desires you to know that she loves you as befits a sister."

Cadfael softened in his hands the stiffened folds of the shirt, where they had dried hard, and drew the linen down over fading lacerations that would leave no scar. Roswitha might be far more deadly. "Draw up your gown now, and if I were you I'd put out the lamp and leave your reading, and sleep." Meriet lay still on his face, saying never a word. Cadfael drew up the blanket over him, and stood looking down at the mute and rigid shape in the bed.

It was no longer quite rigid, the wide shoulders heaved in a suppressed and resented rhythm, the braced forearms were stiff and protective, covering the hidden face. Meriet was weeping. For Roswitha or for Nigel? Or for his own fate?

"Child," said Cadfael, half-exasperated and half-indulgent, "you are nineteen years old, and have not even begun to live, and you think in the first misery of your life that God has abandoned you. Despair is deadly sin, but worse it is mortal folly. The number of your friends is legion, and God is looking your way as attentively as ever he did. And all you have to do to deserve is to wait in patience, and keep up your heart."

Even through his deliberate withdrawal, and angrily-suppressed tears Meriet was listening, so much was clear by his tension and stillness.

"And if you care to know," said Cadfael, almost against his will, and sounding still more exasperated in consequence, "yes, I am, by God's grace, a father. I have a son. And you are the only one but myself who knows it."

And with that he pinched out the wick of the lamp, and in the darkness went to thump on the door to be let out.

It was a question, when Cadfael visited next morning, which of them was the more aloof and wary with the other, each of them having given away rather more than he had intended. Plainly there was to be no more of that. Meriet had put on an austere and composed face, not admitting to any weakness, and Cadfael was gruff and practical, and after a look at the little that was still visible of the damage to his difficult patient, pronounced him in no more need of doctoring, but very well able to concentrate on his reading and make the most of his penitential time for the good of his soul.

"Does that mean," asked Meriet directly, "that you are washing your hands of me?"

"It means I have no more excuse for demanding entry here, when you are supposed to be reflecting on your sins in solitude."

Meriet scowled briefly at the stones of the wall, and then said stiffly: "It is not that you fear I'll take some liberty because of what you were so good as to confide to me? I shall never say word, unless to you and at your instance."

"No such thought ever entered my mind," Cadfael assured him, startled and touched. "Do you think I would have said it to a blabbermouth who would not know a confidence when one was offered him? No, it's simply that I have no warranty to go in and out here without good reason, and I must abide by the rules as you must."

The fragile ice had already melted. "A pity, though," said Meriet, unbending with a sudden smile which Cadfael recalled afterwards as both startlingly sweet and extraordinarily sad. "I reflect on my sins much better when you are here scolding. In solitude I still find myself thinking how much I would like to make Brother Jerome eat his own sandals."

"We'll consider that a confession in itself," said Cadfael, "and one that had better not be made to any other ears. And your penance will be to make do without me until your ten days of mortification are up. I doubt you're incorrigible and past praying for, but we can but try."

He was at the door when Meriet asked anxiously: "Brother Cadfael . . . ?" And when he turned at once: "Do you know what they mean to do with me afterwards?"

"Not to discard you, at all events," said Cadfael, and saw no reason why he should not tell him what was planned for him. It seemed that nothing was changed. The news that he was in no danger of banishment from his chosen field calmed, reassured, placated Meriet; it was all that he wanted to hear. But it did not make him happy.

Cadfael went away discouraged, and was cantankerous with everyone who came in his path for the rest of the day.

CHAPTER SEVEN

HUGH CAME SOUTH FROM THE PEAT-HAGS EMPTY-
handed to his house in Shrewsbury, and sent an invitation to Cadfael to join him at supper on the evening of
his return. To such occasional visits Cadfael had the
most unexceptionable claim, since Giles Beringar, now
some ten months old, was his godson, and a good godfather must keep a close eye on the welfare and
progress of his charge. Of young Giles's physical well
being and inexhaustible energy there could be little
question, but Hugh did sometimes express doubts
about his moral inclinations, and like most fathers, de-
tailed his son's ingenious villainies with respect and
pride.

Aline, having fed and wined her menfolk, and observed with a practised eye the first droop of her son's
eyelids, swept him off out of the room to be put to bed
by Constance, who was his devoted slave, as she had

been loyal friend and servant to his mother from child-hood. Hugh and Cadfael were left alone for a while to exchange such information as they had. But the sum of it was sadly little.

"The men of the moss," said Hugh, "are confident that not one of them has seen hide or hair of a stranger, whether victim or malefactor. Yet the plain fact is that the horse reached the moss, and the man surely cannot have been far away. It still seems to me that he lies somewhere in those peat-pools, and we are never likely to see or hear of him again. I have sent to Canon Eluard to try and find out what he carried on him. I gather he went very well-presented and was given to wearing jewels. Enough to tempt footpads. But if that was the way of it, it seems to be a first venture from farther north, and it may well be that our scourings there have warned off the marauders from coming that way again for a while. There have been no other travellers mo-lested in those parts. And indeed, strangers in the moss would be in some peril themselves. You need to know the safe places to tread. Still, for all I can see, that is what happened to Peter Clemence. I've left a sergeant and a couple of men up there, and the natives are on the watch for us, too."

Cadfael could not but agree that this was the likeli-est answer to the loss of a man. "And yet . . . you know and I know that because one event follows an-other, it is not necessary the one should have caused the other. And yet the mind is so constructed, it can-not break the bond between the two. And here were two events, both unexpected; Clemence visited and departed—for he did depart, not one but four people rode a piece with him and said farewell to him in goodwill—and two days later the younger son of the house declares his intent to take the cowl. There is no sensible connection, and I cannot reeve the two apart."

"Does that mean," demanded Hugh plainly, "that you think this boy may have had a hand in a man's death and be taking refuge in the cloister?"

"No," said Cadfael decidedly. "Don't ask what is in my mind, for all I find there is mist and confusion, but whatever lies behind the mist, I feel certain it is not that. What his motive is I dare not guess, but I do not believe it is blood-guilt." And even as he said and meant it, he saw again Brother Wolstan prone and bleeding in the orchard grass, and Meriet's face fallen into a frozen mask of horror.

"For all that—and I respect what you say—I would like to keep a hand on this strange young man. A hand I can close at any moment if ever I should so wish," said Hugh honestly. "And you tell me he is to go to Saint Giles? To the very edge of town, close to woods and open heaths!"

"You need not fret," said Cadfael, "he will not run. He has nowhere to run to, for whatever else is true, his father is utterly estranged from him and would refuse to take him in. But he will not run because he does not wish to. The only haste he still nurses is to rush into his final vows and be done with it, and beyond deliverance."

"It's perpetual imprisonment he's seeking, then? Not escape?" said Hugh, with his dark head on one side, and a rueful and affectionate smile on his lips.

"Not escape no. From all I have seen," said Cadfael heavily, "he knows of no way of escape, anywhere, for him."

At the end of his penance Meriet came forth from his cell, blinking even at the subdued light of a November morning after the chill dimness within, and was presented at chapter before austere, unrevealing faces to ask pardon for his offences and acknowledge the justice of his penalty, which he did, to Cadfael's relief and admiration, with a calm and dignified bearing and a quiet voice. He looked thinner for his low diet, and his summer brown, smooth copper when he came, had faded into dark, creamy ivory, for though he tanned richly, he had little colour beneath the skin except when enraged. He was docile enough now, or had discovered how to withdraw into himself so far that curiosity, censure and animosity should not be able to move him.

"I desire," he said, "to learn what is due from me and to deliver it faithfully. I am here to be disposed of as may best be fitting."

Well, at any rate he knew how to keep his mouth shut, for evidently he had never let out, even to Brother Paul, that Cadfael had told him what was intended for him. By Isouda's account he must have been keeping his own counsel ever since he began to grow up, perhaps even before, as soon as it burned into his child's heart that he was not loved like his brother, and goaded him to turn mischievous and obdurate to get a little notice from those who undervalued him. Thus setting them ever more against him, and rendering himself ever more outrageously exiled from grace.

And I dared trounce him for succumbing to the first misery of his life, thought Cadfael, remorseful, when half his life has been a very sharp misery.

The abbot was austerely kind, putting behind them past errors atoned for, and explaining to him, what was now asked of him. "You will attend with us this morning," said Radulfus, "and take your dinner in refectory among your brothers. This afternoon Brother Cadfael will take you to the hospice at Saint Giles, since he will be going there to refill the medicine cupboard." And that, at least three days early, was news also to Cadfael, and a welcome indication of the abbot's personal concern. The brother who had shown a close interest in this troubled and troublesome young novice was being told plainly that he had leave to continue his surveillance.

They set forth from the gatehouse side by side in the early afternoon, into the common daily traffic of the high road through the Foregate. Not a great bustle at this hour on a soft, moist, melancholy November day, but always some evidence of human activity, a boy jog-trotting home with a bag on his shoulder and a dog at his heels, a carter making for the town with a load of coppice-wood, an old man leaning on his staff, two sturdy housewives of the Foregate bustling back from the town with their purchases, one of Hugh's officers riding back towards the bridge at a leisurely walk. Meriet opened his eyes wide at everything about him, after ten days of close stone walls and meagre lamp-light. His face was solemn and still, but his eyes de-voured colour and movement hungrily. From the gatehouse to the hospice of Saint Giles was barely half a mile's walk, alongside the enclave wall of the abbey, past the open green of the horse-fair, and along the straight road between the houses of the Foregate, until they thinned out with trees and gardens between, and gave place to the open countryside. And there the low roof of the hospital came into view, and the squat tower of its chapel, on a slight rise to the left of the highway, where the road forked.

Meriet eyed the place as they approached, with pur-poseful interest but no eagerness, simply as the field to which he was assigned.

"How many of these sick people can be housed here?"

"There might be as many as five and twenty at a time, but it varies. Some of them move on, from lazar-house to lazar-house, and make no long stay anywhere. Some come here too ill to go further. Death thins the numbers, and newcomers fill the gaps again. You are not afraid of infection?"

Meriet said: "No," so indifferently that it was almost as if he had said: "Why should I be? What threat can disease possibly be to me?"

"Your Brother Mark is in charge of all?" he asked.

"There is a lay superior, who lives in the Foregate, a decent man and a good manager. And two other helpers. But Mark looks after the inmates. You could be a great help to him if you choose," said Cadfael, "for he's barely older than you, and your company will be very welcome to him. Mark was my right hand and comfort in the herbarium, until he felt it his need to come here and care for the poor and the strays, and now I doubt I shall ever win him back, for he has always some soul here that he cannot leave, and as he loses one he finds another."

He drew in prudently from saying too much in praise of his most prized disciple; but still it came as a surprise to Meriet when they climbed the gentle slope that lifted the hospital clear of the highway, passed through wattled fence and low porch, and came upon Brother Mark sitting at his little desk within. He was furrowing his high forehead over accounts, his lips forming figures silently as he wrote them down on his vellum. His quill needed retrimming, and he had managed to ink his fingers, and by scrubbing bewilderedly in his spiky, straw-coloured fringe of hair had left smudges on both his eyebrow and his crown. Small and slight and plain of face, himself a neglected waif in his childhood, he looked up at them, when they entered the doorway, with a smile of such disarming sweetness that Meriet's firmly-shut mouth fell open, like his guarded eyes, and he stood staring in candid wonder as Cadfael presented him. This little, frail thing, meagre as a sixteen-year-old, and a hungry one at that, was minister to twenty or more sick, maimed, poor, verminous and old!

"I've brought you Brother Meriet," said Cadfael, "as well as this scrip full of goods. He'll be staying with you a while to learn the work here, and you can rely on him to do whatever you ask of him. Find him a corner and a bed, while I fill up your cupboard for you. Then you can tell me if there's anything more you need."

He knew his way here. He left them studying each other and feeling without haste for words, and went to unlock the repository of his medicines, and fill up the shelves. He was in no hurry; there was something about those two, utterly separate through they might be, the one son to a lord of two manors, the other a cottar's orphan, that had suddenly shown them as close kin in his eyes. Neglected and despised both, both of an age, and with such warmth and humility on the one side, and such passionate, and impulsive generosity on the other, how could they fail to come together?

When he had unloaded his scrip, and noted any depleted places remaining on the shelves, he went to find the pair, and followed them at a little distance as Mark led his new helper through hospice and chapel and graveyard, and the sheltered patch of orchard behind, where some of the abler in body sat for part of the day outside, to take the clean air. A household of the indigent and helpless, men, women, even children, forsaken or left orphans, dappled by skin diseases, deformed by accident, leprosy and agues; and a leaven of reasonably healthy beggars who lacked only land,

craft, a place in the orders, and the means to earn their
bread. In Wales, thought Cadfael, these things are better handled, not by charity but by blood-kinship. If a
man belongs to a kinship, who can separate him from
it? It acknowledges and sustains him, it will not let him
be outcast or die of need. Yet even in Wales, the out-
lander without a clan is one man against the world. So
are these runaway serfs, dispossessed cottagers, crippled labourers thrown out when they lose their working
value. And the poor, drab, debased women, some with
children at skirt, and the fathers snug and far, those that
are not honest but dead.

He left them together, and went away quietly with
his empty scrip and his bolstered faith. No need to say
one word to Mark of his new brother's history, let them
make what they could of each other in pure brotherhood, if that term has truly any meaning. Let Mark
make up his own mind, unprejudiced, unprompted, and
in a week we may learn something positive about
Meriet, not filtered through pity.

The last he saw of them they were in the little orchard where the children ran to play; four who could
run, one who hurpled on a single crutch, and one who
at nine years old scuttled on all fours like a small dog,
having lost the toes of both feet through a gangrene
after being exposed to hard frost in a bad winter. Mark
had the littlest by the hand as he led Meriet round the
small enclosure. Meriet had as yet no armoury against
horror, but at least horror in him was not revulsion. He
was stooping to reach a hand to the dog-boy winding

round his feet, and finding him unable to rise, and therefore unwilling to attempt it, he did not hoist the child willy-nilly, but suddenly dropped to his own nimble haunches to bring himself to a comparable level, and squatted there distressed, intent, listening.

It was enough, Cadfael went away content and left them together.

He let them alone for some days, and then made occasion to have a private word with Brother Mark, on the pretext of attending one of the beggars who had a persistent ulcer. Not a word was said of Meriet until Mark accompanied Cadfael out to the gate, and a piece of the way along the road towards the abbey wall.

"And how is your new helper doing?" asked Cadfael then, in the casual tone in which he would have enquired of any other beginning in this testing service.

"Very well," said Mark, cheerful and unsuspicious. "Willing to work until he drops, if I would let him." So he might, of course; it is one way of forgetting what cannot be escaped. "He's very good with the children, they follow him round and take him by the hand when they can." Yes, that also made excellent sense. The children would not ask him questions he did not wish to answer, or weigh him up in the scale as grown men do, but take him on trust and if they liked him, cling to him. He would not need his constant guard with them. "And he does not shrink from the worst disfigurement or the most disgusting tasks," said Mark, "though he is not inured to them as I am, and I know he suffers."

"That's needful," said Cadfael simply. "If he did not suffer he ought not to be here. Cold kindness is only half a man's duty who tends the sick. How do you find him with you—does he speak of himself ever?"

"Never," said Mark, and smiled, feeling no surprise that it should be so. "He has nothing he wishes to say. Not yet."

"And there is nothing you wish to know of him?"

"I'll listen willingly," said Mark, "to anything you think I *should* know of him. But what most matters I know already: that he is by nature honest and sweet clean through, whatever manner of wreck he and other people and ill circumstances may have made of his life. I only wish he were happier. I should like to hear him laugh."

"Not for your need, then," said Cadfael, "but in case of his, you had better know all of him that I know." And forthwith he told it.

"Now I understand," said Mark as the end of it, "why he *would* take his pallet up into the loft. He was afraid that in his sleep he might disturb and frighten those who have more than enough to bear already. I was in two minds about moving up there with him, but I thought better of it. I knew he must have his own good reasons."

"Good reasons for everything he does?" wondered Cadfael.

"Reasons that seem good to him, at any rate. But they might not always be wise," conceded Mark very seriously.

Brother Mark said no word to Meriet about what he had learned, certainly made no move to join him in his self-exile in the loft over the barn, nor offered any comment on such a choice; but he did, on the following three nights, absent himself very quietly from his own bed when all was still, and go softly into the barn to listen for any sound from above. But there was nothing but the long, easy breathing of a man peacefully asleep, and the occasional sigh and rustle as Meriet turned without waking. Perhaps other, deeper sighs at times, seeking to heave away a heavy weight from a heart; but no outcry. At Saint Giles Meriet went to bed tired out and to some consoling degree fulfilled, and slept without dreams.

Among the many benefactors of the leper hospital, the crown was one of the greatest through its grants to the abbey and the abbey's dependencies. There were other lords of manors who allowed certain days for the gathering of wild fruits or dead wood, but in the nearby reaches of the Long Forest the lazar-house had the right to make forays for wood, both for fuel and fencing or other building uses, on four days in the year, one in October, one in November, one in December, whenever the weather allowed, and one in February or March to replenish stocks run down by the winter.

Meriet had been at the hospice just three weeks when the third of December offered a suitably mild day for an expedition to the forest, with early sun and comfortably firm and dry earth underfoot. There had been several dry days, and might not be many more. It was ideal for picking up dead wood, without the extra weight of

damp to carry, and even stacked coppice-wood was fair
prize under the terms. Brother Mark snuffed the air and
declared what was to all intents a holiday. They mar-
shalled two light hand-carts, and a number of woven
slings to bind faggots, put on board a large leather
bucket of food, and collected all the inmates capable of
keeping up with a leisurely progress into the forest.
There were others who would have liked to come, but
could not manage the way and had to wait at home.

From Saint Giles the highway led south, leaving
aside to the left the way Brother Cadfael had taken to
Aspley. Some way past that divide they kept on along
the road, and wheeled right into the scattered copse-
land which fringed the forest, following a good, broad
ride which the carts could easily negotiate. The toeless
boy went with them, riding one of the carts. His weight,
after all, was negligible, and his joy beyond price.
Where they halted in a clearing to collect fallen wood,
they set him down in the smoothest stretch of grass,
and let him play while they worked.

Meriet had set out as grave as ever, but as the morning progressed, so did he emerge from his hiding-place
into muted sunlight, like the day. He snuffed the forest
air, and trod its sward, and seemed to expand, as a dried
shoot does after rain, drawing in sustenance from the
earth on which he strode. There was no one more tireless in collecting the stouter boughs of fallen wood, no
one so agile in binding and loading them. When the
company halted to take meat and drink, emptying the
leather bucket, they were well into the border areas of

the forest, where their pickings would be best, and
Meriet ate his bread and cheese and onion, and drank
his ale, and lay down flat as ground-ivy under the trees,
with the toeless boy sprawled in one arm. Thus deep-
drowned in the last pale grass, he looked like some na-
tive ground-growth burgeoning from the earth,
half-asleep towards the winter, half-wakeful towards
another growing year.

They had gone no more than ten minutes deeper into
the woodland, after their rest, when he checked to look
about him, at the slant of the veiled sun between the
trees, and the shape of the low, lichened outcrop of
rocks on their right.

"Now I know just where we are. When I had my first
pony I was never supposed to come further west than
the highroad from home, let alone venture this far
south-west into the forest, but I often did. There used to
be an old charcoal-burner had a hearth somewhere
here, it can't be far away. They found him dead in his
hut a year and more ago, and there was no son to take
on after him, and nobody wanted to live as lone as he
did. He may have left a cord or two of coppice-wood
stacked to season, that he never lived to burn. Shall we
go and see, Mark? We could do well there."

It was the first time he had ever volunteered even so
innocuous a recollection of his childhood, and the first
time he had shown any eagerness. Mark welcomed the
suggestion gladly.

"Can you find it again? We have a fair load already,
but we can very well cart the best out to the roadside,

and send for it again when we've unloaded the rest. We have the whole day."

"This way it should be," said Meriet, and set off confidently to the left between the trees, lengthening his step to quest ahead of his charges. "Let them follow at their own pace. I'll go forward and find the place. A hollow clearing it was—the stacks must have shelter . . ." His voice and his striding figure dwindled among the trees. He was out of sight for a few minutes before they heard him call, a hail as near pleasure as Mark had ever heard from him.

When Mark reached him he was standing where the trees thinned and fell back, leaving a shallow bowl perhaps forty or fifty paces across, with a level floor of beaten earth and old ash. At the rim, close to them, the decrepit remains of a rough hut of sticks and bracken and earth sagged over its empty log doorway, and on the far side of the arena there were stacked logs of coppicewood, left in the round, and now partially overgrown at the base of the stack with coarse grass and mosses. There was room enough on the prepared floor for two hearths some five long paces each in diameter, and their traces were still plain to be seen, though grass and herbage were encroaching from the edges of the plain, invading even the dead circles of ash with defiant green shoots. The nearer hearth had been cleared after its last burning, and no new stack built there, but on the more distant ring a mound of stacked logs, half burned out and half still keeping its form beneath the layers of grass and leaves and earth, lay flattened and settling.

"He had built his last stack and fired it," said Meriet, gazing, "and then never had time to build its fellow while the first was burning, as he always used to do, nor even to tend the one he had lighted. You see there must have been a wind, after he was dead, and no one by to dress the gap when it began to burn through. All the one side is dead ash, look, and the other only charred. Not much charcoal to be found there, but we might get enough to fill the bucket. And at least he left us a good stock of wood, and well seasoned, too."

"I have no skill in this art," said Mark curiously. "How can such a great hill of wood be got to burn without blazing, so that it may be used as fuel over again?"

"They begin with a tall stake in the middle, and stack dry split logs round it, and then the whole logs, until the stack is made. Then you must cover it with a clean layer, leaves or grass or bracken, to keep out the earth and ash that goes over all to seal it. And to light it, when it's ready, you hoist out the stake to leave a chimney, and drop your first red-hot coals down inside, and good dry sticks after, until it's well afire. Then you cover up the vent, and it burns very slow and hot, sometimes as long as ten days. If there's a wind you must watch it all the while, for if it burns through the whole stack goes up in flames. If there's danger you must patch the place and keep it sealed. There was no one left to do that here."

Their slower companions were coming up through

the trees. Meriet led the way down the slight incline into the hearth, with Mark close at his heels.

"It seems to me," said Mark, smiling, "that you're very well versed in the craft. How did you learn so much about it?"

"He was a surly old man and not well liked," said Meriet, making for the stacked cordwood, "but he was not surly with me. I was here often at one time, until I once helped him to rake down a finished burn, and went home dirtier than even I could account for. I got my tail well leathered, and they wouldn't let me have my pony again until I promised not venture over here to the west. I suppose I was about nine years old—it's a long time ago." He eyed the piled wood with pride and pleasure, and rolled the topmost log from its place, sending a number of frightened denizens scuttling for cover.

They had left one of their hand-carts, already well filled, in the clearing where they had rested at noon. Two of the sturdiest gleaners brought the second weaving between the trees, and the whole company fell gleefully upon the logs and began to load them.

"There'll be half-burned wood still in the stack," said Meriet, "and maybe some charcoal, too, if we strip it." And he was off to the tumbledown hut, and emerged with a large wooden rake, with which he went briskly to attack the misshapen mound left by the last uncontrolled burning. "Strange," he said, lifting his head and wrinkling his nose, "there's still the stink of old burning, who would have thought it could last so long?"

There was indeed a faint stench such as a woodland fire might leave after it had been damped by rain and dried out by wind. Mark could distinguish it, too, and came to Meriet's side as the broad rake began to draw down the covering of earth and leaves from the windward side of the mound. The moist, earthy smell of leaf-mould rose to their nostrils, and half-consumed logs heeled away and rolled down with the rake. Mark walked round to the other side, where the mound had sunk into a weathered mass of grey ash, and the wind had carried its fine dust as far as the rim of the trees. There the smell of dead fire was sharper, and rose in waves as Mark's feet stirred the debris. And surely on this side the leaves still left on the nearest trees were withered as though by scorching.

"Meriet!" called Mark in a low but urgent tone. "Come here to me!"

Meriet looked round, his rake locked in the covering of soil. Surprised but undisturbed, he skirted the ring of ash to come to where Mark stood, but instead of relinquishing the rake he tugged the head after him across the low crest of the mound, and tore down with it a tumble of half-burned logs, rolling merrily down into the ashen grass. It occurred to Mark that this was the first time he had seen his new helper look almost happy, using his body energetically, absorbed in what he was doing and forgetful of his own concerns. "What is it? What have you seen?"

The falling logs, charred and disintegrating, settled in a flurry of acrid dust. Something rolled out to

Meriet's feet, something that was not wood. Blackened, cracked and dried, a leathern shape hardly recognisable at first sight for a long-toed riding shoe, with a tarnished buckle to fasten it across the instep; and protruding from it, something long and rigid, showing gleams of whitish ivory through fluttering, tindery rags of calcined cloth.

There was a long moment while Meriet stood staring down at it without comprehension, his lips still shaping the last word of his blithe enquiry, his face still animated and alert. Then Mark saw the same shocking and violent change Cadfael had once seen, as the brightness of the hazel eyes seemed to collapse inward into total darkness, and the fragile mask of content shrank and froze into horror. He made a very small sound in his throat, a harsh rattle like a man dying, took one reeling step backwards, stumbled in the uneven ground, and dropped cowering into the grass.

CHAPTER EIGHT

IT WAS NO MORE THAN AN INSTANT'S WITHDRAWAL from the unbearable, recoiling into his enfolding arms, shutting out what nevertheless he could not choose but go on seeing. He had not swooned. Even as Mark flew to him, with no outcry to alarm the busy party dismantling the stack of cordwood, he was already rearing his head and doubling his fists grimly into the soil to raise himself. Mark held him with an arm about his body, for he was trembling still when he got to his feet.

"Did you see? Did you see it?" he asked in a whisper. What remained of the half-burned stack was between them and their charges, no one had turned to look in their direction.

"Yes, I saw. I know! We must get them away," said Mark. "Leave this pile as it is, touch nothing more, leave the charcoal. We must just load the wood and start them back for home. Are you fit to go? Can you be as always, and keep your face before them?"

"I can," said Meriet, stiffening, and scrubbed a sleeve over a forehead dewed with a chilly sweat, "I will! But, Mark, if you saw what I saw—we must *know* . . ."

"We do know," said Mark, "you and I both. It's not for us now, this is the law's business, and we must let ill alone for them to see. Don't even look that way again. I saw, perhaps, more than you. I know what is there. What we must do is get our people home without spoiling their day. Now, come and see to loading the cart with me. Can you, yet?"

For answer, Meriet braced his shoulders, heaved in a great breath, and withdrew himself resolutely from the thin arm that still encircled him, "I'm ready!" he said, in a fair attempt at the cheerful, practical voice with which he had summoned them to the hearth, and was off across the level floor to plunge fiercely into the labour of hoisting logs into the cart.

Mark followed him watchfully, and against all temptation contrived to obey his own order, and give no single glance to that which had been uncovered among the ashes. But he did, as they worked, cast a careful eye about the rim of the hearth, where he had also noticed certain circumstances which gave him cause for thought. What he had been about to say to Meriet when the rake fetched down its avalanche was never said.

They loaded their haul, stacking the wood so high

that there was no room for the toeless boy to ride on top of the return journey. Meriet carried him on his back, until the arms that clasped him round the neck fell slack with sleepiness, and he shifted his burden to one arm, so that the boy's tow-coloured head could nod securely on his shoulder. The load on his arm light enough, and warm against his heart. What else he carried unseen, thought Mark watching him with reticent attention, weighed more heavily and struck cold as ice. But Meriet's calm continued rock-firm. The one moment of recoil was over, and there would be no more such lapses.

At Saint Giles Meriet carried the boy indoors, and returned to help haul the carts up the slight slope to the barn, where the wood would be stacked under the low eaves, to be sawn and split later as it was needed.

"I am going now into Shrewsbury," said Mark, having counted all his chicks safely into the coop, tired and elated from their successful foray.

"Yes," said Meriet, without turning from the neat stack he was building, end-outwards between two confining buttresses of wood. "I know someone must."

"Stay here with them. I'll come back as soon as I can."

"I know," said Meriet. "I will. They're happy enough. It was a good day."

Brother Mark hesitated when he reached the abbey gatehouse, for his natural instinct was to take everything first to Brother Cadfael. It was plain that his errand now was to the officers of the king's law in the shire, and urgent, but on the other hand it was Cadfael who had confided Meriet to him, and he was certain in his own mind that the grisly discovery in the charcoal hearth was in some way connected with Meriet. The shock he had felt was genuine, but extreme, his wild recoil too intense to be anything but personal. He had not known, had not dreamed, what he was going to find, but past any doubt he knew it when he found it.

While Mark was hovering irresolute in the arch of the gatehouse Brother Cadfael, who had been sent for before Vespers to an old man in the Foregate who had a bad chest ailment, came behind and clapped him briskly on the shoulder. Turning to find the clemency of heaven apparently presenting him with the answer to his problem, Mark clutched him gratefully by the sleeve, and begged him: "Cadfael, come with me to Hugh Beringar. We've found something hideous in the Long Forest, business for him, surely. I was just by way of praying for you. Meriet was with me—this somehow touches Meriet . . ."

Cadfael fixed him with an acute stare, took him by the arm and turned him promptly towards the town. "Come on then and save your breath to tell the tale but once. I'm earlier back than anyone will expect me, I can stretch my licence an hour or two, for you and for Meriet."

So they were two who arrived at the house near Saint Mary's, where Hugh had settled his family. By luck he was home before supper, and free of his labours for the day. He haled them in warmly, and had wit enough not to offer Brother Mark respite or refreshment until he had heaved his whole anxiety off his narrow chest. Which he did very consideringly, measuring words. He stepped meticulously from fact to fact, as on sure stepping-stones through a perilous stream.

"I called him round to me because I had seen that on the side of that stack where I was, and where the pile was burned out, the wind had carried fine ash right into the trees, and the near branches of the trees were scorched, the leaves browned and withered. I meant to call his attention to these things, for such a fire was no long time ago. Those were this year's leaves scorched brown, that was ash not many weeks old still showing grey. And he came readily, but as he came he held on to the rake and tugged it with him, to bring down the top of the stack, where it had not burned out. So he brought down a whole fall of wood and earth and leaves, and this thing rolled down between, at our feet."

"You saw it plainly," said Hugh gently, "tell us as plainly."

"It is a fashionable long-toed riding shoe," said Mark steadily, "shrunk and dried and twisted by fire, but not consumed. And in it a man's leg-bone, in the ashes of hose."

"You are in no doubt," said Hugh, watching him with sympathy.

"None. I saw projecting from the pile the round

knee-joint from which the shin-bone had parted," said Brother Mark, pale but tranquil. "It so happened I saw it break away. I am sure the man is there. The fire broke through on the other side, a strong wind drove it, and left him, it may be, almost for Christian burial. At least we may collect his bones."

"That shall be done with all reverence," said Hugh, "if you are right. Go on, you have more to tell. Brother Meriet saw what you had seen. What then?"

"He was utterly stricken and shocked. He had spoken of coming there as a child, and helping the old charcoal-burner. I am certain he knew of nothing worse there than what he remembered. I told him first we must get our people home undisturbed, and he did his part valiantly," said Brother Mark. "We have left all as we found it—or as we disturbed it unwitting. In the morning light I can show you the place."

"I think, rather," said Hugh with deliberation, "Meriet Aspley shall do that. But now you have told us what you had to tell, now you may sit down with me and eat and drink a morsel, while we consider this matter."

Brother Mark sat down obediently, sighing away the burden of his knowledge. Grateful for the humblest of hospitality, he was equally unawed by the noblest, and having no pride, he did not know how to be servile. When Aline herself brought him meat and drink, and the same for Cadfael, he received it gladly and simply, as saints accept alms, perpetually astonished and pleased, perpetually serene.

"You said," Hugh pressed him gently over the wine, "that you had cause, in the blown ash and the scorching of the trees, to believe that the fire was of this season, and not from a year ago, and that I accept. Had you other reasons to think so?"

"I had," said Mark simply, "for though we have brought home, to our gain, a whole cord of good coppice-wood, yet not far aside from ours there were two other flattened and whitened shapes in the grass, greener than the one we have now left, but still clear to be seen, which I think must have been bared when the wood was used for this stack. Meriet told me the logs must be left to season. These would have seasoned more than a year, dried out, it may be, too far for what was purposed. No one was left to watch the burning, and the over-dried wood burned through and burst into a blaze. You will see the shapes where the wood lay. You will judge better than I how long since it was moved."

"That I doubt," said Hugh, smiling, "for you seem to have done excellently well. But tomorrow we shall see. There are those can tell to a hair, by the burrowing insects and the spiders, and the tinder fringing the wood. Sit and take your ease a while, before you must return, for there's nothing now can be done before morning."

Brother Mark sat back, relieved, and bit with astonished pleasure into the game pasty Aline had brought him. She thought him underfed, and worried about him because he was so meagre; and indeed he may very well have been underfed, through forgetting to eat while he worried about someone else. There was a great deal of the good woman in Brother Mark, and Aline recognized it.

"Tomorrow morning," said Hugh, when Mark rose to take his leave and make his way back to his charges, "I shall be at Saint Giles with my men immediately after Prime. You may tell Brother Meriet that I shall require him to come with me and show me the place.

That, of course, should occasion no anxiety to an innocent man, since he had been the cause of the discovery in the first place, but it might bring on a very uneasy night for one not entirely innocent, at least of more knowledge than was good for him. Mark could not object to the oblique threat, since his own mind had been working in much the same direction. But in departing he made over again his strongest point in Meriet's defence.

"He led us to the place, for good and sensible reasons, seeing it was fuel we were after. Had he known what he was to find there, he would never have let us near it."

"That shall be borne in mind," said Hugh gravely. "Yet I think you found something more than natural in his horror when he uncovered a dead man. You, after all, are much of his age, and have had no more experience of murder and violence than has he. And I make no doubt you were shaken to the soul—yet not as he was. Granted he knew nothing of this unlawful burial, still the discovery meant to him something more, something worse, than it meant to you. Granted he did not know a body had been so disposed of, may he not, nevertheless, have had knowledge of a body in need of secret disposal, and recognized it when he uncovered it?"

"That is possible," said Mark simply. "It is for you to examine all these things." And he took his leave, and set off alone on the walk back to Saint Giles.

"There's no knowing, as yet," said Cadfael, when Mark was gone, "who or what this dead man may be. He may have nothing to do with Meriet, with Peter Clemence or with the horse straying in the mosses. A live man missing, a dead man found—they need not be one and the same. There's every reason to doubt it. The horse more than twenty miles north of here, the rider's last night halt four miles south-east, and this burning hearth another four miles south-west from there. You'll have hard work linking those into one sequence and making sense of it. He left Aspley travelling north, and one thing's certain by a number of witnesses, he was man alive then. What should he be doing now, not north, but south of Aspley? And his horse miles north, and on the right route he would be taking, bar a little straying at the end?"

"I don't know but I'll be the happier," owned Hugh, "if this turns out to be some other traveller fallen by thieves somewhere, and nothing to do with Clemence, who may well be down in the peat-pools this moment. But do you know of any other gone missing in these parts? And another thing, Cadfael, would common thieves have left him his riding shoes? Or his hose, for that matter? A naked man has nothing left that could benefit his murderers, and nothing by which he may be easily known, two good reasons for stripping him. And again, since he wore long-toed shoes, he was certainly not going far afoot. No sane man would wear them for walking."

A rider without a horse, a saddled horse without a rider, what wonder if the mind put the two together?

"No profit in racking brains," said Cadfael, sighing, "until you've viewed the place, and gathered what there is to be gathered there."

"*We,* old friend! I want you with me, and I think Abbot Radulfus will give me leave to take you. You're better skilled than I in dead men, in how long they may have been dead, and how they died. Moreover, he'll want a watching eye on all that affects Saint Giles, and who better than you? You're waist-deep in the whole matter already, you must either sink or haul clear."

"For my sins!" said Cadfael, somewhat hypocritically. "But I'll gladly come with you. Whatever devil it is that possesses young Meriet is plaguing me by contagion, and I want it exorcized at all costs."

Meriet was waiting for them when they came for him next day, Hugh and Cadfael, a sergeant and two officers, equipped with crows and shovels, and a sieve to sift the ashes for every trace and every bone. In the faint mist of a still morning, Meriet eyed all these preparations with a face stonily calm, braced for everything that might come, and said flatly: "The tools are still there, my lord, in the hut. I fetched the rake from there, Mark will have told you—a corrack, the old man called it." He looked at Cadfael, with the faintest softening in the set of his lips. "Brother Mark said I should be needed. I'm glad he need not go back himself." His voice was in as thorough control as his face; whatever confronted him today, it would not take him by surprise.

They had brought a horse for him, time having its value. He mounted nimbly, perhaps with the only impulse of pleasure that would come his way that day, and led the way down the high road. He did not glance aside when he passed the turning to his own home, but turned on the other hand into the broad ride, and within half an hour had brought them to the shallow bowl of the charcoal hearth. Ground mist lay faintly blue over the shattered mound as Hugh and Cadfael walked round the rim and halted where the log that was no log lay tumbled among the ashes.

The tarnished buckle on the perished leather strap was of silver. The shoe had been elaborate and expensive. Slivers of burned cloth fluttered from the almost fleshless bone.

Hugh looked from the foot to the knee, and on above among the exposed wood for the joint from which it had broken free. "There he should be lying, aligned thus. Whoever put him there did not open a deserted stack, but built this new, and built him into the centre. Someone who knew the method, though perhaps not well enough. We had better take this apart carefully. You may rake off the earth covering and the leaves," he said to his men, "but when you reach the logs we'll hoist them off one by one where they're whole. I doubt he'll be little but bones, but I want all there is of him."

They went to work, raking away the covering on the unburned side, and Cadfael circled the mound to view the quarter from which the destroying wind must have been blowing. Low to the ground a small, arched hole showed in the roots of the pile. He stooped to look more closely, and ran a hand under the hanging leaves that half-obscured it. The hollow continued inward, swallowing his arm to the elbow. It had been built in as the stack was made. He went back to where Hugh stood watching.

"They knew the method, sure enough. There's a vent built in on the windward side to let in a draught. The stack was meant to burn out. But they overdid it. They must have had the vent covered until the stack was well alight, and then opened and left it. It blew too fiercely, and left the windward half hardly more than scorched while the rest blazed. These things have to be watched day and night."

Meriet stood apart, close to where they had tethered the horses, and watched this purposeful activity with an impassive face. He saw Hugh cross to the edge of the arena, where three paler, flattened oblongs in the herbage showed where the wood had been stacked to season. Two of them showed greener than the third, as Mark had said, where new herbage had pierced the layer of dead grass and risen to the light. The third, the one which had supplied such a harvest for the inmates of Saint Giles, lay bleached and flat.

"How long," asked Hugh, "to make this much new growth, and at this season?"

Cadfael pondered, digging a toe into the soft mat of old growth below. "A matter of eight to ten weeks, perhaps. Difficult to tell. And the blown ash might show as long as that. Mark was right, the heat reached the trees. If this floor had been less bare and hard, the fire might have reached them, too, but there was no thick layer of roots and leaf-mould to carry it along the ground."

They returned to where the covering of earth and leaves now lay drawn aside, and the ridged surfaces of logs showed, blackened but keeping their shape. The sergeant and his men laid down their tools and went to work with their hands, hoisting the logs off one by one and stacking them aside out of the way. Slow work; and throughout Meriet stood watching, motionless and mute.

The dead man emerged from his coffin of timber piecemeal after more than two hours of work. He had lain close to the central chimney on the leeward side, and the fire had been fierce enough to burn away all but a few tindery flakes of his clothing, but had passed by too rapidly to take all the flesh from his bones, or even the hair from his head. Laboriously they brushed away debris of charcoal and ash and half-consumed wood from him, but could not keep him intact. The collapse of part of the stack had started his joints and broken him apart. They had to gather up his bones as best they could, and lay them out on the grass until they had, if not the whole man, all but such small bones of finger and wrist as would have to be sifted from the ashes. The skull still retained, above the blackened ruin of a face, the dome of a naked crown fringed with a few wisps and locks of brown hair, cropped short.

But there were other things to lay beside him. Metal is very durable. The silver buckles on his shoes, blackened as they were, kept the form a good workman had given them. There was the twisted half of a tooled leather belt, with another silver buckle, large and elaborate, and traces of silver ornamenting in the leather. There was a broken length of tarnished silver chain attached to a silver cross studded with what must surely be semi-precious stones, though now they were blackened and encrusted with dirt. And one of the men, running fine ash from close to the body through the sieve, came to lay down for examination a finger-bone and the ring it had loosely retained while the flesh was burned from between. The ring bore a large black stone engraved with a design fouled by clotted ash, but which seemed to be a decorative cross. There was also something which had lain within the shattered ribcage, burned almost clean by the fire, the head of the arrow that had killed him.

Hugh stood over the remnants of a man and his death for a long while, staring down with a grim face. Then he turned to where Meriet stood, rigid and still at the rim of the decline.

"Come down here, come and see if you cannot help us further. We need a name for this murdered man. Come and see if by chance you know him."

Meriet came, ivory-faced, drew close as he was ordered, and looked at what lay displayed. Cadfael held off, but at no great distance, and watched and listened. Hugh had not only his work to do, but his own wrung senses to avenge, and if there was some resultant savagery in his handling of Meriet, at least it was not purposeless. For now there was very little doubt of the identity of this dead man they had before them, and the chain that drew Meriet to him was contracting.

"You observe," said Hugh, quite gently and coldly, "that he wore the tonsure, that his own hair was brown, and his height, by the look of his bones, a tall man's. What age would you say, Cadfael?"

"He's straight, and without any of the deformities of ageing. A young man. Thirty he might be, I doubt more."

"And a priest," pursued Hugh mercilessly.

"By the ring, the cross and the tonsure, yes, a priest."

"You perceive our reasoning, Brother Meriet. Have you knowledge of such a man lost hereabouts?"

Meriet continued to stare down at the silent relics that had been a man. His eyes were huge in a face blanched to the palest ivory. He said in a level voice: "I see your reasoning. I do not know the man. How can anyone know him?"

"Not by his visage, certainly. But by his accoutrements, perhaps? The cross, the ring, even the buckles—these could be remembered, if a priest of such years, and so adorned, came into your acquaintance? As a guest, say, in your house?"

Meriet lifted his eyes with a brief and restrained flash of green, and said: "I understand you. There was a priest who came and stayed the night over in my father's house, some weeks ago, before I came into the cloister. But that one travelled on the next morning, northwards, not this way. How could he be here? And how am I, or how are you, to tell the difference between one priest and another, when they are brought down to this?"

"Not by the cross? The ring? If you can say positively that this is *not* the man," said Hugh insinuatingly, "you would be helping me greatly."

"I was of no such account in my father's house," said Meriet with chill bitterness, "to be so close to the honoured guest. I stabled his horse—to that I have testified. To his jewellery I cannot swear."

"There will be others who can," said Hugh grimly. "And as to the horse, yes, I have seen in what comfortable esteem you held each other. You said truly that you are good with horses. If it became advisable to convey the mount some twenty miles or more away from where the rider met his death, who could manage the business better? Ridden or led, he would not give any trouble to you."

"I never had him in my hands but one evening and the morning after," said Meriet, "nor saw him again until you brought him to the abbey, my lord." And though sudden angry colour flamed upward to his brow, his voice was ready and firm, and his temper well in hand.

"Well, let us first find a name for our dead man," said Hugh, and turned to circle the dismembered mound once more, scanning the littered and fouled ground for any further detail that might have some bearing. He pondered what was left of the leather belt, all but the buckle end burned away, the charred remnant extending just far enough to reach a lean man's left hip. "Whoever he was, he carried sword or dagger, here is the loop of the strap by which it hung—a dagger, too light and elegant for a sword. But no sign of the dagger itself. That should be somewhere here among the rubble."

They raked through the debris for a further hour, but found no more of metal or clothing. When he was certain there was nothing more to be discovered, Hugh withdrew his party. They wrapped the recovered bones and the ring and cross reverently in a linen cloth and a blanket, and rode back with them to Saint Giles. There Meriet dismounted, but halted in silence to know what was the deputy-sheriff's will with him.

"You will be remaining here at the hospice?" asked Hugh, eyeing him impartially. "Your abbot has committed you to this service?"

"Yes, my lord. Until or unless I am recalled to the abbey, I shall be here." It was said with emphasis, not merely stating a fact, but stressing that he felt himself to have taken vows already, and not only his duty of obedience but his own will would keep him here.

"Good! So we know where to find you at need. Very well, continue your work here without hindrance, but subject to your abbot's authority, hold yourself also at my disposal."

"So I will, my lord. So I do," said Meriet, and turned on his heel with a certain drear dignity, and stalked away up the incline to the gate in the wattle fence.

"And now, I suppose," sighed Hugh, riding on towards the Foregate with Cadfael beside him, "you will be at odds with me for being rough with your fledgling. Though I give you due credit, you held your tongue very generously."

"No," said Cadfael honestly, "he's none the worse for goading. And there's no blinking it, suspicion drapes itself round him like cobwebs on an autumn bush."

"It *is* the man, and he knows that it is. He knew it as soon as he raked out the shoe and the foot within it. That, and not the mere matter of some unknown man's ugly death, was what shook him almost out of his wits.

He knew—quite certainly he knew—that Peter Clemence was dead, but just as certainly he did *not* know what had been done with the body. Will you go with me so far?"

"So far," said Cadfael ruefully, "I have already gone. An irony, indeed, that he led them straight to the place, when for once he was thinking of nothing but finding his poor folk fuel for the winter. Which is on the doorstep this very evening, unless my nose for weather fails me."

The air had certainly grown still and chill, and the sky was closing down upon the world in leaden cloud. Winter had delayed, but was not far away.

"First," pursued Hugh, harking back to the matter in hand, "we have to affix a name to these bones. That whole household at Aspley saw the man, spent an evening in his company, they must all know these gems of his, soiled as they may be now. It might put a rampaging cat among pigeons if I sent to summon Leoric here to speak as to his guest's cross and ring. When the birds fly wild, we may pick up a feather or two."

"But for all that," said Cadfael earnestly, "I should not do it. Say never a probing word to any, leave them lulled. Let it be known we've found a murdered man, but no more. If you let out too much, then the one with guilt to hide will be off and out of reach. Let him think all's well, and he'll be off his guard. You'll not have forgotten, the older boy's marriage is set for the twenty-first of this month, and two days before that the whole clan of them, neighbours, friends and all, will be gathering in our guest-halls. Bring them in, and you have everyone in your hand. By then we may have the means to divine truth from untruth. And as for proving that this is indeed Peter Clemence—not that I'm in doubt!—did you not tell me that Canon Eluard intends to come back to us on the way south from Lincoln, and let the king go without him to Westminster?"

"True, so he said he would. He's anxious for news to take back to the bishop at Winchester, but it's no good news we have for him."

"If Stephen means to spend his Christmas in London, then Canon Eluard may very well be here before the wedding party arrives. He knew Clemence well, they've both been close about Bishop Henry. He should be your best witness."

"Well, a couple of weeks can hardly hurt Peter Clemence now," agreed Hugh wryly. "But have you noticed, Cadfael, the strangest thing in all this coil? Nothing was stolen from him, everything burned with him. Yet more than one man, more than two, worked at building that pyre. Would you not say there was a voice in authority there, that would not permit theft though it had been forced to conceal murder? And those who took his orders feared him—or at the least minded him—more than they coveted rings and crosses."

It was true. Whoever had decreed that disposal of Peter Clemence had put it clean out of consideration that his death could be the work of common footpads and thieves. A mistake, if he hoped to set all suspicion at a distance from himself and his own people. That rigid honesty had mattered more to him, whoever he was, than safety. Murder was within the scope of his understanding, if not of his tolerance; but not theft from the dead.

CHAPTER NINE

FROST SET IN THAT NIGHT, HERALDING A WEEK OF hard weather. No snow fell, but a blistering east wind scoured the hills, wild birds ventured close to human habitations to pick up scraps of food, and even the woodland foxes came skulking a mile closer to the town. And so did some unknown human predator who had been snatching the occasional hen from certain outlying runs, and now and then a loaf of bread from a kitchen. Complaints began to be brought in to the town provost of thefts from the garden stores outside the walls, and to the castle of poultry taken from homesteads at the edge of Foregate, and not by foxes or other vermin. One of the foresters from the Long Forest brought in a tale of a gutted deer lost a month ago, with evidence enough that the marauder was in possession of a good knife. Now the cold was driving someone living wild nearer to the town, where nights could be spent warmer in byre or barn than in the bleak woods.

King Stephen had detained his sheriff at Shropshire in attendance about his person that autumn, after the usual Michaelmas accounting, and taken him with him in the company now paying calculated courtesies to the earl of Chester and William of Roumare in Lincoln, so that this matter of the henhouse marauder, along with all other offences against the king's peace and good order, fell into Hugh's hands. "As well!" said Hugh, "for I'd just as lief keep the Clemence affair mine without interference, now it's gone so far."

He was well aware that he had not too much time left in which to bring it to a just end single-handed, for if the king meant to be back in Westminster for Christmas, then the sheriff might return to his shire in a very few days. And certainly this wild man's activities seemed to be centred on the eastern fringe of the forest, which was engaging Hugh's interest already for a very different reason.

In a country racked by civil war, and therefore hampered in keeping ordinary law and order, everything unaccountable was being put down to outlaws living wild; but for all that, now and then the simplest explanation turns out to be the true one. Hugh had no such expectations in this case, and was greatly surprised when one of his sergeants brought in to the castle wards in triumph the thief who had been living off the more unwary inhabitants of the Foregate. Not because of the man himself, who was very much what might have been expected, but because of the dagger and sheath which had been found on him, and were handed over as proof of his villainies. There were even traces of dried blood, no doubt from someone's pullet or goose, engrained in the grooved blade.

It was a very elegant dagger, with rough gems in the hilt, so shaped as to be comfortable to the hand, and its sheath of metal covered with tooled leather had been blackened and discoloured by fire, the leather frayed away for half its length from the tip. An end of thin leather strap still adhered to it. Hugh had seen the loop from which it, or its fellow, should have depended.

In the bleak space of the inner ward he jerked his head towards the anteroom of the hall, and said: "Bring him within." There was a good fire in there, and a bench to sit on. "Take off his chains," said Hugh, after one look at the wreck of a big man, "and let him sit by the fire. You may keep by him, but I doubt if he'll give you any trouble."

The prisoner could have been an imposing figure, if he had still had flesh and sinew on his long, large bones, but he was shrunken by starvation, and with nothing but rags on him in this onset of winter. He could not be old, his eyes and his shock of pale hair were those of a young man, his bones, however starting from his flesh, moved with the live vigour of youth. Close to the fire, warmed after intense cold, he flushed and dilated into something nearer approaching his proper growth. But his face, blue-eyed, hollow-cheeked, stared in mute terror upon Hugh. He was like a wild thing in a trap, braced taut, waiting for a bolt-hole. Ceaselessly he rubbed at his wrists, just loosed from the heavy chains.

"What is your name?" asked Hugh, so mildly that the creature stared and froze, afraid to understand such a tone.

"What do men call you?" repeated Hugh patiently.

"Harald, my lord. I'm named Harald." The large frame produced a skeletal sound, deep but dry and remote. He had a cough that perforated his speech uneasily, and a name that had once belonged to a king, and that within the memory of old men still living, men of his own fair colouring.

"Tell me how you came by this thing, Harald. For it's a rich man's weapon, as you must know. See the craftsmanship of it, and the jeweller's work. Where did you find such a thing?"

"I didn't steal it," said the wretch, trembling. "I swear I didn't! It was thrown away, no one wanted it . . ."

"Where did you find it?" demanded Hugh more sharply.

"In the forest, my lord. There's a place where they burn charcoal." He described it, stammering and blinking, voluble to hold off blame. "There was a dead fire there, I took fuel from it sometimes, but I was afraid to stay so near the road. The knife was lying in the ashes, lost or thrown away. Nobody wanted it. And I needed a knife . . ." "He shook, watching Hugh's impassive face with frightened blue eyes. "It was not stealing . . . I never stole but to keep alive, my lord, I swear it."

He had not been a very successful thief, even so, for he had barely kept body and soul together. Hugh regarded him with detached interest, and no particular severity.

"How long have you been living wild?"

"Four months it must be, my lord. But I never did violence, nor stole anything but food. I needed a knife for my hunting . . ."

Ah, well, thought Hugh, the king can afford a deer here and there. This poor devil needs it more than Stephen does, and Stephen in his truest mood would give it to him freely. Aloud he said: "A hard life for a man, come wintertime. You'll do better indoors with us for a while, Harald, and feed regularly, if not on venison." He turned to the sergeant, who was standing warily by. "Lock him away. Let him have blankets to wrap him. And see to it he eats—but none too much to start with or he'll gorge and die on us." He had known it happen among the wretched creatures in flight the previous winter from the storming of Worcester, starving on the road and eating themselves to death when they came to shelter. "And use him well!" said Hugh sharply as the sergeant hauled up his prisoner. "He'll not stand rough handling, and I want him. Understood?"

The sergeant understood it as meaning this was the wanted murderer, and must live to stand his trial and take his ceremonial death. He grinned, and abated his hold on the bony shoulder he gripped. "I take your meaning, my lord."

They were gone, captor and captive, off to a securely locked cell where the outlaw Harald, almost certainly a runaway villein, and probably with good reason, could at least be warmer than out in the woods, and get his meals, rough as they might be, brought to him without hunting.

Hugh completed his daily business about the castle, and then went off to find Brother Cadfael in his workshop, brewing some aromatic mixture to soothe ageing throats through the first chills of the winter. Hugh sat back on the familiar bench against the timber wall, and accepted a cup of one of Cadfael's better wines, kept for his better acquaintances.

"Well, we have our murderer safely under lock and key," he announced, straight-faced, and recounted what had emerged. Cadfael listened attentively, for all he seemed to have his whole mind on his simmering syrup.

"Folly!" he said then, scornfully. His brew was bubbling too briskly, he lifted it to the side of the brazier.

"Of course folly," agreed Hugh heartily. "A poor wretch without a rag to his covering or a crust to his name, kill a man and leave him his valuables, let alone his clothes? They must be about of a height, he would have stripped him naked and been glad of such cloth. And build the clerk single-handed into that stack of timber? Even if he knew how such burnings are managed, and I doubt if he does. . . . No, it is beyond belief.

He found the dagger, just as he says. What we have here is some poor soul pushed so far by a heavy-handed lord that he's run for it. And too timid, or too sure of his lord's will to pursue him, to risk walking into the town and seeking work. He's been loose four months, picking up what food he could where he could."

"You have it all clear enough, it seems," said Cadfael, still brooding over his concoction, though it was beginning to settle in the pot, gently hiccuping. "What is it you want of me?"

"My man has a cough, and a festered wound on his forearm, I judge a dog's bite, somewhere he lifted a hen. Come and sain it for him, and get out of him whatever you can, where he came from, who is his master, what is his trade. We've room for good craftsmen of every kind in the town, as you know, and have taken in several, to our gain and theirs. This may well be another as useful."

"I'll do that gladly," said Cadfael, turning to look at his friend with a very shrewd eye. "And what has he to offer you in exchange for a meal and a bed? And maybe a suit of clothes, if you had his inches, as by your own account you have not. I'd swear Peter Clemence could have topped you by a hand's length."

"This fellow certainly could," allowed Hugh, grinning. "Though sidewise even I could make two of him as he is now. But you'll see for yourself, and no doubt be casting an eye over all your acquaintance to find a man whose cast-offs would fit him. As for what use I have for him, apart from keeping him from starving to death—my sergeant is already putting it about that our wild man is taken, and I've no doubt he won't omit the matter of the dagger. No need to frighten the poor devil worse than he's been frightened already by charging him, but if the world outside has it on good authority that our murderer is safe behind bars, so much the better. Everyone can breathe more freely—notably the murderer. And a man off his guard, as you said, may make a fatal slip."

Cadfael considered and approved. So desirable an ending, to have an outlaw and a stranger, who mattered to nobody, blamed for whatever evil was done locally; and one week now to pass before the wedding party assembled, all with minds at ease.

"For that stubborn lad of yours at Saint Giles," said Hugh very seriously, "knows what happened to Peter Clemence, whether he had any hand in it, or no."

"Knows," said Brother Cadfael, equally gravely, "or thinks he knows."

He went up through the town to the castle that same afternoon, bespoken by Hugh from the abbot as healer even to prisoners and criminals. He found the prisoner Harald in a cell at least dry with a stone bench to lie on, and blankets to soften it and wrap him from the cold, and that was surely Hugh's doing. The opening of the door upon his solitude occasioned instant mute alarm, but the appearance of a Benedictine habit both astonished and soothed him, and to be asked to show his

hurts was still deeper bewilderment, but softened into
wonder and hope. After long loneliness, where the
sound of a voice could mean nothing but threat, the
fugitive recovered his tongue rustily but gratefully, and
ended in a flood of words like floods of tears, draining
and exhausting him. After Cadfael left him he stretched
and eased into prodigious sleep.

Cadfael reported to Hugh before leaving the castle
wards.

"He's a farrier, he says a good one. It may well be
true, it is the only source of pride he has left. Can you
use such? I've dressed his bite with a lotion of hound's-
tongue, and anointed a few other cuts and grazes he
has. I think he'll do well enough. Let him eat little but
often for a day or two or he'll sicken. He's from some
way south, by Gretton. He says his lord's steward took
his sister against her will, and he tried to avenge her.
He was not good at murder," said Cadfael wryly, "and
the ravisher got away with a mere graze. He may be
better at farriery. His lord sought his blood and he
ran—who could blame him?"

"Villein?" asked Hugh resignedly.

"Surely."

"And sought, probably vindictively. Well, they'll
have a vain hunt if they hunt him into Shrewsbury castle, we can hold him securely enough. And you think
he tells truth?"

"He's too far gone to lie," said Cadfael. "Even if
lying came easily, and I think this is a simple soul who
leans to truth. Besides, he believes in my habit. We

have still a reputation, Hugh, God send we may deserve
it."

"He's within a charter town, if he is in prison," said
Hugh with satisfaction, "and it would be a bold lord
who would try to take him from the king's hold. Let his
master rejoice in thinking the poor wretch held for murder, if that gives him pleasure. We'll put it about, then,
that our murderer's taken, and watch for what follows."

The news went round, as news does, from gossip to
gossip, those within the town parading their superior
knowledge to those without, those who came to market
in town or Foregate carrying their news to outer villages and manors. As the word of Peter Clemence's
disappearance had been blown on the wind, and after it
news of the discovery of his body in the forest, so did
every breeze spread abroad the word that his killer was
already taken and in prison in the castle, found in possession of the dead man's dagger, and charged with his
murder. No more mystery to be mulled over in taverns
and on street-corners, no further sensations to be hoped
for. The town made do with what it had, and made the
most of it. More distant and isolated manors had to wait
a week or more for the news to reach them.

The marvel was that it took three whole days to
reach Saint Giles. Isolated though the hospice was,
since its inmates were not allowed nearer the town for
fear of contagion, somehow they usually seemed to get
word of everything that was happening almost as soon
as it was common gossip in the streets; but this time the

system was slow in functioning. Bother Cadfael had given anxious thought to consideration of what effect the news was likely to have upon Meriet. But there was nothing to be done about that but to wait and see. No need to make a point of bringing the story to the young man's ears deliberately, better let it make its way to him by the common talk, as to everyone else.

So it was not until two lay servants came to deliver the hospital's customary loaves from the abbey bakery, on the third day, that word of the arrest of the runaway villein Harald came to Meriet's ears. By chance it was he who took in the great basket and unloaded the bread in the store, helped by the two bakery hands who had brought it. For his silence they made up in volubility.

"You'll be getting more and more beggars coming in for shelter, brother, if this cold weather sets in in earnest. Hard frost and an east wind again, no season to be on the roads."

Civil but taciturn, Meriet agreed that winter came hard on the poor.

"Not that they're all honest and deserving," said the other, shrugging. "Who knows what you're taking in sometimes? Rogues and vagabonds as likely as not, and who's to tell the difference?"

"There's one you might have got this week past that you can well do without," said his fellow, "for you might have got a throat cut in the night, and whatever's worth stealing made away with. But you're safe from him, at any rate, for he's locked up in Shrewsbury castle till he comes to his trial for murder."

"For killing a priest, at that! He'll pay for it with his own neck, surely, but that's poor reparation for a priest."

Meriet had turned, stiffly attentive, staring at them with frowning eyes. "For killing a priest? What priest? Who is this you speak of?"

"What, have you not heard yet? Why, the bishop of Winchester's chaplain that was found in the Long Forest. A wild man who's been preying on the houses outside the town killed him. It's what I was saying, with winter coming on sharp now you might have had him shivering and begging at your door here, and with the priest's own dagger under his ragged coat ready for you."

"Let me understand you," said Meriet slowly. "You say a man is taken for that death? Arrested and charged with it?"

"Taken, charged, gaoled, and as good has hanged," agreed his informant cheerfully. "That's one you need not worry your head about, brother."

"What man is he? How did this come about?" asked Meriet urgently.

They told him, in strophe and antistrophe, pleased to find someone who had not already heard the tale.

"And waste of time to deny, for he had the dagger on him that belonged to the murdered man. Found it, he said, in the charcoal hearth there, and a likely tale that makes."

Staring beyond them, Meriet asked, low-voiced:

"What like is he, this fellow? A local man? Do you know his name?"

That they could not supply, but they could describe him. "Not from these parts, some runaway living rough, a poor starving wretch, swears he's never done worse than steal a little bread or an egg to keep himself alive, but the foresters say he's taken their deer in his time. Thin as a fence-pale, and in rags, a desperate case . . ."

They took their basket and departed, and Meriet went about his work in dead, cold silence all that day. A desperate case—yes, so it sounded. As good as hanged! Starved and runaway and living wild, thin to emaciation . . .

He said no word to Brother Mark, but one of the brightest and most inquisitive of the children had stretched his ears in the kitchen doorway and heard the exchanges, and spread the news through the household with natural relish. Life in Saint Giles, however sheltered, could be tedious, it was none the worse for an occasional sensation to vary the routine of the day. The story came to Brother Mark's ears. He debated whether to speak or not, watching the chill mask of Meriet's face, and the inward state of his hazel eyes. But at last he did venture a word.

"You have heard, they have taken up a man for the killing of Peter Clemence?"

"Yes," said Meriet, leaden-voiced, and looked through him and far away.

"If there is no guilt in him," said Mark emphatically, "there will no harm come to him."

But Meriet had nothing to say, nor did it seem fitting to Mark to add anything more. Yet he did watch his friend from that moment with unobtrusive care, and fretted to see how utterly he had withdrawn into himself with this knowledge that seemed to work in him like poison.

In the darkness of the night Mark could not sleep. It was some time now since he had stolen across to the barn by night, to listen intently at the foot of the ladder stair that led up into the loft, and take comfort in the silence that meant Meriet was deeply asleep; but on this night he made that pilgrimage again. He did not know the true cause and nature of Meriet's pain, but he knew that it was heart-deep and very bitter. He rose with careful quietness, not to disturb his neighbours, and made his way out to the barn.

The frost was not so sharp that night, the air had a stillness and faint haze instead of the piercing starry glitter of past nights. In the loft there would be warmth enough, and the homely scents of timber, straw and grain, but also great loneliness for that inaccessible sleeper who shrank from having neighbours, for fear of frightening them. Mark had wondered lately whether he might not appeal to Meriet to come down and rejoin his fellowmen, but it would not have been easy to do without alerting that austere spirit to the fact that his slumbers had been spied upon, however benevolently, and Mark had never quite reached the point of making the assay.

He knew his way in pitch darkness to the foot of the

steep stairway, a mere step-ladder unprotected by any rail. He stood there and held his breath, nose full of the harvest-scent of the barn. Above him the silence was uneasy, stirred by slight tremors of movement. He thought first that sleep was shallow, and the sleeper turning in his bed to find a posture from which he could submerge deeper into peace. Then he knew that he was listening to Meriet's voice, withdrawn into a strange distance but unmistakable, without distinguishable words, a mere murmur, but terrible in its sustained argument between one need and another need, equally demanding. Like some obdurate soul drawn apart by drivers' horses, torn limb from limb. And yet so slight and faint a sound, he had to strain his ears to follow it.

Brother Mark stood wretched, wondering whether to go up and either awake this sleeper, if indeed he slept, or lie by him and refuse to leave him if he was awake. There is a time to let well or ill alone, and a time to go forward into forbidden places with banners flying and trumpets sounding, and demand a surrender. But he did not know if they were come to that extreme. Brother Mark prayed, not with words, but by somehow igniting a candle-flame within him that burned immensely tall, and sent up the smoke of his entreaty, which was all for Meriet.

Above him in the darkness a foot stirred in the small, dry dust of chaff and straw, like mice venturing forth by night. Soft steps moved overhead, even and slow. In the dimness below, softened now by filtering starlight, Mark stared upward, and saw the darkness stir and swirl. Something suave and pale dipped from the yawning trap, and reached for the top rung of the ladder; a naked foot. Its fellow followed, stooping a rung lower. A voice, still drawn back deep into the body that leaned at the head of the stair, said distantly but clearly: "No I will not suffer it!"

He was coming down, he was seeking help. Brother Mark breathed gratitude, and said softly into the dimness above him: "Meriet! I am here!" Very softly, but it was enough.

The foot seeking its rest on the next tread balked and stepped astray. There was a faint, distressed cry, weak as a bird's and then an awakened shriek, live and indignant in bewilderment. Meriet's body folded sidelong and fell, hurtling, half into Brother Mark's blindly extended arms, and half askew from him with a dull, deflating thud to the floor of the barn. Mark clung desperately to what he held, borne down by the weight, and lowered it as softly as he might, feeling the limbs fold together to lie limp and still. There was a silence but for his own labouring breath.

With anguished hands he felt about the motionless body, stooped his ear to listen for breathing and the beat of the heart, touched a smooth cheek and the thick thatch of dark hair, and drew his fingers away warm and sticky with blood. "Meriet!" he urged, whispering close to a deaf ear, and knew that Meriet was far out of reach.

Mark ran for lights and help, but even at this pass was careful not to alarm the whole dortoir, but only to coax out of their sleep two of the most able-bodied and willing of his flock, who slept close to the door, and could withdraw without disturbing the rest. Between them they brought a lantern, and examined Meriet on the floor of the barn, still out of his senses. Mark had partially broken his fall, but his head had struck the sharp edge of the step-ladder, and bore a long graze that ran diagonally across his right temple and into his hair which bled freely, and he had fallen with his right foot twisted awkwardly beneath him.

"My fault, my fault!" whispered Mark wretchedly, feeling about the limp body for broken bones. "I startled him awake. I didn't know he was asleep, I thought he was coming to me of his own will . . ."

Meriet lay oblivious and let himself be handled as they would. There seemed to be no fractures, but there might well be sprains, and his head wound bled alarmingly. To move him as little as need be they brought down his pallet from the loft, and set it below in the barn where he lay, so that he might have quiet from the rest of the household. They bathed and dressed his head and lifted him gently into his cot with an added brychan for warmth, injury and shock making him very cold to the touch. And all the while his face, beneath the swathing bandage, was remote and peaceful and pale as Mark had never seen it before, his trouble for these few hours stricken out of him.

"Go now and get your own rest," said Brother Mark to his concerned helpers. "There's nothing more we can do at this moment. I shall sit with him. If I need you I'll call you."

He trimmed the lantern to burn steadily, and sat beside the pallet all the rest of the night. Meriet lay mute and motionless until past the dawn, though his breathing perceptibly lengthened and grew calmer as he passed from senselessness into sleep, but his face remained bloodless. It was past Prime when his lips began to twitch and his eyelids to flutter, as if he wished to open them, but had not the strength. Mark bathed his face, and moistened the struggling lips with water and wine.

"Lie still," he said, with a hand cupping Meriet's cheek. "I am here—Mark. Be troubled by nothing, you are safe here with me." He was not aware that he had meant to say that. It was promising infinite blessing, and what right had he to claim any such power? And yet the words had come to him unbidden.

The heavy eyelids heaved, fought for a moment with the unknown weight holding them closed, and parted upon a reflected flame in desperate green eyes. A shudder passed through Meriet's body. He worked a dry mouth and got out faintly: "I must go—I must tell them . . . Let me up!"

The effort he made to rise was easily suppressed by a hand on his breast; he lay helpless but shaking.

"I must go! Help me!"

"There is nowhere you need go," said Mark, leaning over him. "If there is any message you wish sent to any man, lie still, and only tell me. You know I will do it faithfully. You had a fall, you must lie still and rest."

"Mark . . . It is you?" He felt outside his blankets blindly, and Mark took the wandering hand and held it. "It *is* you," said Meriet, sighing. "Mark—the man they've taken . . . for killing the bishop's clerk . . . I must tell them . . . I must go to Hugh Beringar . . ."

"Tell me," said Mark, "and you have done all. I will see done whatever you want done, and you may rest. What is it I am to tell Hugh Beringar?" But in his heart he already knew.

"Tell him he must let this poor soul go . . . Say he never did that slaying. Tell him I *know*! Tell him," said Meriet, his dilated eyes hungry and emerald-green on Mark's attentive face, "that I confess my mortal sin . . . that it was I who killed Peter Clemence. I shot him down in the woods, three miles and more from Aspley. Say I am sorry, so to shame my father's house."

He was weak and dazed, shaking with belated shock, the tears sprang from his eyes, startling him with their unexpected flood. He gripped and wrung the hand he held. "Promise! Promise you will tell him so . . ."

"I will, and bear the errand myself, no other shall," said Mark, stooping low to straining, blinded eyes to be seen and believed. "Every word you give me I will deliver. If you will also do a good and needful thing for yourself and for me, before I go. Then you may sleep more peacefully."

The green eyes cleared in wonder, staring up at him. "What thing is that?"

Mark told him, very gently and firmly. Before he had
the words well out, Meriet had wrenched away his
hand and heaved his bruised body over in the bed, turning his face away. "No!" he said in a low wail of distress. "No, I will not! No . . ."

Mark talked on, quietly urging what he asked, but
stopped when it was still denied, and with ever more
agitated rejection. "Hush!" he said then placatingly.
"You need not fret so. Even without it, I'll do your errand, every word. You be still and sleep."

He was instantly believed; the body stiff with resistance softened and eased. The swathed head turned towards him again; even the dim light within the barn
caused his eyes to narrow and frown. Brother Mark put
out the lantern, and drew the brychans close. Then he
kissed his patient and penitent, and went to do his errand.

Brother Mark walked the length of the Foregate and
across the stone bridge into the town, exchanging the
time of day with all he met, enquired for Hugh
Beringar at his house by Saint Mary's, and walked on
undismayed and unwearied when he was told that the
deputy-sheriff was already at the castle. It was by way
of a bonus that Brother Cadfael happened to be there
also, having just emerged from applying another dress-
ing to the festered wound in the prisoner's forearm.
Hunger and exposure are not conducive to ready heal-
ing, but Harald's hurts were showing signs of yielding
to treatment. Already he had a little more flesh on his

long, raw bones, and a little more of the texture of youth in his hollow cheeks. Solid stone walls, sleep without constant fear, warm blankets and three rough meals a day were a heaven to him.

Against the stony ramparts of the inner ward, shut off from even what light there was in this muted morning, Brother Mark's diminutive figure looked even smaller, but his grave dignity was in no way diminished. Hugh welcomed him with astonishment, so unexpected was he in this place, and haled him into the anteroom of the guard, where there was a fire burning, and torchlight, since full daylight seldom penetrated there to much effect.

"I'm sent with a message," said Brother Mark, going directly to his goal, "to Hugh Beringar, from Brother Meriet. I've promised to deliver it faithfully word for word, since he cannot do it himself, as he wanted to do. Brother Meriet learned only yesterday, as did we all at Saint Giles, that you have a man held here in prison for the murder of Peter Clemence. Last night, after he had retired, Meriet was desperately troubled in his sleep, and rose and walked. He fell from the loft, sleeping, and is now laid in his bed with a broken head and many bruises, but he has come to himself, and I think with care he'll take no grave harm. But if Brother Cadfael would come and look at him I should be easier in my mind."

"Son, with all my heart!" said Cadfael, dismayed. "But what was he about, wandering in his sleep? He never left his bed before in his fits. And men who do commonly tread very skillfully, even where a waking man would not venture."

"So he might have done," owned Mark, sadly wrung, "if I had not spoken to him from below. For I thought he was well awake, and coming to ask comfort and aid, but when I called his name he stepped at fault, and cried out and fell. And now he is come to himself. I know where he was bound, even in his sleep, and on what errand. For that errand he has committed to me, now he is helpless, and I am here to deliver it."

"You've left him safe?" asked Cadfael anxiously, but half-ashamed to doubt whatever Brother Mark thought fit to do.

"There are two good souls keeping an eye on him, but I think he will sleep. He has unloaded his mind upon me, and here I discharge the burden," said Brother Mark, and he had the erect and simple solitude of a priest, standing small and plain between them and Meriet. "He bids me say to Hugh Beringar that he must let this prisoner go, for he never did that slaying with which he is charged. He bids me say that he speaks of his own knowledge, and confesses to his own mortal sin, for it was he who killed Peter Clemence. Shot him down in the woods, says Meriet, more than three miles north of Aspley. And he bids me say also that he is sorry, so to have disgraced his father's house."

He stood fronting them, wide-eyed and open-faced as was his nature, and they stared back at him with withdrawn and thoughtful faces. So simple an ending! The son, passionate of nature and quick to act, kills, the father, upright and austere yet jealous of his ancient honour, offers the sinner a choice between the public contumely that will destroy his ancestral house, or the lifelong penance of the cloister, and his father's-son prefers his personal purgatory to shameful death, and the degradation of his family. And it could be so! It could answer every question.

"But of course," said Brother Mark, with the exalted confidence of angels and archangels, and the simplicity of children, "it is not true."

"I need not quarrel with what you say," said Hugh mildly, after a long and profound pause for thought, "if I ask you whether you speak only on belief in Brother Meriet—for which you may feel you have good cause—or from knowledge by proof? How do you know he is lying?"

"I do know by what I know of him," said Mark firmly, "but I have tried to put that away. If I say he is no such person to shoot down a man from ambush, but rather to stand square in his way and challenge him hand to hand, I am saying what I strongly believe. But I was born humble, out of this world of honour, how should I speak to it with certainty? No, I have tested him. When he told me what he told me, I said to him that for his soul's comfort he should let me call our chaplain, and as a sick man make his confession to him and seek absolution. And he would not do it," said Mark, and smiled upon them. "At the very thought he shook and turned away. When I pressed him, he was in great agitation. For he can lie to me and to you, to the king's law itself, for a cause that seems to him good enough," said Mark, "but he will not lie to his confessor, and through his confessor to God."

THE DEVIL'S NOVICE 194

CHAPTER TEN

AFTER LONG AND SOMBRE CONSIDERATION, HUGH said: "For the moment, it seems, this boy will keep, whatever the truth of it. He is in his bed with a broken head, and not likely to stir for a while, all the more if he believes we have accepted what, for whatever cause, he wishes us to believe. Take care of him, Mark, and let him think he has done what he set out to do. Tell him he can be easy about this prisoner of ours, he is not charged, and no harm will come to him. But don't let it be put abroad that we're holding an innocent man who is in no peril of his life. Meriet may know it. Not a soul outside. For the common ear, we have our murderer safe in hold."

One deceit partnered another deceit, both meant to some good end; and if it seemed to Brother Mark that deceit ought not to have any place in the pilgrimage after truth, yet he acknowledged the mysterious uses of all manner of improbable devices in the workings of the purposes of God, and saw the truth reflected even in lies. He would let Meriet believe his ordeal was ended and his confession accepted, and Meriet would sleep without fears or hopes, without dreams, but with the drear satisfaction of his voluntary sacrifice, and grow well again to a better, an unrevealed world.

"I will see to it," said Mark, "that only he knows. And I will be his pledge that he shall be at your disposal whenever you need him."

"Good! then go back now to your patient, Cadfael and I will follow you very shortly."

Mark departed, satisfied, to trudge back through the town and out along the Foregate. When he was gone, Hugh stood gazing eye to eye with Brother Cadfael, long and thoughtfully. "Well?"

"It's a tale that makes excellent sense," said Cadfael, "and a great part of it most likely true. I am of Mark's way of thinking, I do not believe the boy has killed. But the rest of it? The man who caused that fire to be built and kindled had force enough to get his men to do his will and keep his secret. A man well-served, well-feared, perhaps even well-loved. A man who would neither steal anything from the dead himself, nor allow any of his people to do so. All committed to the fire. Those who worked for him respected and obeyed him. Leoric Aspley is such a man, and in such a manner he might behave, if he believed a son of his had murdered from ambush a man who had been a guest in his house. There would be no forgiveness. If he protected the murderer from the death due, it might well be for the sake of his name, and only to serve a lifetime's penance."

He was remembering their arrival in the rain, father and son, the one severe, cold and hostile, departing without the kiss due between kinsmen, the other submissive and dutiful, but surely against his nature, at once rebellious and resigned. Feverish in his desire to shorten his probation and be imprisoned past deliverance, but in his sleep fighting like a demon for his liberty. It made a true picture. But Mark was absolute that Meriet had lied.

"It lacks nothing," said Hugh, shaking his head. "He has said throughout that it was his own wish to take the cowl—so it might well be; good reason, if he was offered no other alternative but the gallows. The death came there, soon after leaving Aspley. The horse was taken far north and abandoned, so that the body should be sought only well away from where the man was killed. But whatever else the boy knows, he did not know that he was leading his gleaners straight to the place where the bones would be found, and his father's careful work undone. I take Mark's word for that, and by God, I am inclined to take Mark's word for the rest. But if Meriet did not kill the man, why should he so accept condemnation and sentence? Of his own will!"

"There is but one possible answer," said Cadfael. "To protect someone else."

"Then you are saying that he knows who the murderer is."

"Or thinks he knows," said Cadfael. "For there is veil on veil here hiding these people one from another, and it seems to me that Aspley, if he has done this to his son, believes he knows beyond doubt that the boy is guilty. And Meriet, since he has sacrificed himself to a life against which his whole spirit rebels, and now to shameful death, must be just as certain of the guilt of that other person whom he loves and desires to save. But if Leoric is so wildly mistaken, may not Meriet also be in error?"

"Are we not all?" said Hugh, sighing. "Come, let's go and see this sleep-walking penitent first, and—who knows?—if he's bent on confession, and has to lie to accomplish it, he may let slip something much more to our purpose. I'll say this for him, he was not prepared to let another poor devil suffer in his place, or even in the place of someone dearer to him than himself. Harald has fetched him out of his silence fast enough."

Meriet was sleeping when they came to Saint Giles. Cadfael stood beside the pallet in the barn, and looked down upon a face strangely peaceful and childlike, exorcised of its devil. Meriet's breathing was long and deep and sweet. It was believable that here was a tormented sinner who had made confession and cleansed his breast, and found all thing hereafter made easy. But he would not repeat his confession to a priest. Mark had a very powerful argument there.

"Let him rest," said Hugh, when Mark, though reluctantly, would have awakened the sleeper. "We can wait." And wait they did, the better part of an hour, until Meriet stirred and opened his eyes. Even then Hugh would have him tended and fed and given drink before he consented to sit by him and hear what he had to say. Cadfael had looked him over, and found nothing wrong that a few days of rest would not mend, though he had turned an ankle and foot under him in falling, and would find it difficult and painful to put any weight upon it for some time. The blow on the head had shaken his wits sadly, and his memory of recent days might be hazy, though he held fast to the one more distant memory which he so desired to declare. The gash crossing his temple would soon heal; the bleeding had already stopped.

His eyes, in the dim light within the barns, shone darkly green, staring up dilated and intent. His voice was faint but resolute, as he repeated with slow emphasis the confession he had made to Brother Mark. He was bent on convincing, very willing and patient in dredging up details. Listening, Cadfael had to admit to himself, with dismay, that Meriet was indeed utterly convincing. Hugh must also be thinking so.

He questioned, slowly and evenly: "You watched the man ride away, with your father in attendance, and made no demur. Then you went out with your bow—mounted or afoot?"

"Mounted," said Meriet with fiery readiness; for if he had gone on foot, how could he have circled at speed, and been ahead of the rider after his escort had left him to return home? Cadfael remembered Isouda saying that Meriet had come home late that afternoon with his father's party, though he had not ridden out with them. She had not said whether he was mounted when he returned or walking; that was something worth probing.

"With murderous intent?" Hugh pursued mildly. "Or did this thing come on you unawares? For what can you have had against Master Clemence to warrant his death?"

"He had made far too free with my brother's bride," said Meriet. "I did hold it against him—a priest, playing the courtier, and so sure of his height about us. A manorless man, with only his learning and his patron's name for lands and lineage, and looking down upon us, as long rooted as we are. On grievance for my brother . . ."

"Yet your brother made no move to take reparation," said Hugh.

"He was gone to the Lindes, to Roswitha . . . He had escorted her home the night before, and I am sure he had quarrelled with her. He went out early, he did not even see the guest leave, he went to make good whatever was ill between those two . . . He never came home," said Meriet, clearly and firmly, "until late in the evening, long after all was over."

True, by Isouda's account, thought Cadfael. After all was over, and Meriet brought home a convicted murderer, to reappear only after he had chosen of his own will to ask admittance to the cloister, and was prepared to go forth on his parole, and so declare himself, an oblate to the abbey, fully aware of what he was doing. So he had told his very acute and perceptive playmate, in calm control of himself. He was doing what he wished to do.

"But you, Meriet, you rode ahead of Master Clemence. With murder in mind?"

"I had not thought," said Meriet, hesitating for the first time. "I went alone . . . But I was angry."

"You went in haste," said Hugh, pressing him, "if you overtook the departing guest, and by a roundabout way, if you passed and intercepted him, as you say."

Meriet stretched and stiffened in his bed, large eyes straining on his questioner. He set his jaw. "I did hasten, though not for any deliberate purpose. I was in thick covert when I was aware of him riding towards me, in no hurry. I drew and loosed upon him. He fell . . ." Sweat broke on the pallid brow beneath his bandages. He closed his eyes.

"Let be!" said Cadfael, quiet at Hugh's shoulder. "He has enough."

"No," said Meriet strongly. "Let me make an end. He was dead when I stooped over him. I had killed him. And my father took me so, redhanded. The hounds—he had hounds with him—they scented me and brought him down upon me. He has covered up for my sake, and for the sake of an honoured name, what I did, but for whatever he may have done that is unlawful, to keep me man alive, I take the blame upon me, for I am the cause of it. But he would not condone. He promised me cover for my forfeit life, if I would accept banishment from the world and take myself off into the cloister. What was done afterwards no one ever told me. I did by my own will and consent accept my penalty. I even hoped . . . and I have tried . . . But set down all that was done to my account, and let me pay all."

He thought he had done, and heaved a great sigh out of him, Hugh also sighed and stirred as if about to rise, but then asked carelessly: "At what hour was this, Meriet, that your father happened upon you in the act of murder?"

"About three in the afternoon," said Meriet indifferently, falling headlong into the trap.

"And Master Clemence set out soon after Prime? It took him a great while," said Hugh with deceptive mildness, "to ride somewhat over three miles."

Meriet's eyes, half-closed in weariness and release from tension, flared wide open in consternation. It cost him a convulsive struggle to master voice and face, but he did it, hoisting up out of the well of his resolution and dismay a credible answer. "I cut my story too short, wanting it done. When this thing befell it cannot have been even mid-morning. But I ran from him and let him lie, and wandered the woods in dread of what I'd done. But in the end I went back. It seemed better to hide him in the thick coverts off the pathways, where he could lie undiscovered, and I might come by night and bury him. I was in terror, but in the end I went back. I am not sorry," said Meriet at the end, so simply that somewhere in those last words there must be truth. But he had never shot down any man. He had come upon a dead man lying in his blood, just as he had balked and stood aghast at the sight of Brother Wolstan bleeding at the foot of the apple tree. A three-mile ride from Aspley, yes, thought Cadfael with certainty, but well into the autumn afternoon, when his father was out with hawk and hound. "I am not sorry," said Meriet again, quite gently. "It's good that I was taken so. Better still that I have now told you all."

Hugh rose, and stood looking down at him with an unreadable face. "Very well! You should not yet be moved, and there is no reason you should not remain here in Brother Mark's care. Brother Cadfael tells me you would need crutches if you tried to walk for some days yet. You'll be secure enough where you are."

"I would give you my parole," said Meriet sadly, "but I doubt if you would take it. But Mark will, and I will submit myself to him. Only—the other man—you will see he goes free?"

"You need not fret, he is cleared of all blame but a little thieving to fill his belly, and that will be forgotten. It is to your own case you should be giving thought," said Hugh gravely. "I would urge you receive a priest and make your confession."

"You and the hangman can be my priests," said Meriet, and fetched up from somewhere a wry and painful smile.

"He is lying and telling truth in the selfsame breath," said Hugh with resigned exasperation on the way back along the Foregate. "Almost surely what he says of his father's part is truth, so he was caught, and so he was both protected and condemned. That is how he came to you, willing-unwilling. It accounts for all the to-and-fro you have had with him, waking and sleeping. But it does not give us our answer to who killed Peter Clemence, for it's as good as certain Meriet did not. He had not even thought of that glaring error in the time of day, until I prodded him with it. And considering the shock it gave him, he did pretty well at accounting for it. But far too late. To have made that mistake was enough. Now what is our best way? Supposing we should blazon it abroad that young Aspley has confessed to the murder, and put his neck in a noose? If he is indeed sacrificing himself for someone else, do you think that person would come forward and loose the knot and slip his own neck in it, as Meriet has for him?"

With bleak conviction Cadfael said: "No. If he let him go unredeemed into one hell to save his own sweet skin, I doubt if he'd lift a hand to help him down the gallows. God forgive me if I misjudge him, but on that conscience there'll be no relying. And you would have committed yourself and the law to a lie for nothing, and brought the boy deeper into grief. No. We have still a little time, let things be. In two or three days more this wedding party will be with us in the abbey, and Leoric Aspley could be brought to answer for his own part, but since he's truly convinced Meriet is guilty, he can hardly help us to the real murderer.

Make no move to bring him to account, Hugh, until after the marriage. Let me have him to myself until then. I have certain thoughts concerning this father and son."

"You may have him and welcome," said Hugh, "for as things are I'm damned if I know what to do with him. His offence is rather against the church than against any law I administer. Depriving a dead man of Christian burial and the proper rites due to him is hardly within my writ. Aspley is a patron of the abbey, let the lord abbot be his judge. The man I want is the murderer. You, I know, want to hammer it into that old tyrant's head that he knows his younger son so poorly that mere acquaintances of a few weeks have more faith in the lad, and more understanding of him, than his sire has. And I wish you success. As for me, Cadfael, I'll tell you what troubles me most. I cannot for my life see what cause anyone in these parts, Aspley or Linde or Foriet or who you will, had to wish Peter Clemence out of the world. Shoot him down for being too bold and too ingratiating with the girl? Foolery! The man was leaving, none of them had seen much of him before, none need ever see him again, and the bridegroom's only concern, it seems, was to make his peace with his bride after too sharp reproaches. Kill for such a cause? Not unless a man ran utterly mad. You tell me the girl will flutter her lashes at every admirer, but none has ever died for it. No, there is, there must be, another cause, but for my life I cannot see what it can be."

It had troubled Cadfael, too. Minor brawls of one evening over a girl, and over too assiduous compliments to her, not affronts, a mere bubble in one family's hitherto placid life—no, men do not kill for such trivial causes. And no one had ever yet suggested a deeper quarrel with Peter Clemence. His distant kinsmen knew him but slightly, their neighbours not at all. If you find a new acquaintance irritating, but know he remains for only one night, you bear with him tolerantly, and wave him away from your doorsill with a smile, and breathe the more easily thereafter. But you do not skulk in woods where he must pass, and shoot him down.

But if it was not the man himself, what else could there be to bring him to his death? His errand? He had not said what it was, at least while Isouda was by to hear. And even if he had, what was there in that to make it necessary to halt him? A civil diplomatic mission to two northern lords, to secure their allegiance to Bishop Henry's efforts for peace. A mission Canon Eluard had since pursued successfully, to such happy effect that he had now conducted his king thither to seal the accord, and by this time was accompanying him south again to keep his Christmas in high content. There could be nothing amiss there. Great men have their private plans, and may welcome at one time a visit they repel at another, but here was the proof of the approach, and a reasonably secure Christmas looming.

Back to the man, and the man was harmless, a passing kinsman expanding and preening himself under a family roof, then passing on.

No personal grudge, then. So what was left but the common hazard of travel, the sneak-thief and killer loose in the wild places, ready to pull a man from his horse and bludgeon his head to pulp for the clothes he wore, let alone a splendid horse and a handful of jew-ellery? And that was ruled out, because Peter Clemence had not been robbed, not of a silver buckle, not of a jewelled cross. No one had benefited in goods or gear from his death, even the horse had been turned loose in the mosses with his harness untouched.

"I have wondered about the horse," said Hugh, as though he had been following Cadfael's thoughts.

"I, too. The night after you brought the beast back to the abbey, Meriet called him in his sleep. Did they ever tell you that? Barbary, Barbary—and he whistled after him. His devil whistled back to him, the novices said. I wonder if he came, there in the woods, or if Leoric had to send out men after him later? I think he would come to Meriet. When he found the man dead, his next thought would be for the beast, he went call-ing him."

"The hounds may well have picked up his voice," said Hugh ruefully, "before ever they got his scent. And brought his father down on him."

"Hugh, I have been thinking. The lad answered you very valiantly when you fetched him up hard against that error in time. But I do not believe it had dawned on him at all what it meant. See, if Meriet had simply blundered upon a lone body dead in the forest, with no sign to turn his suspicions towards any man, all he would then have known was that Clemence had ridden but a short way before he was shot. Then how could the boy know or even guess by whom? But if he chanced upon some other soul trapped as he was, stooped over the dead, or trying to drag him into hiding—someone close and dear to him—then he has not realized, even now, that this someone else came to this spot in the forest, even as he himself did, at least six hours too late to be the murderer!"

On the eighteenth day of December Canon Eluard rode into Shrewsbury in very good conceit of himself, having persuaded his king into a visit which had turned out conspicuously well, and escorted him thus far south again towards his customary London Christmas, before leaving him in order to diverge westward in search of news of Peter Clemence. Chester and Lincoln, both earls now in name as well as in fact, had made much of Stephen, and pledged him their unshakable loyalty, which he in turn had recognized with gifts of land as well as titles. Lincoln castle he retained in his own hand, well-garrisoned, but the city and the shire were open to his new earl. The atmosphere in Lincoln had been of holiday and ease, aided by clement weather for December. Christmas in the northeast bade fair to be a carefree festival.

Hugh came down from the castle to attend on the canon and exchange the news with him, though it was a very uneven exchange. He had brought with him the relics of Peter Clemence's jewels and harness, cleaned of their encrusted filth of ash and soil, but discoloured by the marks of fire. The dead man's bones reposed now in a lead-lined coffin in the mortuary chapel of the abbey, but the coffin was not yet sealed. Canon Eluard had it opened for him, and gazed upon the remains within, grim-faced but unwincing.

"Cover him," he said, and turned away. There was nothing there that could ever again be known as any man. The cross and ring were a very different matter.

"This I do know. This I have commonly seen him wearing," said Eluard, with the cross in the palm of his hand. Over the silver surface the coloured sheen of tarnish glimmered, but the gems shone clear. "This is certainly Clemence," said Eluard heavily. "It will be grievous news for my bishop. And you have some fellow in hold for this crime?"

"We have a man in prison, true," said Hugh, "and have let it be noised abroad that he is the man, but in truth I must tell you that he is not charged, and almost certainly never will be. The worst known of him is a little thieving here and there, from hunger, and on that I continue to hold him. But a murderer I am sure he is not." He told the story of his search, but said no word of Meriet's confession. "If you intend to rest here two or three days before riding on, there may yet be more news to take with you."

It was in his mind as he said it that he was a fool to promise any such thing, but his thumbs had pricked,

and the words were out. Cadfael had business with
Leoric Aspley when he came, and the imminent gathering here of all those closest about Peter Clemence's
last hours seemed to Hugh like the thickening and low-
ering of a cloud before the storm breaks and the rain
falls. If the rain refused to fall, then after the wedding
Aspley should be made to tell all that he knew, and
probe after what he did not know, taking into account
such small matters as those six unrecorded hours, and
the mere three miles Clemence had ridden before he
met his death.

"Nothing can restore the dead," said Canon Eluard
sombrely, "but it is only just and right that his murderer should be brought to account. I trust that may yet
be done."

"And you'll be here yet a few days? You're not in
haste to rejoin the king?"

"I go to Winchester, not Westminster. And it will be
worth waiting a few days to have somewhat more to
tell the bishop concerning this grievous loss. I confess
to being in need of a brief rest, too, I am not so young
as once I was. Your sheriff still leaves you to carry the
care of the shire alone, by the way. King Stephen
wishes to retain him in his company over the feast,
they go directly to London."

That was by no means unwelcome news to Hugh.
The business he had begun he was strongly minded to
finish, and two minds bent to the same task, the one
more impatient than the other, do not make for good

results. "And you are content with your visit," he said. "Something, at least, has gone well."

"It was worth all the travelling," said Eluard with satisfaction. "The king can be easy in his mind about the north, Ranulf and William between them have every mile of it well in hand, it would be a bold man who would meddle with their order. His Grace's castellan in Lincoln is on the best of terms with the earls and their ladies. And the messages I bear to the bishop are gracious indeed. Yes, it was well worth the miles I've ridden to secure it."

On the following day the wedding party arrived in modest manorial state, to apartments prepared for them in the abbey guest-halls: the Aspleys, the Lindes, the heiress of Foriet, and a great rout of their invited guests from all the neighbouring manors down the fringes of the forest. All but the common hall and dortoir for the pedlars and pilgrims and birds of passage was given over to the party. Canon Eluard, the abbot's guest, took a benevolent interest in the bright bustle from his privileged distance. The novices and the boys looked on in eager curiosity, delighted at any distraction in their ordered lives. Prior Robert allowed himself to be seen about the court and the cloisters at his most benign and dignified, always at his best where there were ceremonies to be patronized and a patrician audience to appreciate and admire him; and Brother Jerome made himself even more than usually busy and authoritative among the novices and lay servants. In the stable-yard there was great activity, and all the stalls were filled. Brothers who had kin among the guests were allowed to receive them in the parlour. A great wave of admiration and interest swept through the courts and the gardens, all the more gaily because the weather, though crisp and very cold, was clear and fine, and daylight lasted late towards evening.

Cadfael stood with Brother Paul at the corner of the cloister and watched them ride in in their best travelling array, with pack-ponies bringing their wedding finery. The Lindes came first. Wulfric Linde was a fat, flabby, middle-aged man of amiable, lethargic face, and Cadfael could not choose but wonder what his dead lady must have been like, to make it possible for the pair of them to produce two such beautiful children. His daughter rode a pretty, cream-coloured palfrey, smilingly aware of all the eyes upon her, and keeping her own eyes tantalizingly lowered, in an appearance of modesty which gave exaggerated power to every flashing sidelong glance. Swathed warmly in a fine blue cloak that concealed all but the rosy oval of her face, she still knew how to radiate beauty, and oh, she knew, how well she knew, that she had at least forty pairs of innocent male eyes upon her, marvelling at what strange delights were withheld from them. Women of all ages, practical and purposeful, went in and out regularly at these gates, with complaint, appeal, request and gift, and made no stir and asked no tribute. Roswitha came armed in knowledge of her power, and delighted in the disquiet she brought with her. There would be some strange dreams among Brother Paul's novices.

Close behind her, and for a moment hard to recognize, came Isouda Foriet on a tall, spirited horse. Groomed and shod and well-mounted, her hair netted and uncovered to the light, a bright russet like autumn leaves, with her hood tossed back on her shoulders and her back straight and lissom as a birch-tree, Isouda rode without artifice, and needed none. As good as a boy! As good as the boy who rode beside her, with a hand stretched out to her bridle-hand, lightly touching. Neighbours, each with a manor to offer, would it be strange if Janyn's father and Isouda's guardian planned to match them? Excellently matched in age, in quality, having known each other from children, what could be more suitable? But the two most concerned still chattered and wrangled like brother and sister, very easy and familiar together. And besides, Isouda had other plans.

Janyn carried with him, here as elsewhere, his light, comely candour, smiling round him with pleasure on all he saw. Sweeping a bright glance round all the watching faces, he recognized Brother Cadfael, and his face lit up engagingly as he gave him a marked inclination of his fair head.

"He knows you," said Brother Paul, catching the gesture.

"The bride's brother—her twin. I encountered him when I went to talk with Meriet's father. The two families are close neighbours."

"A great pity," said Paul sympathetically, "that Brother Meriet is not well enough to be here. I am sure he would wish to be present when his brother marries, and to wish them God's blessing. He cannot walk yet?"

All that was known of Meriet among these who had done their best for him was that he had had a fall, and was laid up with a lingering weakness and a twisted foot.

"He hobbles with a stick," said Cadfael. "I would not like him to venture far as he is. In a day or two we shall see how far we may let him try his powers."

Janyn was down from his saddle with a bound, and attentive at Isouda's stirrup as she made to descend. She laid a hand heartily on his shoulder and came down like a feather, and they laughed together, and turned to join the company already assembled. After them came the Aspleys, Leoric as Cadfael had imagined and seen him, bolt-upright body and soul, appearing tall as a church column in his saddle; an irate, intolerant, honourable man, exact to his responsibilities, absolute on his privileges. A demi-god to his servants, and one to be trusted provided they in turn were trustworthy; a god to his sons. What he had been to his dead wife could scarcely be guessed, or what she had felt towards her second boy. The admirable firstborn, close at his father's elbow, vaulted out of his tall saddle like a bird lighting, large, vigorous and beautiful. At every move Nigel did honour to his progenitors and his name. Cloistered young men watching him murmured admiration, and well they might.

"Difficult," said Brother Paul always sensitive to youth and its obscure torments, "to be second to such a one."

"Difficult indeed," said Cadfael ruefully.

Kinsmen and neighbours followed, small lords and their ladies, self-confident folk, commanding limited realms, perhaps, but absolute within them, and well able to guard their own. They alighted, their grooms led away the horses and ponies, the court gradually emptied of the sudden blaze of colour and animation, and the fixed and revered order continued unbroken, with Vespers drawing near.

Brother Cadfael went to his workshop in the herbarium after supper to fetch certain dried herbs needed by Brother Petrus, the abbot's cook, for the next day's dinner, when the Aspleys and the Lindes were to dine with Canon Eluard at the abbot's table. Frost was setting in again for the night, the air was crisp and still and the sky starry, and even the smallest sound rang like a bell in the pure darkness. The footsteps that followed him along the hard earth path between the pleached hedges were very soft, but he heard them; someone small and light of foot, keeping her distance, one sharp ear listening for Cadfael's guiding steps ahead, the other pricked back to make sure no others followed behind. When he opened the door of his hut and passed within, his pursuer halted, giving him time

to strike a spark from his flint and light his little lamp.
Then she came into the open doorway, wrapped in a
dark cloak, her hair loose on her neck as he had first
seen her, the cold stinging her cheeks into rose-red,
and the flame of the lamp making stars of her eyes.

"Come in, Isouda," said Cadfael placidly, rustling
the bunches of herbs that dangled from the beams
above. "I've been hoping to find a means of talking
with you. I should have known you would make your
own occasion."

"But I mustn't stay long," she said, coming in and
closing the door behind her. "I am supposed to be
lighting a candle and putting up prayers in the church
for my father's soul."

"Then should you not be doing that?" said Cadfael,
smiling. "Here, sit and be easy for the short time you
have, and whatever you want of me, ask."

"I have lit my candle," she said, seating herself on
the bench by the wall, "it's there to be seen, but my father was a fine man, and God will take good care of
his soul without any interference from me. And I need
to know what is really happening to Meriet."

"They'll have told you that he had a bad fall, and
cannot walk as yet?"

"Brother Paul told us so. He said it would be no
lasting harm. Is it so? Will he be well again surely?"

"Surely he will. He got a gash on the head in his
fall, but that's already healed, and his wrenched foot
needs only a little longer rest, and it will bear him
again as well as ever. He's in good hands, Brother

Mark is taking care of him, and Brother Mark is his staunch friend. Tell me, how did his father take the word of his fall?"

"He kept a severe face," she said, "though he said he grieved to hear it, so coldly, who would believe him? But for all that, he does grieve."

"He did not ask to visit him?"

She made a disdainful face at the obstinacy of men. "Not he! He has given him to God, and God must fend for him. He will not go near him. But I came to ask you if you will take *me* there to see him."

Cadfael stood earnestly considering her for a long moment, and then sat down beside her and told her all that had happened, all that he knew or guessed. She was shrewd, gallant and resolute, and she knew what she wanted and was ready to fight for it. She gnawed a calculating lip when she heard that Meriet had confessed to murder, and glowed in proud acknowledgement when Cadfael stressed that she was the sole privileged person, besides himself and Mark and the law, to be apprised of it, and to know, to her comfort, that it was not believed.

"Sheer folly!" she said roundly. "I thank God you see through him as through gauze. And his fool of a father *believes* it? But he never has known him, he never has valued or come close to him, from the day Meriet was born. And yet he's a fair-minded man, I own it, he would not knowingly do any man wrong. He must have urgent cause to believe this. And Meriet cause just as grave to leave him in the mistake—even while he certainly must be holding it against him that he's so ready to believe evil of his own flesh and blood. Brother Cadfael, I tell you, I never before saw so clearly how like those two are, proud and stubborn and solitary, taking to themselves every burden that falls their way, shutting out kith and kin and liegemen and all. I could knock their two fool crowns together. But what good would that do, without an answer that would shut both their mouths—except on penitence?"

"There will be such an answer," said Cadfael, "and if ever you do knock their heads together, I promise you both shall be unshaven. And yes, tomorrow I will take you to practise upon the one of them, but after dinner—for before it, I aim to bring your Uncle Leoric to visit his son, whether he will or no. Tell me, if you know, what are their plans for the morrow? They have yet one day to spare before the marriage."

"They mean to attend High Mass," she said, sparkling hopefully, "and then we women will be fitting gowns and choosing ornaments, and putting a stitch in here and there to the wedding clothes. Nigel will be shut out of all that, until we go to dine with the lord abbot, and I think he and Janyn intend to go into town for some last trifles. Uncle Leoric may be left to himself after Mass. You might snare him then, if you catch your time."

"I shall be watching for it," Cadfael assured her. "And after the abbot's dinner, if you can absent yourself, then I will take you to Meriet."

She rose joyfully when she thought it high time to

leave, and she went forth valiantly, certain of herself and her stars, and her standing with the powers of heaven. And Cadfael went to deliver his selected herbs to Brother Petrus, who was already brooding over the masterpieces he would produce the next day at noon.

After High Mass on the morning of the twentieth of December the womenfolk repaired to their own apartments, to make careful choice of the right array for dining with the abbot. Leoric's son and his son's bosom friend went off on foot into the town, his guests dispersed to pay local visits for which this was rare opportunity, and make purchases of store for their country manors while they were close to the town, or to burnish their own finery for the morrow. Leoric walked briskly in the frosty air the length of the gardens, round fish-ponds and fields, down to the Meole brook, fringed with delicate frost like fine lace, and after that as decisively vanished. Cadfael had waited to give him time to be alone, as plainly he willed to be, and then lost sight of him, to find him again in the mortuary chapel where Peter Clemence's coffin, closed now and richly draped, waited for Bishop Henry's word as to its disposal. Two new, fine candles burned on a branched candlestick at the head, and Leoric Aspley was on his knees on the flagstones at the foot. His lips moved upon silent, methodical prayers, his open eyes were fixed unflinchingly upon the bier. Cadfael knew then that he was on firm ground. The candles might have been simply any courtly man's offering to a dead kinsman, however distant, but the grim and grievous face, silently acknowledging a guilt not yet confessed or atoned for, confirmed the part he had played in denying this dead man burial, and pointed plainly at the reason.

Cadfael withdrew silently, and waited for him to come forth. Blinking as he emerged into daylight again, Leoric found himself confronted by a short, sturdy, nut-brown brother who stepped into his path and addressed him ominously, like a warning angel blocking the way:

"My lord, I have an urgent errand to you. I beg you to come with me. You are needed. Your son is mortally ill."

It came so suddenly and shortly, it struck like a lance. The two young men had been gone half an hour, time for the assassin's stroke, for the sneak-thief's knife, for any number of disasters. Leoric heaved up his head and snuffed the air of terror, and gasped aloud: "My son . . . ?"

Only then did he recognize the brother who had come to Aspley on the abbot's errand. Cadfael saw hostile suspicion flare in the deep-set, arrogant eyes, and forestalled whatever his antagonist might have had to say.

"It's high time," said Cadfael, "that you remembered you have two sons. Will you let one of them die uncomforted?"

CHAPTER ELEVEN

LEORIC WENT WITH HIM; STRIDING IMPATIENTLY, suspiciously, intolerantly, yet continuing to go with him. He questioned, and was not answered. When Cadfael said simply: "Turn back, then, if that's your will, and make your own peace with God and him!" Leoric set his teeth and his jaw, and went on.

At the rising path up the grass-slope to Saint Giles he checked, but rather to take stock of the place where his son served and suffered than out of any fear of the many contagions that might be met within. Cadfael brought him to the barn, where Meriet's pallet was still laid, and Meriet at this moment was seated upon it, the stout staff by which he hobbled about the hospice braced upright in his right hand, and his head leaned upon its handle. He would have been about the place as best he might since Prime, and Mark must have banished him to an interval of rest before the midday meal. He was not immediately aware of them, the light within the barn being dim and mellow, and subject to passing shadows. He looked several years older than the silent and submissive youth Leoric had brought to the abbey a postulant, almost three months earlier.

His sire, entering with the light sidelong, stood gazing. His face was closed and angry, but the eyes in it stared in bewilderment and grief, and indignation, too, at being led here in this fashion when the sufferer had no mark of death upon him, but leaned resigned and quiet, like a man at peace with his fate.

"Go in," said Cadfael at Leoric's shoulder, "and speak to him."

It hung perilously in the balance whether Leoric would not turn, thrust his deceitful guide out of the way, and stalk back by the way he had come. He did cast a black look over his shoulder and make to draw back from the doorway; but either Cadfael's low voice or the stir of movement had reached and startled Meriet. He raised his head and saw his father. The strangest contortion of astonishment, pain, and reluctant and grudging affection twisted his face. He made to rise respectfully and fumbled it in his haste. The crutch slipped out of his hand and thudded to the floor, and he reached for it, wincing.

Leoric was before him. He crossed the space between in three long, impatient strides, pressed his son back to the pallet with a brusque hand on his shoulder, and restored the staff to his hand, rather as one exasperated by clumsiness than considerate of distress. "Sit!" he said gruffly. "No need to stir. They tell me you have had a fall, and cannot yet walk well."

"I have come to no great harm," said Meriet, gazing up at him steadily. "I shall be fit to walk very soon. I take it kindly that you have come to see me, I did not expect a visit. Will you sit, sir?"

No, Leoric was too disturbed and too restless, he gazed about him at the furnishings of the barn, and only by rapid glimpses at his son. "This life—the way you consented to—they tell me you have found it hard to come to terms with it. You put your hand to the plough, you must finish the furrow. Do not expect me to take you back again." His voice was harsh but his face was wrung.

"My furrow bids fair to be a short one, and I daresay I can hold straight to the end of it," said Meriet sharply. "Or have they not told you, also, that I have confessed the thing I did, and there is no further need for you to shelter me?"

"You have confessed . . ." Leoric was at a loss. He passed a long hand over his eyes, and stared, and shook. The boy's dead calm was more confounding than any passion could have been.

"I am sorry to have caused you so much labour and pain to no useful end," said Meriet. "But it was necessary to speak. They were making a great error, they had charged another man, some poor wretch living wild, who had taken food here and there. You had not heard that? Him, at least, I could deliver. Hugh Beringar has assured me no harm will come to him. You would not have had me leave him in his peril? Give your blessing to this act, at least."

Leoric stood speechless some minutes, his tall body palsied and shaken as though he struggled with his own demon, before he sat down abruptly beside his son on the creaking pallet, and clamped a hand over Meriet's hand; and though his face was still marble-hard, and the very gesture of his hand like a blow, and his voice when he finally found words still severe and harsh, Cadfael nevertheless withdrew from them quietly, and drew the door to after him. He went aside and sat in the porch, not so far away that he could not hear the tones of the two voices within, though not their words, and so placed that he could watch the doorway. He did not think he would be needed any more, though at times the father's voice rose in helpless rage, and once or twice Meriet's rang with a clear and obstinate asperity. That did not matter, they would have been lost without the sparks they struck from each other.

After this, though Cadfael, let him put on indifference as icily as he will, I shall know better.

He went back when he judged it was time, for he had much to say to Leoric for his own part before the hour of the abbot's dinner. Their rapid and high-toned exchanges ceased as he entered, what few words they still had to say came quietly and lamely.

"Be my messenger to Nigel and to Roswitha. Say

that I pray their happiness always. I should have liked to be there to see them wed," said Meriet steadily, "but that I cannot expect now."

Leoric looked down at him and asked awkwardly: "You are cared for here? Body and soul?"

Meriet's exhausted face smiled, a pale smile but warm and sweet. "As well as ever in my life. I am very well-friended, here among my peers. Brother Cadfael knows!"

And this time, at parting, it fell out not quite as once before. Cadfael had wondered. Leoric turned to go, turned back, wrestled with his unbending pride a moment, and then stooped almost clumsily and very briefly, and bestowed on Meriet's lifted cheek a kiss that still resembled a blow. Fierce blood mantled at the smitten cheekbone as Leoric straightened up, turned, and strode from the barn.

He crossed towards the gate mute and stiff, his eyes looking inwards rather than out, so that he struck shoulder and hip against the gatepost, and hardly noticed the shock.

"Wait!" said Cadfael. "Come here with me into the church, and say whatever you have to say, and so will I. We still have time."

In the little single-aisled church of the hospice, under its squat tower, it was dim and chill, and very silent. Leoric knotted veined hands and wrung them, and turned in formidable quiet anger upon his guide. "Was this well done, brother? Falsely you brought me here! You told me my son was mortally ill."

"So he is," said Cadfael. "Have you not his own word for it how close he feels his death? So are you, so are we all. The disease of mortality is in us from the womb, from the day of our birth we are on the way to our death. What matters is how we conduct the journey. You heard him. He has confessed to the murder of Peter Clemence. Why have you not been told that, without having to hear it from Meriet? Because there was no one to tell you else but Brother Mark, or Hugh Beringar, or myself, for no one else knows. Meriet believes himself to be watched as a committed felon, that barn his prison. Now *I* tell you, Aspley, that it is not so. There is not one of us three who have heard his avowal, but is heart-sure he is lying. You are the fourth, his father, and the only one to believe in his guilt."

Leoric was shaking his head violently and wretchedly. "I wish it were so, but I know better. Why do you say he is lying? What proof can you have for your trust, compared with that I have for my certainty?"

"I will give you one proof for my trust," said Cadfael, "in exchange for all your proofs of your certainty. As soon as he heard there was another man accused, Meriet made his confession of guilt to the law, which can destroy his body. But resolutely he refused then and refuses still to repeat that confession to a priest, and ask penance and absolution for a sin he has not committed. That is why I believe him guiltless. Now show me, if you can, as strong a reason why you should believe him guilty."

The lofty, tormented grey head continued its anguished motions of rejection. "I wish to God you were right and I wrong, but I know what I saw and what I heard. I never can forget it. Now that I must tell it openly, since there's an innocent man at stake, and Meriet to his honour has cleansed his breast, why should I not tell it first to you? My guest was gone on his way safely, it was a day like any other day. I went out for exercise with hawk and hounds, and three besides, my chaplain and huntsman, and a groom, honest men all, they will bear me out. There's thick woodland three miles north from us, a wide belt of it. It was the hounds picked up Meriet's voice, no more than a distant call to me until we got nearer and I knew him. He was calling Barbary and whistling for him—the horse that Clemence rode. It may have been the whistle the hounds caught first, and went eager but silent to find Meriet. By the time we came on him he had the horse tethered—you'll have heard he has a gift. When we burst in on him, he had the dead man under the arms, and was dragging him deep into a covert off the path. An arrow in Peter's breast, and bow and quiver on Meriet's shoulder. Do you want more? When I cried out on him, what had he done?— he never said word to deny. When I ordered him to return with us, and laid him under lock and key until I could consider such a shame and horror, and know my way, he never said nay to it, but submitted to all.

When I told him I would keep him man alive and cover up his mortal sin, but on conditions, he accepted life and withdrawal, I do believe, as much for our name's sake as for his own life, but he chose."

"He did choose, he did far more than accept," said Cadfael, "for he told Isouda what he told us all, later, that he came to us of his own will, at his own desire. Never has he said that he was forced. But go on, tell me your own part."

"I did what I had promised him, I had the horse led far to the north, by the way Clemence should have ridden, and there turned loose in the mosses, where it might be thought his rider had foundered. And the body we took secretly, with all that was his, and my chaplain read the rites over him with all reverence, before we laid him within a new stack on the charcoal-burner's old hearth, and fired it. It was ill-done and against my conscience, but I did it. Now I will answer for it. I shall not be sorry to pay whatever is due."

"Your son has taken care," said Cadfael hardly, "to claim to himself, along with the death, all that you have done to conceal it. But he will not confess lies to his confessor, as mortal a sin as hiding truth."

"But why?" demanded Leoric wildly. "Why should he so yield and accept all, if he had an answer for me? Why?"

"Because the answer he had for you would have been too hard for you to bear, and unbearable also to him. For love, surely," said Brother Cadfael. "I doubt if he has had his proper fill of love all his life, but those who most hunger for it do most and best deliver it."

"I have loved him," protested Leoric, raging and writhing, "though he has been always so troublous a soul, for ever going contrary."

"Going contrary is one way of getting your notice," said Cadfael ruefully, "when obedience and virtue go unregarded. But let that be. You want instances. This spot where you came upon him, it was hardly more than three miles from your manor—what, forty minutes' ride? And the hour when you came there was well on in the afternoon. How many hours had Clemence lain there dead? And suddenly there is Meriet toiling to hide the dead body, and whistling up the straying horse left riderless. Even if he had run in terror, and wandered the woods fevered over his deed, would he not have dealt with the horse before he fled? Either lashed him away to ride wild, or caught and ridden him far off. What was he doing there calling and tethering the horse, and hiding the body, all those hours after the man must have died? Did you never think of that?"

"I thought," said Leoric, speaking slowly now, wide-eyed, urgent upon Cadfael's face, "as you have said, that he had run in terror from what he had done, and come back, late in the day, to hide it from all eyes."

"So he has said now, but it cost him a great heave

of the heart and mind to fetch that excuse up out of the well."

"Then what," whispered Leoric, shaking now with mingled hope and bewilderment, and very afraid to trust, "what has moved him to accept so dreadful a wrong? How could he do such an injury to me and to himself?"

"For fear, perhaps, of doing you a greater. And for love of someone he had cause to doubt, as you found cause to doubt him. Meriet has a great store of love to give," said Brother Cadfael gravely, "and you would not allow him to give much of it to you. He has given it elsewhere, where it was not repelled, however it may have been undervalued. Have I to say to you again, that you have two sons?"

"No!" cried Leoric in a muted howl of protest and outrage, towering taller in his anger, head and shoulders above Cadfael's square, solid form. "That I will not hear! You presume! It is impossible!"

"Impossible for your heir and darling, yet instantly believable in his brother? In this world all men are fallible, and all things are possible."

"But I tell you I saw him hiding his dead man, and sweating over it. If he had happened on him innocently by chance he would not have had cause to conceal the death, he would have come crying it aloud."

"Not if he happened innocently on someone dear to him as brother or friend stooped over the same horrid task. You believe what you saw, why should not Meriet also believe what he saw? You put your own soul in peril to cover up what you believed he had done, why should not he do as much for another? You promised silence and concealment at a price—and that protection offered to him was just as surely protection for another—only the price was still to be exacted from Meriet. And Meriet did not grudge it. Of his own will he paid it—that was no mere consent to your terms, he wished it and tried to be glad of it, because it bought free someone he loved. Do you know of any other creature breathing that he loves as he loves his brother?"

"This is madness!" said Leoric, breathing hard like a man who has run himself half to death. "Nigel was the whole day with the Lindes, Roswitha will tell you, Janyn will tell you. He had a falling-out to make up with the girl, he was off to her early in the morning, and came home only late in the evening. He knew nothing of that day's business, he was aghast when he heard of it."

"From Linde's manor to that place in the forest is no long journey for a mounted man," said Cadfael relentlessly. "How if Meriet found him busy and bloodied over Clemence's body, and said to him: Go, get clean away from here, leave him to me—go and be seen elsewhere all this day. I will do what must be done. What then?"

"Are you truly saying," demanded Leoric in hoarse whisper, "that Nigel killed the man? Such a crime against hospitality, against kinship, against his nature?"

"No," said Cadfael. "But I am saying that it may be true that Meriet did so find him, just as you found Meriet. Why should what was such plain proof to you be any less convincing to Meriet? Had he not overwhelming reason to believe his brother guilty, to fear him guilty, or no less terrible, to dread that he might be convinced in innocence? For bear this ever in mind, if you could be mistaken in giving such instant credence to what you saw, so could Meriet. For those lost six hours still stick in my craw, and how to account for them I don't yet know."

"Is it possible?" whispered Leoric, shaken and wondering. "Have I so wronged him? And my own part—must I not go straight to Hugh Beringar and let him judge? In God's name, what are we to do, to set right what can be righted?"

"You must go, rather, to Abbot Radulfus's dinner," said Cadfael, "and be such a convivial guest as he expects, and tomorrow you must marry your son as you have planned. We are still groping in the dark, and have no choice but to wait for enlightenment. Think of what I have said, but say no word of it to any other. Not yet. Let them have their wedding day in peace."

But for all that he was certain then, in his own mind, that it would not be in peace.

Isouda came to find him in his workshop in the herbarium. He took one look at her, forgot his broodings, and smiled. She came in the austere but fine array she had thought suitable for dining with abbots, and catching the smile and the lighting of Cadfael's eyes, she relaxed into her impish grin and opened her cloak wide, putting off the hood to let him admire her.

"You think it will do?"

Her hair, too short to braid, was bound about her brow by an embroidered ribbon fillet, just such a one as Meriet had hidden in his bed in the dortoir, and below the confinement it clustered in a thick mane of curls on her neck. Her dress was an over-tunic of deep blue, fitting closely to the hip and there flowing out in gentle folds, over a long-sleeved and high-necked cotte of a pale rose-coloured wool. Exceedingly grown-up, not at all the colours or the cut to which a wild child would fly, allowed for once to dine with the adults. Her bearing, always erect and confident, had acquired a lordly dignity to go with the dress, and her gait as she entered was princely. The close necklace of heavy natural stones, polished but not cut, served beautifully to call the eye to the fine carriage of her head. She wore no other ornaments.

"It would do for me," said Cadfael simply, "if I were a green boy expecting a hoyden known from a child. Are you as unprepared for him, I wonder, as he will be for you?"

Isouda shook her head until the brown curls danced, and settled again into new and distracting patterns on her shoulders. "No! I've thought of all you've told me, and I know my Meriet. Neither you nor he need fear. I can deal!"

"Then before we go," said Cadfael, "you had better be armed with everything I have gleaned in the meantime." And he sat down with her and told. She heard him out with a serious but tranquil face, unshaken.

"Listen, Brother Cadfael, why should he *not* come to see his brother married, since things are as you say? I know it would not be a kindness, not yet, to tell him he's *known* as an innocent and deceives nobody, it would only set him agonizing for whoever it is he's hiding. But you know him now. If he's given his parole, he'll not break it, and he's innocent enough, God knows, to believe that other men are as honest as he, and will take his word as simply as he gives it. He would credit it if Hugh Beringar allowed even a captive felon to come to see his brother married."

"He could not yet walk so far," said Cadfael, though he was captivated by the notion.

"He need not. I would send a groom with a horse for him. Brother Mark could come with him. Why not? He could come early, and cloaked, and take his place privately where he could watch. Whatever follows," said Isouda with grave determination, "for I am not such a fool as to doubt there's grief here somehow for their house—whatever follows, I want *him* brought forth into daylight, where he belongs. Or whatever faces may be fouled! For his is fair enough, and so I want it shown."

"So do I," said Cadfael heartily, "so do I!"

"Then ask Hugh Beringar if I may send for him to come. I don't know—I feel there may be need of him, that he has the right to be there, that he should be there."

"I will speak to Hugh," said Cadfael. "And now, come, let's be off to Saint Giles before the light fails."

They walked together along the Foregate, veered right at the bleached grass triangle of the horse-fair, and out between scattered houses and green fields to the hospice. The shadowy, skeleton trees made lace patterns against a greenish, pallid sky thinning to frost.

"This is where even lepers may go for shelter?" she said, climbing the gentle grassy slope to the boundary fence. "They medicine them here, and do their best to heal? That is noble!"

"They even have their successes," said Cadfael. "There's never any want of volunteers to serve here, even after a death. Mark may have gone far to heal your Meriet, body and soul."

"When I have finished what he has begun," she said with a sudden shining smile, "I will thank him properly. Now where must we go?"

Cadfael took her directly to the barn, but at this hour it was empty. The evening meal was not yet due, but the light was too far gone for any activity out-doors. The solitary low pallet stood neatly covered with its dun blanket.

"This is his bed?" she asked, gazing down at it with a meditative face.

"It is. He had it up in the loft above, for fear of disturbing his fellows if he had bad dreams, and it was here he fell. By Mark's account he was on his way in his sleep to make confession to Hugh Beringar, and get him to free his prisoner. Will you wait for him here? I'll find him and bring him to you."

Meriet was seated at Brother Mark's little desk in the anteroom of the hall, mending the binding of a service book with a strip of leather. His face was grave in concentration on his task, his fingers patient and adroit. Only when Cadfael informed him that he had a visitor waiting in the barn was he shaken by sudden agitation. Cadfael he was used to, and did not mind, but he shrank from showing himself to others, as though he carried a contagion.

"I had rather no one came," he said, torn between gratitude for an intended kindness and reluctance to have to make the effort of bearing the consequent pain. "What good can it do, now? What is there to be said? I've been glad of my quietness here." He gnawed a doubtful lip and asked resignedly: "Who is it?"

"No one you need fear," said Cadfael, thinking of Nigel, whose brotherly attentions might have proved too much to bear, had they been offered. But they had not. Bridegrooms have some excuse for putting all other business aside, certainly, but at least he should have asked after his brother. "It is only Isouda."

Only Isouda! Meriet drew relieved breath. "Isouda has thought of me? That was kind. But—does she know? That I am a confessed felon. I would not have her in a mistake . . ."

"She does know. No need to say word of that, and neither will she. She would have me bring her because she has a loyal affection for you. It won't cost you much to spend a few minutes with her, and I doubt if you'll have to do much talking, for she will do the most of it."

Meriet went with him, still a little reluctantly, but not greatly disturbed by the thoughts of having to bear the regard, the sympathy, the obstinate championship, perhaps, of a child playmate. The children among his beggars had been good for him, simple, undemanding, accepting him without question. Isouda's sisterly fondness he could meet in the same way, or so he supposed.

She had helped herself to the flint and tinder in the box beside the cot, struck sparks, and kindled the wick of the small lamp, setting it carefully on the broad stone placed for it, where it would be safe from contact with any drifting straw, and shed its mellow, mild light upon the foot of the bed, where she had seated herself. She had put back her cloak to rest only upon her shoulders and frame the sober grandeur of her gown, her embroidered girdle, and the hands folded in her lap. She lifted upon Meriet as he entered the discreet, age-old smile of the Virgin in one of the more worldly paintings of the Annunciation, where the angel's embassage is patently superfluous, for the lady has known it long before.

Meriet caught his breath and halted at gaze, seeing this grown lady seated calmly and expectantly upon his bed. How could a few months so change anyone? He had meant to say gently but bluntly, "You should not have come here," but the words were never uttered. There she sat in possession of herself and of place and time, and he was almost afraid of her, and of the sorry changes she might find in him, thin, limping, outcast, no way resembling the boy who had run wild with her no long time ago. But Isouda rose, advanced upon him with hands raised to draw his head down to her, and kissed him soundly.

"Do you know you've grown almost handsome? I'm sorry about your broken head," she said, lifting a hand to touch the healed wound, "but this will go, you'll bear no mark. Someone did good work closing that cut. You may surely kiss me, you are not a monk yet."

Meriet's lips, still and chill against her cheek, suddenly stirred and quivered, closing in helpless passion. Not for her as a woman, not yet, simply as a warmth, a kindness, someone coming with open arms and no questions or reproaches. He embraced her inexpertly, wavering between impetuosity and shyness of this transformed being, and quaked at the contact.

"You're still lame," she said solicitously. "Come and sit down with me. I won't stay too long, to tire you, but I couldn't be so near without coming to see

you again. Tell me about this place," she ordered,
drawing him down to the bed beside her. "There are
children here, too, I heard their voices. Quite young
children."

Spellbound, he began to tell her in stumbling, broken phrases about Brother Mark, small and fragile
and indestructible, who had the signature of God
upon him and longed to become a priest. It was not
hard to talk about his friend, and the unfortunates
who were yet fortunate in falling into such hands.
Never a word about himself or her, while they sat
shoulder to shoulder, turned inwards towards each
other, and their eyes ceaselessly measured and noted
the changes wrought by this season of trial. He forgot
that he was a man self-condemned, with only a brief
but strangely tranquil life before him, and she a
young heiress with a manor double the value of Aspley, and grown suddenly beautiful. They sat immured
from time and unthreatened by the world; and Cadfael slipped away satisfied, and went to snatch a word
with Brother Mark, while there was time. She had her
finger on the pulse of the hours, she would not stay
too long. The art was to astonish, to warm, to quicken
an absurd but utterly credible hope, and then to depart.

When she thought fit to go, Meriet brought her
from the barn by the hand. They had both a high
colour and bright eyes, and by the way they moved
together they had broken free from the first awe, and
had been arguing as of old; and that was good. He

stooped his cheek to be kissed when they separated, and she kissed him briskly, gave him a cheek in exchange, said he was a stubborn wretch as he always had been, and yet left him exalted almost into content, and herself went away cautiously encouraged.

"I have as good as promised him I will send my horse to fetch him in good time tomorrow morning," she said, when they were reaching the first scattered houses of the Foregate.

"I have as good as promised Mark the same," said Cadfael. "But he had best come cloaked and quietly. God, he knows if I have any good reason for it, but my thumbs prick and I want him there, but unknown to those closest to him in blood."

"We are troubling too much," said the girl buoyantly, exalted by her own success. "I told you long ago, he is mine, and no one else will have him. If it is needful that Peter Clemence's slayer must be taken, to give Meriet to me, then why fret, for he will be taken."

"Girl," said Cadfael, breathing in deeply, "you terrify me like an act of God. And I do believe you will pull down the thunderbolt."

In the warmth and soft light in their small chamber in the guest-hall after supper, the two girls who shared a bed sat brooding over their plans for the morrow. They were not sleepy, they had far too much on their minds to wish for sleep. Roswitha's maid-servant, who attended them both, had gone to her bed an hour ago; she was a raw country girl, not entrusted with the choice of jewels, ornaments and perfumes for a marriage. It would be Isouda who would dress her friend's hair, help her into her gown, and escort her from guest-hall to church and back again, withdrawing the cloak from her shoulders at the church door, in this December cold, restoring it when she left on her lord's arm, a new-made wife.

Roswitha had spread out her wedding gown on the bed, to brood over its every fold, consider the set of the sleeves and the fit of the bodice, and wonder whether it would not be the better still for a closer clasp to the gilded girdle.

Isouda roamed the room restlessly, replying carelessly to Roswitha's dreaming comments and questions. They had the wooden chests of their possessions, leather-covered, stacked against one wall, and the small things they had taken out were spread at large on every surface; bed, shelf and chest. The little box that held Roswitha's jewels stood upon the press beside the guttering lamp. Isouda delved a hand idly into it, plucking out one piece after another. She had no great interest in such adornments.

"Would you wear the yellow mountain stones?" asked Roswitha, "to match with this gold thread in the girdle?"

Isouda held the amber pebbles to the light and let them run smoothly through her fingers. "They would suit well. But let me see what else you have here. You've never shown me the half of these." She was fingering them curiously when she caught the buried gleam of coloured enamels, and unearthed from the very bottom of the box a large brooch of the ancient ring-and-pin kind, the ring with its broad, flattened terminals intricately ornamented with filigree shapes of gold framing the enamels, sinuous animals that became twining leaves if viewed a second time, and twisted back into serpents as she gazed. The pin was of silver, with a diamond-shaped head engraved with a formal flower in enamels, and the point projected the length of her little finger beyond the ring, which filled her palm. A princely thing, made to fasten the thick folds of a man's cloak. She had begun to say: "I've never seen this . . ." before she had it out and saw it clearly. She broke off then, and the sudden silence caused Roswitha to look up. She rose quickly, and came to plunge her own hand into the box and thrust the brooch to the bottom again, out of sight.

"Oh, not that!" she said with a grimace. "It's too heavy, and so old-fashioned. Put them all back, I shall need only the yellow necklace and the silver hair-combs." She closed the lid firmly, and drew Isouda back to the bed, where the gown lay carefully outspread. "See here, there are a few frayed stitches in the embroidery, could you catch them up for me? You are a better needlewoman than I."

With a placid face and steady hand Isouda sat down and did as she was asked, and refrained from casting another glance at the box that held the brooch. But when the hour of Compline came, she snapped off her thread at the final stitch, laid her work aside and announced that she was going to attend the office. Roswitha, already languidly undressing for bed, made no move to dissuade, and certainly none to join her.

Brother Cadfael left the church after Compline by the south porch, intending only to pay a brief visit to his workshop to see that the brazier, which Brother Oswin had been using earlier, was safely out, everything securely stoppered, and the door properly closed to conserve what warmth remained. The night was starry and sharp with frost, and he needed no other light to see his way by such familiar paths. But he had got no further than the archway into the court when he was plucked urgently by the sleeve, and a breathless voice whispered in his ear: "Brother Cadfael, I must talk to you!"

"Isouda! What is it? Something has happened?" He drew her back into one of the carrels of the scriptorium; no one else would be stirring there now, and in the darkness the two of them were invisible, drawn back into the most sheltered corner. Her face at his shoulder was intent, a pale oval afloat above the darkness of her cloak.

"Happened, indeed! You *said* I might pull down the thunderbolt. I have found something," she said, rapid and low in his ear, "in Roswitha's jewel box. Hidden at the bottom. A great ring-brooch, very old and fine, in gold and silver and enamels, the kind men made long before ever the Normans came. As big as the palm of my hand, with a long pin. When she saw what I had, she came and thrust it back into the box and closed the lid, saying that was too heavy and old-fashioned to wear. So I let it pass, and never said word of what I knew. I doubt if she understands what it is, or how whoever gave it to her came by it, though I think he must have warned her not to wear or show it, not yet . . . Why else should she be so quick to put it out of my sight? Or else simply she doesn't like it—I suppose it might be no more than that. But *I* know what it is and where it came from, and so will you when I tell you . . ." She had run out of breath in her haste, and panted soft warmth against his cheek, leaning close. "I have seen it before, as she may not have done. It was I who took the cloak from him and carried it within, to the chamber we made ready for him. Fremund brought in his saddle-bags, the cloak I carried . . . and this brooch was pinned in the collar."

Cadfael laid a hand over the small hand that gripped his sleeve, and asked, half-doubting, half-convinced already: "Whose cloak? Are you saying this thing belonged to Peter Clemence?"

"I *am* saying it. I will swear it."

"You are sure it must be the same?"

"I am sure. I tell you I carried it in, I touched, I admired it."

"No, there could not well be two such," he said,

and drew breath deep. "Of such rare things I doubt there were ever made two alike."

"Even if there were, why should both wander into this shire? But no, surely every one was made for a prince or a chief and never repeated. My grandsire had such a brooch, but not near so fine and large, he said it came from Ireland, long ago. Besides, I remember the very colours and the strange beasts. It is the same. And she has it!" She had a new thought, and voiced it eagerly. "Canon Eluard is still here, he knew the cross and ring, he will surely know this, and he can swear to it. But if that fails, so can I, and I will. Tomorrow—how must we deal tomorrow? For Hugh Beringar is not here to be told, and the time so short. It rests with us. Tell me what I can best do?"

"So I will," said Cadfael slowly, his hand firm over hers, "when you have told me one more most vital thing. This brooch—it is whole and clean? No stain, no discolouration anywhere upon it, on metals or enamels? Not even thin edges where such discolourings may have been cleaned away?"

"No!" said Isouda after a sudden brief silence, and drew in understanding breath. "I had not thought of that! No, it is as it was made, bright and perfect. Not like the others . . . No, *this* has *not* been through the fire."

CHAPTER TWELVE

THE WEDDING DAY DAWNED CLEAR, BRIGHT AND very cold. A flake or two of frozen snow, almost too fine to be seen but stinging on the cheek, greeted Isouda as she crossed the court for Prime, but the sky was so pure and lofty that it seemed there would be no fall. Isouda prayed earnestly and bluntly, rather demanding help from heaven than entreating it. From the church she went to the stable-yard, to give orders that her groom should go with her horse and bring Meriet at the right time, with Mark in attendance, to see his brother married. Then she went to dress Roswitha, braid her hair and dress it high with the silver combs and gilt net, fasten the yellow necklace about her throat, walk round her and twitch every fold into place. Uncle Leoric, whether avoiding this cloistered abode of women or grimly preoccupied with the divergent fortunes of his two sons, made no appearance until it was time for him to proceed to his place in the church, but Wulfric Linde hovered in satisfied admiration of his daughter's beauty, and did not seem to find this over-womaned air hard to breathe. Isouda had a mild, tolerant regard for him; a silly, kind man, competent at getting good value out of a manor, and reasonable with his tenants and villeins, but seldom looking beyond, and always the last to know what his children or neighbours were about.

Somewhere, at this same time, Janyn and Nigel were certainly engaged in the same archaic dance, making the bridegroom ready for what was at the same time triumph and sacrifice.

Wulfric studied the set of Roswitha's bliaut, and turned her about fondly to admire her from every angle. Isouda withdrew to the press, and let them confer contentedly, totally absorbed, while she fished up by touch, from the bottom of the casket, the ancient ring-brooch that had belonged to Peter Clemence, and secured it by the pin in her wide oversleeve.

The young groom Edred arrived at Saint Giles with two horses, in good time to bring Meriet and Brother Mark to the dim privacy within the church before the invited company assembled. In spite of his natural longing to see his brother wed, Meriet had shrunk from being seen to be present, an accused felon as he was, and a shame to his father's house. So he had said when Isouda promised him access, and assured him that Hugh Beringar would allow the indulgence and accept his prisoner's sworn word not to take advantage of such clemency; the scruple had suited Isouda's purpose then and was even more urgently welcome now. He need not make himself known to anyone, and no one should recognize or even notice him. Edred would bring him early, and he could be safely installed in a dim corner of the choir before ever the guests came in, some withdrawn place where he could see and not be seen. And when the married pair left, and the guests after them, then he could follow unnoticed and return to his prison with his gentle gaoler, who was necessary as friend, prop in case of need, and witness, though Meriet knew nothing of the need there might well be of informed witnesses.

"And the lady of Foriet orders me," said Edred cheerfully, "to tether the horses outside the precinct, ready for when you want to return. Outside the gatehouse I'll hitch them until the rest have gone in, if you so please. You won't mind, brothers, if I take an hour or so free while you're within? There's a sister of mine has a house along the Foregate, a small cot for her and her man." There was also a girl he fancied, in the hovel next door, but that he did not feel it necessary to say.

Meriet came forth from the barn strung taut like an overtuned lute, his cowl drawn forward to hide his face. He had discarded his stick, except when overtired at the end of the day, but he still went a little lame on his sprained foot. Mark kept close at his elbow, watching the sharp, lean profile that was honed even finer by the dark backcloth of the cowl, a face lofty-browed, high-nosed, fastidious.

"Should I so intrude upon him?" wondered Meriet, his voice thin with pain. "He has not asked after me," he said, aching, and turned his face away, ashamed of so complaining.

"You should and you must," said Mark firmly. "You promised the lady, and she has put herself out to make your visit easy. Now let her groom mount you, you have not yet the full use of that foot, you cannot spring."

Meriet gave way, consenting to borrow a hand to get into the saddle. "And that's her own riding horse you have there," said Edred, looking up proudly at the tall young gelding. "And a stout little horse-woman she is, and thinks the world of him. There's not many she'd let into a saddle on *that* back, I can tell you."

It occurred to Meriet, somewhat late, to wonder if he was not trying Brother Mark too far, in enforcing him to clamber aboard a beast strange and possibly fearsome to him. He knew so little of this small, tireless brother, only what he was, not at all what he had been aforetime, nor how long he had worn the habit; there were those children of the cloister who had been habited from infancy. But Brother Mark set foot briskly enough in the stirrup, and hoisted his light weight into the saddle without either grace or difficulty.

"I grew up on a well-farmed yardland," he said, noting Meriet's wide eye. "I have had to do with horses from an infant, not your high-bred stock, but farm-drudges. I plod like them, but I can stay up, and I can get my beast where he must go. I began very early," he said, remembering long hours half-asleep and sagging in the fields, a small hand clutching the stones in his bag, to sling at the crows along the furrow.

They went out along the Foregate thus, two mounted brothers of the Benedictines with a young groom trotting alongside. The winter morning was young, but the human traffic was already brisk, husbandmen out to feed their winter stock, housewives shopping, late packmen humping their packs, children running and playing, everybody quick to make use of a fine morning, where daylight was in any case short, and fine mornings might be few. As brothers of the abbey, they exchanged greetings and reverences all along the way.

They lighted down before the gatehouse, and left the horses with Edred to bestow as he had said. Here in the precinct where he had sought entry, for whatever reason of his own and counter-reason of his father's, Meriet hung irresolute, trembling, if Mark had not taken him by the arm, and drawn him within. Through the great court, busy enough but engrossed, they made their way into the blessed dimness and

chill of the church, and if any noticed them they
never wondered at two brothers going cowled and in
a hurry on such a frosty morning.

Edred, whistling, tethered the horses as he had said
he would, and went off to visit his sister and the girl
next door.

Hugh Beringar, not a wedding guest, was nevertheless as early on the scene as were Meriet and Mark,
nor did he come alone. Two of his officers loitered
unobtrusively among the shifting throng in the great
court, where a number of the curious inhabitants of
the Foregate had added themselves to the lay servants, boys and novices, and the various birds of passage lodged in the common hall. Cold though it
might be, they intended to see all there was to be
seen. Hugh kept out of sight in the anteroom of the
gatehouse, where he could observe without himself
being observed. Here he had within his hand all those
who had been closest to the death of Peter Clemence.
If this day's ferment did not cast up anything fresh,
then both Leoric and Nigel must be held to account,
and made to speak out whatever they knew.

In compliment to a generous patron of the abbey,
Abbot Radulfus himself had elected to conduct the
marriage service, and that ensured that his guest
Canon Eluard should also attend. Moreover, the
sacrament would be at the high altar, not the parish
altar, since the abbot was officiating, and the choir
monks would all be in their places. That severed

Hugh from any possibility of a word in advance with Cadfael. A pity, but they knew each other well enough by now to act in alliance even without pre-arrangement.

The leisurely business of assembly had begun already, guests crossed from hall to church by twos and threes, in their best. A country gathering, not a court one, but equally proud and of lineage as old or older. Compassed about with a great cloud of witnesses, equally Saxon and Norman, Roswitha Linde would go to her bridal. Shrewsbury had been given to the great Earl Roger almost as soon as Duke William became king, but many a manor in the outlying countryside had remained with its old lord, and many a come-lately Norman lordling had had the sense to take a Saxon wife, and secure his gains through blood older than his own, and a loyalty not due to himself.

The interested crowd shifted and murmured, craning to get the best view of the passing guests. There went Leoric Aspley, and there his son Nigel, that splendid young man, decked out to show him at his best, and Janyn Linde in airy attendance, his amused and indulgent smile appropriate enough in a good-natured bachelor assisting at another young man's loss of liberty. That meant that all the guests should now be in their places. The two young men halted at the door of the church and took their stand there.

Roswitha came from the guest-hall swathed in her fine blue cloak, for her gown was light for a winter morning. No question but she was beautiful, Hugh thought, watching her sail down the stone steps on Wulfric's plump, complacent arm. Cadfael had reported her as quite unable to resist drawing all men after her, even elderly monks of no attraction or presence. She had the audience of her life now, lined up on either side of her unhurried passage to the church, gaping in admiration. And in her it seemed as innocent and foolish as an over-fondness for honey. To be jealous of her would be absurd.

Isouda Foriet, demure in eclipse behind such radiance, walked after the bride, bearing her gilded prayer-book and ready to attend on her at the church door, where Wulfric lifted his daughter's hand from his own arm, and laid it in the eager hand Nigel extended to receive it. Bride and groom entered the church porch together, and there Isouda lifted the warm mantle from Roswitha's shoulders and folded it over her own arm, and so followed the bridal pair into the dim nave of the church.

Not at the parish altar of Holy Cross, but at the high altar of Saint Peter and Saint Paul, Nigel Aspley and Roswitha Linde were made man and wife.

Nigel made his triumphal way from the church by the great west door which lay just outside the enclave of the abbey, close beside the gatehouse. He had Roswitha ceremoniously by the hand, and was so blind and drunk with his own pride of possession that it was doubtful if he was aware even of Isouda herself standing in the porch, let alone of the cloak she spread in her hands and draped over Roswitha's shoulders, as bride and groom reached the chill brightness of the frosty noon outside. After them streamed the proud fathers and gratified guests; and if Leoric's face was unwontedly grey and sombre for such an occasion, no one seemed to remark it; he was at all times an austere man.

Nor did Roswitha notice the slight extra weight on her left shoulder of an ornament intended for a man's wear. Her eyes were fixed only on the admiring crowd that heaved and sighed with approbation at sight of her. Here outside the wall the throng had grown, since everyone who had business or a dwelling along the Foregate had come to stare. Not here, thought Isouda, following watchfully, not here will there be any response, here all those who might recognize the brooch are walking behind her, and Nigel is as oblivious as she. Only when they turn in again at the gatehouse, having shown themselves from the parish door, will there be anyone to take heed. And if Canon Eluard fails me, she thought resolute, then *I* shall speak out, my word against hers or any man's.

Roswitha was in no hurry; her progress down the steps, across the cobbles of the forecourt to the gateway and so within to the great court, was slow and stately, so that every man might stare his fill. That was a blessed chance, for in the meantime Abbot Radulfus and Canon Eluard had left the church by transept and cloister, and stood to watch benevolently by the stair to the guest-hall, and the choir monks had followed them out to disperse and mingle with the fringe of the crowd, aloof but interested.

Brother Cadfael made his way unobtrusively to a post close to where the abbot and his guest stood, so that he could view the advancing pair as they did. Against the heavy blue cloth of Roswitha's cloak the great brooch, aggressively male, stood out brilliantly. Canon Eluard had broken off short in the middle of some quiet remark in the abbot's ear, and his beneficent smile faded, and gave place to a considering and intent frown, as though at this slight distance his vision failed to convince him he was seeing what indeed he saw.

"But that . . . ," he murmured, to himself rather than to any other. "But no, how can it be?"

Bride and groom drew close, and made dutiful reverence to the dignitaries of the church. Behind them came Isouda, Leoric, Wulfric, and all the assembly of their guests. Under the arch of the gatehouse Cadfael saw Janyn's fair head and flashing blue eyes, as he loitered to exchange a word with someone in the Foregate crowd known to him, and then came on with his light, springing step, smiling.

Nigel was handing his wife to the first step of the stone stairway when Canon Eluard stepped forward and stood between, with an arresting motion of his hand. Only then, following his fixed gaze, did Roswitha look down at the collar of her cloak, which swung loose on her shoulders, and see the glitter of enamelled colours and the thin gold outlines of fabulous beasts, entwined with sinuous leaves.

"Child," said Eluard, "may I look more closely?" He touched the raised threads of gold, and the silver head of the pin. She watched in wary silence, startled and uneasy, but not yet defensive or afraid. "That is a beautiful and rare thing you have there," said the canon, eyeing her with a slight, uncertain frown. "Where did you get it?"

Hugh had come forth from the gatehouse and was watching and listening from the rear of the crowd. At the corner of the cloister two habited brothers watched from a distance. Pinned here between the watchers round the west door and the gathering now halted inexplicably here in the great court, and unwilling to be noticed by either, Meriet stood stiff and motionless in shadow, with Brother Mark beside him, and waited to return unseen to his prison and refuge.

Roswitha moistened her lips, and said with a pale smile: "It was a gift to me from a kinsman."

"Strange!" said Eluard, and turned to the abbot with a grave face. "My lord abbot, I know this brooch well, too well ever to mistake it. It belonged to the bishop of Winchester, and he gave it to Peter Clemence—to that favoured clerk of his household whose remains now lie in your chapel."

Brother Cadfael had already noted one remarkable circumstance. He had been watching Nigel's face ever since that young man had first looked down at the adornment that was causing so much interest, and until this moment there had been no sign whatever that the brooch meant anything to him. He was glancing from Canon Eluard to Roswitha, and back again, a puzzled frown furrowing his broad forehead and a faint, questioning smile on his lips, waiting for someone to enlighten him. But now that its owner had been named, it suddenly had meaning for him, and a grim and frightening meaning at that. He paled and stiffened, staring at the canon, but though his throat and lips worked, either he found no words or thought better of those that he had found, for he remained mute. Abbot Radulfus had drawn close on one side, and Hugh Beringar on the other.

"What is this? You recognize this gem as belonging to Master Clemence? You are certain?"

"As certain as I was of those possessions of his which you have already shown me, cross and ring and dagger, which had gone through the fire with him. This he valued in particular as the bishop's gift. Whether he was wearing it on his last journey I cannot say, but it was his habit, for he prized it."

"If I may speak, my lord," said Isouda clearly from behind Roswitha's shoulder, "I *do* know that he was wearing it when he came to Aspley. The brooch was in his cloak when I took it from him at the door and carried it to the chamber prepared for him, and it was in his cloak also when I brought it out to him the next morning when he left us. He did not need the cloak for riding, the morning was warm and fine. He had it slung over his saddle-bow when he rode away."

"In full view, then," said Hugh sharply. For cross and ring had been left with the dead man and gone to the fire with him. Either time had been short and flight imperative, or else some superstitious awe had deterred the murderer from stripping a priest's gems of office from his very body, though he had not scrupled to remove this one fine thing which lay open to his hand. "You observe, my lords," said Hugh, "that this jewel seems to show no marks of damage. If you will allow us to handle and examine it . . . ?"

Good, thought Cadfael, reassured, I should have known Hugh would need no nudging from me. I can leave all to him now.

Roswitha made no move either to allow or prevent, as Hugh unpinned the great brooch from its place. She looked on with a blanched and apprehensive face, but said never a word. No, Roswitha was not entirely innocent in the matter; whether she had known what this gift was and how come by or not, she had certainly understood that it was perilous and not to be shown—not yet! Perhaps not here? And after their marriage they were bound for Nigel's northern manor. Who was likely to know it there?

"This has never seen the fire," said Hugh, and handed it to Canon Eluard for confirmation. "Everything else the man had was burned with him. Only this one thing was taken from him before ever those reached him who built him into his pyre. And only one person, last to see him alive, first to see him dead, can have taken this from his cloak as he lay, and that was his murderer." He turned to Roswitha, who stood pale to translucency, like a woman of ice, staring at him with wide and horrified eyes.

"Who gave it to you?"

She cast one rapid glance around her, and then as suddenly took heart, and drawing breath deep, she answered loudly and clearly: "Meriet!"

Cadfael awoke abruptly to the realization that he possessed knowledge which he had not yet confided to Hugh, and if he waited for the right challenge to this bold declaration from other lips he might wait in vain, and lose what had already been gained. For most of those here assembled, there was nothing incredible in this great lie she had just told, nothing even surprising, considering the circumstances of Meriet's entry into the cloister, and the history of the devil's novice within these walls. And she had clutched at the brief general hush as encouragement, and was enlarging boldly: "He was always following me with his dog's eyes. I didn't want his gifts, but I took it to be kind to him. How could I know where he got it?"

"When?" demanded Cadfael loudly, as one having authority. "*When* did he give you this gift?"

"When?" She looked round, hardly knowing where the question had come from, but hasty and positive in answering it, to hammer home conviction. "It was the day after Master Clemence left Aspley—the day after he was killed—in the afternoon. He came to me in your paddock at Linde. He pressed me so to take it . . . I did not want to hurt him . . ." From the tail of his eye Cadfael saw that Meriet had come forth from his shadowy place and drawn a little nearer, and Mark had followed him anxiously though without attempting to restrain him. But the next moment all eyes were drawn to the tall figure of Leoric Aspley, as he came striding and shouldering forward to tower over his son and his son's new wife.

"Girl," cried Leoric, "think what you say! Is it well to lie? *I know* this cannot be true." He swung about vehemently, encountering in turn with his grieved, grim eyes abbot and canon and deputy-sheriff. "My lords all, what she says is false. My part in this I will confess, and accept gladly whatever penalty is due from me. For this I know, I brought home my son Meriet, that same day that I brought home the dead body of my guest and kinsman, and having cause, or so I thought, to believe my son the slayer, I laid him under lock and key from that hour, until I had considered, and he had accepted, the fate I decreed for him. From late afternoon of the day Peter Clemence died, all the next day, and until noon of the third, my son Meriet was close prisoner in my house. He never visited this girl. He never gave her this gift, for he never had it in his possession. Nor did he ever lift hand against my guest and his kinsman, now it is shown! God forgive me that ever I credited it!"

"I am not lying!" shrilled Roswitha, struggling to recover the belief she had felt within her grasp. "A mistake only—I mistook the day! It was the third day he came . . ."

Meriet had drawn very slowly nearer. From deep within his shadowing cowl great eyes stared, examining in wonder and anguish his father, his adored brother and his first love, so frantically busy twisting knives in him. Roswitha's roving, pleading eyes met his, and she fell mute like a songbird shot down in flight, and shrank into Nigel's circling arms with a wail of despair.

Meriet stood motionless for a long moment, then he turned on his heel and limped rapidly away. The motion of his lame foot was as if at every step he shook off dust.

"Who gave it to you?" asked Hugh, with pointed and relentless patience.

All the crowd had drawn in close, watching and listening, they had not failed to follow the logic of what had passed. A hundred pairs of eyes settled gradually and remorselessly upon Nigel. He knew it, and so did she.

"No, no, no!" she cried, turning to wind her arms fiercely about her husband. "It was not my lord—not Nigel! It was my brother gave me the brooch!"

On the instant everyone present was gazing round in haste, searching the court for the fair head, the blue eyes and light-hearted smile, and Hugh's officers were burrowing through the press and bursting out at the gate to no purpose. For Janyn Linde had vanished silently and circumspectly, probably by cool and un-hurried paces from the moment Canon Eluard first noticed the bright enamels on Roswitha's shoulder. And so had Isouda's riding-horse, the better of the two hitched outside of the gatehouse for Meriet's use. The porter had paid no attention to a young man sauntering innocently out and mounting without haste. It was a youngster of the Foregate, bright-eyed and knowing, who informed the sergeants that a young gentleman had left by the gate, as long as a quarter of an hour earlier, unhitched his horse, and ridden off along the Foregate, not towards the town. Modestly enough to start with said the shrewd urchin, but he was into a good gallop by the time he reached the corner at the horse-fair and vanished.

From the chaos within the great court, which must be left to sort itself out without his aid, Hugh flew to the stables, to mount himself and the officers he had with him, send for more men, and pursue the fugitive; if such a word might properly be applied to so gay and competent a malefactor as Janyn.

"But why, in God's name, why?" groaned Hugh, tightening girths in the stable-yard, and appealing to Brother Cadfael, busy at the same task beside him. "Why should he kill? What can he have had against the man? He had never so much as seen him, he was not at Aspley that night. How in the devil's name did he even know the looks of the man he was waiting for?

"Someone had pictured him for him—and he knew

the time of his departure and the road he would take, that's plain." But all the rest was still obscure, to Cadfael as to Hugh.

Janyn was gone, he had plucked himself gently out of the law's reach in excellent time, forseeing that all must come out. By fleeing he had owned to his act, but the act itself remained inexplicable.

"Not the man," fretted Cadfael to himself, puffing after Hugh as he led his saddled horse at a trot up to the court and the gatehouse. "Not the man, then it must have been his errand, after all. What else is there? But why should anyone wish to prevent him from completing his well-intentioned ride to Chester, on the bishop's business? What harm could there be to any man in that?"

The wedding party had scattered indecisively about the court, the involved families taking refuge in the guest-hall, their closest friends loyally following them out of sight, where wounds could be dressed and quarrels reconciled without witnesses from the common herd. More distant guests took counsel, and some withdrew discreetly, preferring to be at home. The inhabitants of the Foregate, pleased and entertained and passing dubiously reliable information hither and yon and adding to it as it passed, continued attentive about the gatehouse.

Hugh had his men mustered and his foot in the stirrup when the furious pounding of galloping hooves, rarely heard in the Foregate, came echoing madly along the enclave wall, and clashed in over the cobbles of the gateway. An exhausted rider, sweating on a lathered horse, reined to a slithering, screaming stop on the frosty stones, and fell rather than dismounted into Hugh's arms, his knees giving under him. All those left in the court, Abbot Radulfus and Prior Robert among them, came closing in haste about the newcomer, foreseeing desperate news.

"Sheriff Prestcote," panted the reeling messenger, "or who stands here for him—from the lord bishop of Lincoln, in haste, and pleads for haste . . ."

"I stand here for the sheriff," said Hugh. "Speak out! What's the lord bishop's urgent word for us?"

"That you should call up all the king's knight-service in the shire," said the messenger, bracing himself strongly, "for in the north-east there's black treason, in despite of his Grace's head. Two days after the lord king left Lincoln, Ranulf of Chester and William of Roumare made their way into the king's castle by a subterfuge and have taken it by force. The citizens of Lincoln cry out to his Grace to rescue them from an abominable tyranny, and the lord bishop has contrived to send out a warning, through tight defences, to tell his Grace of what is done. There are many of us now, riding every way with the word. It will be in London by nightfall."

"King Stephen was there but a week or more ago," cried Canon Eluard, "and they pledged their faith to him. How is this possible? They promised a strong chain of fortresses across the north."

"And that they have," said the envoy, heaving at

breath, "but not for King Stephen's service, nor the empress's neither, but for their own bastard kingdom in the north. Planned long ago, when they met and called all their castellans to Chester in September, with links as far south as here, and garrisons and constables ready for every castle. They've been gathering young men about them everywhere for their ends . . ."

So that was the way of it! Planned long ago, in September, at Chester, where Peter Clemence was bound with an errand from Henry of Blois, a most untimely visitor to intervene where such a company was gathered in arms and such a plot being hatched. No wonder Clemence could not be allowed to ride on unmolested and complete his embassy. And with links as far south as here!

Cadfael caught at Hugh's arm. "They were two in it together, Hugh. Tomorrow this newly-wed pair were to be on their way north to the very borders of Lincolnshire—it's Aspley has the manor there, not Linde. Secure Nigel, while you can! If it's not already too late!"

Hugh turned to stare for an instant only, grasped the force of it, dropped his bridle and ran, beckoning his sergeants after him to the guest-hall. Cadfael was close at his heels when they broke in upon a demoralized wedding party, bereft of gaiety, appetite of spirits, draped about the untouched board in burdened converse more fitting a wake than a wedding. The bride wept desolately in the arms of a stout matron,

with three or four other women clucking and cooing
around her. The bridegroom was nowhere to be seen.

"He's away!" said Cadfael. "While we were in the
stable-yard, no other chance. And without her! The
bishop of Lincoln got his message out of a tightly-
sealed city at least a day too soon."

There was no horse tethered outside the gatehouse,
when they recalled the possibility and ran to see.
Nigel had taken the first opportunity of following his
fellow-conspirator towards the lands, offices and
commands William of Roumare had promised them,
where able young men of martial achievements and
small scruples could carve out a fatter future than in
two modest Shropshire manors on the edge of the
Long Forest.

CHAPTER THIRTEEN

THERE WAS NEW AND SENSATIONAL MATTER FOR
gossip now, and the watchers in the Foregate, having
taken in all that stretched ears and sharp eyes could
command, went to spread the word further, and there
was planned rebellion in the north, a bid to set up a private kingdom for the earls of Chester and Lincoln, that
the fine young men of the wedding company were in
the plot from long since, and were fled because the
matter had come to light before they could make an or-
derly withdrawal as planned. The lord bishop of Lincoln, no very close friend of King Stephen, had
nevertheless found Chester and Roumare still more ob-
jectionable, and bestirred himself to smuggle out word
to the king and implore rescue, for himself and his city.

The comings and goings about bridge and abbey
were watched avidly. Hugh Beringar, torn two ways,
had delegated the pursuit of the traitors to his sergeants,

while he rode at once to the castle to send out the call to the knight-service of the shire to be ready to join the force which King Stephen would certainly be raising to besiege Lincoln, to begin commandeering mounts enough for his force, and see that all that was needed in the armoury was in good order. The bishop's messenger was lodged at the abbey, and his message sped on its way by another rider to the castles in the south of the shire. In the guest-hall the shattered company and the deserted bride remained invisible, shut in with the ruins of their celebration.

All this, and the twenty-first day of December barely past two in the afternoon! And what more was to happen before night, who could guess, when things were rushing along at such a speed?

Abbot Radulfus had reasserted his domestic rule, and the brothers went obediently to dinner in the refectory at his express order, somewhat later than usual. The horarium of the house could not be altogether abandoned even for such devastating matters as murder, treason and man-hunt. Besides, as Brother Cadfael thoughtfully concluded, those who had survived this upheaval to gain, instead of loss, might safely be left to draw breath and think in peace, before they must encounter and come to new terms. And those who had lost must have time to lick their wounds. As for the fugitives, the first of them had a handsome start, and the second had benefited by the arrival of even more shocking news to gain a limited breathing-space, but for all that, the hounds were on their trail, well aware now what route to take, for Aspley's northern manor lay somewhere south of Newark, and anyone making for it must set forth by the road to Stafford. Somewhere in the heathland short of that town, dusk would be closing on the travellers. They might think it safe to lodge overnight in the town. They might yet be overtaken and brought back.

On leaving the refectory Cadfael made for his normal destination during the afternoon hours of work, the hut in the herb garden where he brewed his mysteries. And they were there, the two young men in Benedictine habits, seated quietly side by side on the bench against the end wall. The very small spark of the brazier glowed faintly on their faces. Meriet leaned back against the timbers in simple exhaustion, his cowl thrust back on his shoulders, his face shadowy. He had been down into the very profound of anger, grief and bitterness, and surfaced again to find Mark still constant and patient beside him; and now he was at rest, without thought or feeling, ready to be born afresh into a changed world, but not in haste. Mark looked as he always looked, mild, almost deprecatory, as though he pleaded a fragile right to be where he was, and yet would stand to it to the death.

"I thought I might find you here," said Brother Cadfael, and took the little bellows and blew the brazier into rosy life, for it was none too warm within there. He closed and barred the door to keep out even the draught that found its way through the chinks. "I doubt if you'll have eaten," he said, feeling along the shelf behind the door. "There are oat cakes here and some apples, and I think I have a morsel of cheese. You'll be the better for a bite. And I have a wine that will do you no harm either."

And behold, the boy was hungry! So simple it was. He was not long turned nineteen, and physically hearty, and he had eaten nothing since dawn. He began listlessly, docile to persuasion, and at the first bite he was alive again and ravenous, his eyes brightening, the glow of the blown brazier gilding and softening hollow cheeks. The wine, as Cadfael had predicted, did him no harm at all. Blood flowed through him again, with new warmth and urgency.

He said not one word of brother, father or lost love. It was still too early. He had heard himself falsely accused by one of them, falsely suspected by another, and what by the third? Left to pursue his devoted and foolish self-sacrifice, without a word to absolve him. He had a great load of bitterness still to shake from his heart. But praise God, he came to life for food and ate like a starved schoolboy. Brother Cadfael was greatly encouraged.

In the mortuary chapel, where Peter Clemence lay in his sealed coffin on his draped bier, Leoric Aspley had chosen to make his confession, and entreated Abbot Radulfus to be the priest to hear it. On his knees on the flagstones, by his own choice, he set forth the story as he had known it, the fearful discovery of his younger son labouring to drag a dead man into cover and hide him from all eyes, Meriet's tacit acceptance of the guilt, and his own reluctance to deliver up his son to death, or let him go free.

"I promised him I would deal with his dead man, even at the peril of my soul, and he should live, but in perpetual penance out of the world. And to that he agreed and embraced his penalty, as I now know or fear that I now know, for love of his brother, whom he had better reason for believing a murderer than ever I had for crediting the same guilt to Meriet. I am afraid, father, that he accepted his fate as much for my sake as for his brother's, having cause, to my shame, to believe—no, to know!—that I built all on Nigel and all too little upon him, and could live on after writing him out of my life, though the loss of Nigel would be my death. As now he is lost indeed, but I can and I will live. Therefore my grievous sin against my son Meriet is not only this doubt of him, this easy credence of his crime and his banishment into the cloister, but stretches back to his birth in lifelong misprizing.

"And as to my sin against you, father, and against this house, that also I confess and repent, for so to dispose of a suspect murderer and so to enforce a young man without a true vocation, was vile towards him and towards this house. Take that also into account, for I would be free of all my debts.

"And as to my sin against Peter Clemence, my guest and my kinsman, in denying him Christian burial to protect the good name of my own house, I am glad now that the hand of God made use of my own abused son to uncover and undo the evil I have done. Whatever penance you decree for me in that matter, I shall add to it an endowment to provide Masses for his soul for as long as my own life continues . . ."

As proud and rigid in confessing faults as in correcting them in his son, he unwound the tale to the end, and to the end Radulfus listened patiently and gravely, decreed measured terms by way of amends, and gave absolution.

Leoric arose stiffly from his knees, and went out in unaccustomed humility and dread, to look for the one son he had left.

The rapping at the closed and barred door of Cadfael's workshop came when the wine, one of Cadfael's three-year-old brews, had begun to warm Meriet into a hesitant reconciliation with life, blurring the sharp memories of betrayal. Cadfael opened the door, and into the mellow ring of light from the brazier stepped Isouda in her grown-up wedding finery, crimson and rose and ivory, a silver fillet round her hair, her face solemn and important. There was a taller shape behind her in the doorway, shadowy against the winter dusk.

"I thought we might find you here," she said, and the light gilded her faint, secure smile. "I am a herald. You have been sought everywhere. Your father begs you to admit him to speech with you."

Meriet had stiffened where he sat, knowing who stood behind her. "That is not the way I was ever summoned to my father's presence," he said, with a fading spurt of malice and pain. "In his house things were not conducted so."

"Very well then," said Isouda, undisturbed. "Your father *orders* you to admit him here, or I do in his behalf, and you had better be sharp and respectful about it."

And she stood aside, eyes imperiously beckoning Brother Cadfael and Brother Mark, as Leoric came into the hut, his tall head brushing the dangling bunches of dried herbs swinging from the beams.

Meriet rose from the bench and made a slow, hostile but punctilious reverence, his back stiff as pride itself, his eyes burning. But his voice was quiet and secure as he said: "Be pleased to come in. Will you sit, sir?"

Cadfael and Mark drew away one on either side, and followed Isouda into the chill of the dusk. Behind them they heard Leoric say, very quietly and humbly: "You will not now refuse *me* the kiss?"

There was a brief and perilous silence; then Meriet said hoarsely: "Father . . ." and Cadfael closed the door.

In the high and broken heathland to the southwest of the town of Stafford, about this same hour, Nigel Aspley rode headlong into a deep copse, over thick, tussocky turf, and all but rode over his friend, neighbour and fellow-conspirator, Janyn Linde, cursing and sweating over a horse that went deadly lame upon a hind foot after treading askew and falling in the rough ground. Nigel cried recognition with relief, for he had small appetite for venturesome enterprises alone, and lighted down to look what the damage might be. But Isouda's horse limped to the point of foundering, and manifestly could go no further.

"You?" cried Janyn. "You broke through, then? God curse this damned brute, he's thrown me and crippled himself." He clutched at his friend's arm. "What have you done with my sister? Left her to answer for all? She'll run mad!"

"She's well enough and safe enough, we'll send for her as soon as we may . . . *You* to cry out on me!" flared Nigel, turning on him hotly. "*You* made your escape in good time, and left the pair of us in mire to the brows. Who sank us in this bog in the first place? Did *I* bid you kill the man? All I asked was that you send a rider ahead to give warning, have them put everything out of sight quickly before he came. They could have done it! How could *I* send? The man was lodged there in our house, I had no one to send who would not be missed . . . But you—*you* had to shoot him down . . ."

"I had the hardihood to make all certain, where you would have flinched," spat Janyn, curling a contemptuous lip. "A rider would have got there too late. I made sure the bishop's lackey should never get there."

"And left him lying! Lying in the open ride!"

"For you to be fool enough to run there as soon as I told you!" Janyn hissed derisive scorn at such weakness of will and nerve. "If you'd let him lie, who was ever to know who struck him down? But you must take fright, and rush to try and hide him, who was far better not hidden. And fetch your poor idiot brother down on you, and your father after him! That ever I broached such high business to such a broken reed!"

"Or I ever listened to such a plausible tempter!" fretted Nigel wretchedly. "Now here we are helpless. This creature cannot go—you see it! And the town above a mile distant, and night coming . . ."

"And I had a head start," raged Janyn, stamping the thick, blanched grass, "and fortune ahead of me, and the beast had to founder! And you'll be off to pick up the prizes due to both of us—you who crumple at the first threat! God's curse on the day!"

"Hush your noise!" Nigel turned his back despairingly, stroking the lame horse's sweating flank. "I wish to God I'd never in life set eyes on you, to come to this pass, but I'll not leave you. If you must be dragged back—you think they'll be far behind us now?—we'll go back together. But let's at least *try* to reach Stafford. Let's leave this one tethered to be found, and ride and run by turns with the other . . ."

His back was still turned when the dagger slid in between his ribs from behind, and he sagged and folded, marvelling, not yet feeling any pain, but only the withdrawal of his life and force, that laid him almost softly in the grass. Blood streamed out from his wound and warmed his side, flowing round to fire the ground beneath him. He tried to raise himself, and could not stir a hand.

Janyn stood a moment looking down at him dispassionately. He doubted if the wound itself was fatal, but judged it would take less than half an hour for his sometime friend to bleed to death, which would do as well. He spurned the motionless body with a careless foot, wiped his dagger on the grass, and turned to mount the horse Nigel had ridden. Without another glance behind he dug in his heels and set off at a rapid canter towards Stafford, between the darkening trees.

Hugh's officers, coming at speed some ten minutes later, found half-dead man and lamed horse, and divided their forces, two men riding on to try to overtake Janyn, while the remaining pair salvaged both man and beast, bestowed Isouda's horse at the nearest holding, and carried Nigel back to Shrewsbury, pallid, swathed and senseless, but alive.

". . . he promised us advancement, castles and commands—William of Roumare. It was when Janyn went north with me at midsummer to view my manor—it was Janyn persuaded me." Nigel brought out the sorry, broken fragments of his confession late in the dusk of the following day, in his wits again and half-wishing he were not. So many eyes round his bed, his father erect and ravaged of face at the foot, staring upon his heir with grieved eyes, Roswitha kneeling at his right side, tearless now, but bloated with past weeping, Brother Cadfael and Brother Edmund the infirmarer watchful from the shadows in case their patient tried his strength too far too soon. And on his left Meriet, back in cotte and hose, stripped of the black habit which had never fitted or suited him, and looking strangely taller, leaner and older than when he had first put it on. His eyes, aloof and stern as his father's, were the first Nigel's waking, wandering stare had encountered. There was no knowing what went on in the mind behind them.

"We have been his men from that time on . . . We knew the time set for the strike at Lincoln. We meant to ride north after our marriage, Janyn with us—but

Roswitha did not know! And now we have lost. Word came through too soon . . ."

"Come to the death-day," said Hugh, standing at Leoric's shoulder.

"Yes—Clemence. At supper he let out what his business was. And they were there in Chester, all their constables and castellans . . . in the act! When I took Roswitha home I told Janyn, and begged him to send a rider ahead at once, through the night, to warn them. He swore he would . . . I went there next morning early, but he was not there, he never came until past noon, and when I asked if all was well, he said, very well! For Peter Clemence was dead in the forest, and the gathering in Chester safe enough. He laughed at me for being in dread. Let him lie, he said, who'll be the wiser, there are footpads everywhere . . . But I was afraid! I went to find him, to hide him away until night . . ."

"And Meriet happened upon you in the act," said Hugh, quietly prompting.

"I had cut away the shaft, the better to move him. There was blood on my hands—what else could he think? I swore it was not my work, but he did not believe me. He told me, go quickly, wash off the blood, go back to Roswitha, stay the day out, I will do what must be done. For our father's sake, he said . . . he sets such store on you, he said, it would break his heart . . . And I did as he said! A jealous killing, he must have thought . . . he never knew what I had— what we had—to cover up. I went from him and left him to be taken in guilt that was none of his . . ."

Tears sprang in Nigel's eyes. He groped out blindly for any hand that would comfort him with a touch, and it was Meriet who suddenly dropped to his knees and took it. His face remained obstinately stern and ever more resembling his father's, but still he accepted the fumbling hand and held it firmly.

"Only late at night, when I went home, then I heard . . . How could I speak? It would have betrayed all . . . all . . . When Meriet was loosed out to us again, when he had given his pledge to take the cowl, then I did go to him," pleaded Nigel feebly. "I did offer . . . He would not let me meddle. He said he was resolved and willing, and I must let things be . . ."

"It is true," said Meriet. "I did so persuade him. Why make bad worse?"

"But he did not know of treason . . . I repent me," said Nigel, wringing at the hand he held in his, and subsiding into his welcome weakness, refuge from present harassment. "I do repent of what I have done to my father's house . . . and most of all to Meriet . . . If I live, I will make amends . . ."

"He'll live," said Cadfael, glad to escape from that dolorous bedside into the frosty air of the great court, and draw deep breaths to breathe forth again in silver mist. "Yes, and make good his present losses by mustering for King Stephen, if he can bear arms by the time his Grace moves north. It cannot be till after the feast, there's an army to raise. And though I'm sure young Janyn meant murder, for it seems to come easily to him as smiling, his dagger went somewhat astray, and has done no mortal harm. Once we've fed and rested him, and made good the blood he's lost, Nigel will be his own man again, and do his devoir for whoever can best vantage him. Unless you see fit to commit him for this treason?"

"In this mad age," said Hugh ruefully, "what is treason? With two monarchs in the field, and a dozen petty kings like Chester riding the tide, and even such as Bishop Henry hovering between two or three loyalties? No, let him lie, he's small chaff, only a half-hearted traitor, and no murderer at all—that I believe, he would not have the stomach."

Behind them Roswitha emerged from the infirmary, huddling her cloak about her against the cold, and crossed with a hasty step towards the guest-hall. Even after abasement, abandonment and grief she had the resilience to look beautiful, though these two men, at least, she could now pass by hurriedly and with averted eyes.

"Handsome is as handsome does," said Brother Cadfael somewhat morosely, looking after her. "Ah, well, they deserve each other. Let them end or mend together."

Leoric Aspley requested audience of the abbot after Vespers of that day.

"Father, there are yet two matters I would raise with you. There is this young brother of your fraternity at Saint Giles, who has been brother indeed to my son Meriet, beyond his brother in blood. My son tells me it is the heart's wish of Brother Mark to be a priest. Surely he is worthy. Father, I offer whatever moneys may be needed to provide him the years of study that will bring him to his goal. If you will guide, I will pay all, and be his debtor still."

"I have myself noted Brother Mark's inclination," said the abbot, "and approved it. He has the heart of the matter in him. I will see him advanced, and take your offer willingly."

"And the second thing," said Leoric, "concerns my sons, for I have learned by good and by ill that I have two, as a certain brother of this house has twice found occasion to remind me, and with good reason. My son Nigel is wed to a daughter of a manor now lacking another heir, and will therefore inherit through his wife, if he makes good his reparation for faults confessed. Therefore I intend to settle my manor of Aspley to my younger son Meriet. I mean to make my intent known in a charter, and beg you to be one of my witnesses."

"With my goodwill," said Radulfus, gravely smiling, "and part with him gladly, to meet him in another fashion, outside this pale which never was meant to contain him."

Brother Cadfael betook himself to his workshop that night before Compline, to make his usual nightly check that all was in order there, the brazier fire either out or so low that it presented no threat, all the vessels not in use tidied away, his current wines contentedly bubbling, the lids on all his jars and the stoppers in all his flasks and bottles. He was tired but tranquil, the world about him hardly more chaotic than it had been two days ago, and in the meantime the innocent delivered, not without great cost. For the boy had worshipped the easy, warm, kind brother so much more pleasing to the eye and so much gifted in graces and physical accomplishments than ever he could be, so much more loved, so much more vulnerable and frail, if only the soul showed through. Worship was over now, but compassion and loyalty, even pity, can be just as enchanting. Meriet had been the last to leave Nigel's sick-room. Strange to think that it must have cost Leoric a great pang of jealousy to leave him there so long, fettered to his brother and letting his father go. They had still some fearful lunges of adjustment to make between those three before all would be resolved.

Cadfael sat down with a sigh in his dark hut, only a glowing spark in the brazier to keep him company. A quarter of an hour yet before Compline. Hugh was away home at last, shutting out for tonight the task of levying men for the king's service. Christmas would come and go, and Stephen would move almost on its heels—that mild, admirable, lethargic soul of generous inclinations, stung into violent action by a blatantly treasonous act. He could move fast when he chose, his trouble was that his animosities died young. He could not really hate. And somewhere in the north, far towards his goal now, rode Janyn Linde, no doubt still smiling, whistling, light of heart, with his two unavoidable dead men behind him, and his sister, who had been nearer to him than any other human creature, nonetheless shrugged off like a split glove. Hugh would have Janyn Linde in his levelled eye, when he came with Stephen to Lincoln. A light young man with heavy enormities to answer for, and all to be paid, here or hereafter. Better here.

As for the villein Harald, there was a farrier on the town side of the western bridge willing to take him on, and as soon as the flighty public mind had forgotten him he would be quietly let out to take up honest work there. A year and a day in a charter borough, and he would be a free man.

Unwittingly Cadfael had closed his eyes for a few drowsing moments, leaning well back against his timber wall, with legs stretched out before him and ankles comfortably crossed. Only the momentarily chill draught penetrated his half-sleep, and caused him to open his eyes. And they were there before him, standing hand in hand, very gravely smiling, twin images of indulgence to his age and cares, the boy become a man and the girl become what she had always been in the bud, a formidable woman. There was only the glow-worm spark of the dying brazier to light them, but they shone most satisfactorily.

Isouda loosed her playfellow's hand and came forward to stoop and kiss Cadfael's furrowed russet cheek.

"Tomorrow early we are going home. There may be no chance then to say farewell properly. But we shall not be far away. Roswitha is staying with Nigel, and will take him home with her when he is well."

The secret light played on the planes of her face, rounded and soft and strong, and found frets of scarlet in her mane of hair. Roswitha had never been as beautiful as this, the burning heart was wanting.

"We do love you!" said Isouda impulsively, speaking for both after her confident fashion, "you and Brother Mark!" She swooped to cup his sleepy face in her hands for an instant, and quickly withdrew to surrender him generously to Meriet.

He had been out in the frost with her, and the cold had stung high colour into his cheeks. In the warmer air within the hut his dark, thick thatch of hair, still blessedly untonsured, dangled thawing over his brow, and he looked somewhat as Cadfael had first seen him, lighting down in the rain to hold his father's stirrup, stubborn and dutiful, when those two, so perilously alike, had been at odds over a mortal issue. But the face beneath the damp locks was mature and calm now, even resigned, acknowledging the burden of a weaker brother in need of loyalty. Not for his disastrous acts, but for his poor, faulty flesh and spirit.

"So we've lost you," said Cadfael. "If ever you'd come by choice I should have been glad for you, we can do with a man of action to leaven us. Brother Jerome needs a hand round his over-voluble throat now and again."

Meriet had the grace to blush and the serenity to smile. "I've made my peace with Brother Jerome, very civilly and humbly, you would have approved. I *hope* you would! He wished me well, and said he would continue to pray for me."

"Did he, indeed!" In one who might grudgingly forgive an injury to his person, but seldom one to his dignity, that was handsome, and should be reckoned as credit to Jerome. Or was it simply that he was heartily glad to see the back of the devil's novice, and giving devout thanks after his own fashion?

"I was very young and foolish," said Meriet, with a sage's indulgence for the green boy he had been, hugging to his grieving heart the keepsake of a girl he would live to hear unload upon him shamelessly the guilt of murder and theft. "Do you remember," asked Meriet, "the few times I've ever called you 'brother'? I was trying hard to get into the way of it. But it was not what I felt, or what I wanted to say. And now in the end it seems it's Mark I shall have to call 'father,' though he's the one I shall always think of as a brother. I was in need of fathering, more ways than one. This once, will you let me so claim and so call you as . . . as I would have liked to then . . . ?"

"Son Meriet," said Cadfael, rising heartily to embrace him and plant the formal kiss of kinship resoundingly on a cheek frostily cool and smooth, "you're of my kin and welcome to whatsoever I have whenever you need it. And bear in mind, I'm Welsh, and that's a lifelong tie. There, are you satisfied?"

His kiss was returned, very solemnly and fervently, by cold lips that burned into ardent heat as they touched. But Meriet had yet one more request to make, and clung to Cadfael's hand as he advanced it.

"And will you, while he's here, extend the same goodness to my brother? For his need is greater than mine ever was."

Withdrawn discreetly into shadow, Cadfael thought he heard Isouda utter a brief, soft spurt of laughter, and after it heave a resigned sigh; but if so, both escaped Meriet's ears.

"Child," said Cadfael, shaking his head over such obstinate devotion, but very complacently, "you are either an idiot or a saint, and I am not in the mood at present to have much patience with either. But for the sake of peace, yes, I will, I will! What I can do, I'll do. There, be off with you! Take him away girl, and let me put out the brazier and shut up my workshop or I shall be late for Compline!"